WAR
JOURNEY

Center Point
Large Print

Also by Fred Grove and available from
Center Point Large Print:

Trouble Hunter

**This Large Print Book carries the
Seal of Approval of N.A.V.H.**

WAR JOURNEY

Fred Grove

CENTER POINT LARGE PRINT
THORNDIKE, MAINE

This Center Point Large Print edition is published
in the year 2016 by arrangement with
Golden West Literary Agency.

First US edition: Doubleday
First UK edition: Universal Tandem

The text of this Large Print edition is unabridged.
In other aspects, this book may vary
from the original edition.
Printed in the United States of America
on permanent paper.
Set in 16-point Times New Roman type.

ISBN: 978-1-68324-011-2 (hardcover)
ISBN: 978-1-68324-015-0 (paperback)

Library of Congress Cataloging-in-Publication Data

Names: Grove, Fred, author.
Title: War journey / Fred Grove.
Description: Center Point Large Print edition. | Thorndike, Maine :
Center Point Large Print, 2016. | ©1971
Identifiers: LCCN 2016009750| ISBN 9781683240112 (hardcover :
alk. paper) | ISBN 9781683240150 (pbk. : alk. paper)
Subjects: LCSH: Large type books. | GSAFD: Western stories.
Classification: LCC PS3557.R7 W368 2016 | DDC 813/.54—dc23
LC record available at http://lccn.loc.gov/2016009750

To Paul Patterson,
who knows his Texas
and so generously
shared that knowledge.

Chapter 1

These round-shouldered humps of the granitic Wichitas fascinated him, for passing among them now he was discovering much bounty concealed from the distant eye, beguiled by purple haze and heat waves. Grassy benches rising like great steps up the jaws of the broad gap through which he rode. Stands of oaks and blackjacks—maples in the draws; now and then a stately cottonwood, which meant a spring close by. Stubby cedars in their dark-green cloaks.

The wind on his face felt light and sweet-scented, faintly cool, here where the uncropped tall grasses of the prairie and those of the short-grass country joined in a borderland of emerald profusion. Far ahead, southwest, the mountains fell away to heat-glazed flats and the occasional stub of a sentry peak.

Paul Benedict drew a long breath, savoring the grass smells once more, his delighted eye imagining the vivid details in water colors. An intrusion erased the forming scene. He gave a start, suddenly missing Shadler, and he glanced back and saw the guide dragging behind again. Damnation! Even from here his shiftless manner was pronounced, slouched in the saddle, hat brim pulled low over his whiskered face, meaty shoulders humped. All day he had kept up a nervous turning and looking.

Shadler caught up after a wait and before Paul could voice his annoyance, the guide grumbled, "Figure we'd better head back."

"Back!" Paul echoed, more astonished than angry. "Before we find White Tail's peaceful Kiowas?"

Shadler shrugged. In two days of travel he had seldom given Paul a direct answer, and now he threw a jumpy look around and set his brown jaws to grinding on the bulge of an enormous tobacco cud. His greasy black hair (his one pride, Paul had observed), the ends plaited with little strings of beaver skin, hung to the shoulders of his buckskin shirt, stained dark with sweat. Shadler pressed a grimy hand to his hair, stroking it; still looking off, he said, "Ain't gonna find 'em, 'pears like. Figured they'd be camped right around here."

Paul didn't like his tone. "Shadler," he said, "I came all the way from Baltimore to paint Indians in their primitive state. I don't propose to turn back at the first hitch in plans."

"You tellin' me what I know?" Shadler retorted. Usually the older man showed an air of braggadocio; even that seemed to have deserted him.

Paul wished now that he had curbed his impatience instead of hiring the first loud-talking white man pointed out to him at the Fort Sill Hotel as a guide. Still, Shadler was convincing and he looked the part as much as any frontiersman pictured in Leslie's *Illustrated Magazine*—the waterfall of his black mane of hair, stiff with grease, the magnificent wing-spread of his black mustache, his broad hat and his fringed buckskin shirt reeking of wood-smoke, his rusty brown pantaloons and beauti-fully beaded moccasins, and his meek Caddo Indian wife, a silent, unblinking shape bundled in long-skirted calico, sitting like a frozen image on the porch, waiting for her white lord to finish his talk. Impressed, Paul had sketched them both and given the woman a silver dollar.

"I see no signs of any recent Indian encamp-ment," said Paul, dubiously.

Shadler spat. "By God, I'll show you," he said and saddled away. Paul followed, unconvinced. Presently the guide drew rein, grumbling, "That suit you, yer majesty?"

Paul saw blanched circles where hide tipis had stood, and cracked bones and tattered bits of hide, and the blackened holes of campfires dug in the center of the circles, and mounds of ashes. Except the campfire remains had sunken, long-ago looks, and the grass seemed too high for a recent camp-site.

"You found White Tail here a short time ago?" Shadler nodded and jutted his jaw and Paul, unable to restrain his doubt, said, "The camp looks old even to me, parlor-bred."

9

Shadler didn't bat an eye. "Rained a few days back. Grass grows fast out here. An' remember— an Indian's like the wind."

The man's gall! He could look at you straight and improvise a story without the slightest change of expression. Paul felt a weary frustration. "See that big cottonwood yonder? I'm going to sketch there a while."

"Jim-dandy with me," Shadler said, and suddenly he was obliging, too obliging. He stroked his hair. "I'll take me a little looksee to the north. Maybe old White Tail moved camp thereabouts."

"Maybe," Paul said, "maybe," letting Shadler see his skepticism. "When you come back, I want to talk about going out on the plains."

Leading the pack mule, Paul rode to the cottonwood and sat a spell, listening to the musical rustling of the spangled leaves in the gentle breeze. He staked the mule and looked back, obeying a growing mistrust. Shadler was still in sight, riding through a break in the gap. As the guide faded from view, a sharpening suspicion disturbed Paul and he mounted and followed. At the opening he looked north for motion and saw none; looking to the east, he picked up at once the wedge of a hurrying horseman.

His anger burst. It was Shadler quirting his horse, and there was no doubt as to his destination. He was sneaking off to the settlement at the fort. He had his guide money, paid in advance, and he was afraid.

Paul spurred after him, his firm intention to bring the man back. Just as suddenly he changed his mind. Why not consider it a fortunate riddance? Paul could find his way back. He would return to the cottonwood and sketch, afterward choose a camp for tonight. Perhaps he could even convert a sketch or two to water colors; in the morning he would rise early and be at his work when first light touched fire to these craggy mountaintops.

One thought bothered him. It wasn't so much Shadler's inexcusable desertion and his masquerading as a guide, but Shadler's evident fear, even though they had seen no Indians nor recent Indian sign.

With a sense of relief, Paul rode back to the cottonwood. He took a folding camp chair from the mule pack, and with his sketchbook on his lap began drawing the distant, placid flats, filling in the isolated peaks and the broken slopes of the long gap clothed in rich grass and shaggy timber, capped with rocky crowns.

At times he paused to observe the clean sky. It was, beyond doubt, the softest and clearest blue of his memory, and he felt content simply to gaze at it for long moments, mouth parted. The next time he scanned the flats he detected, to his intense delight, bands of buffalo freckling the short-grassed sea.

Excitement possessed him. He must, he must include them, though they would show up as no more than dark-brown dots. He sketched rapidly, using deft, bold strokes, yet mindful of detail, hurrying to get down all that his eyes could observe, thinking that back at the settlement or, later, in his home studio, he could render his field sketches into finished water colors. But suddenly he itched to capture the perfect sky on paper. Not weeks hence, but *now.* Rising, impatient, he dug into his pack and selected a crayon of soft blue. He must have the sky this very instant or he would lose it forever.

Working furiously, he finished the sketch. Earlier that day he and Shadler had chanced upon a white-tail doe and her fawn; for an interval they stood as motionless as if they were painted on canvas. That serene scene seemed to float before his eyes again, in bold relief, and he started roughing it in.

He lost all measure of time. An idle breeze rustled the pages of his sketchbook. He smoothed the working page and continued, engrossed, at peace as he had never been before.

A noise invaded his concentration. A muffled ruffling which, very suddenly, sounded quite close behind him. He frowned at the interruption, annoyed, deciding that Shadler had come back, which, however, did not seem logical; and so he sat a bit longer, his pencil busy, reluctant to lose his mood.

But the precious moment was broken. He flung around and then he flinched and became oddly still, his eyes widening on slow-walking horses and bronze riders, their half-naked bodies shining like greased metal in the afternoon sunlight.

Shadler wasn't among them.

Still, he reasoned, his mind racing, these Indians could be part of White Tail's peaceful band. He stood and smiled at them, as he had at the stoic Kiowas and Comanches drawing rations at the agency south of the fort.

No expression crossed these high-boned faces, yet neither had the so-called reservation Indians responded. He held up his right hand in greeting. Again nothing. No sign. The Indians came on.

Now, with a pinched-off intake of breath, he noted their weapons. Circular shields hanging from rawhide-covered saddles. Some Indians carrying lances and bows, and those with the bows had arrows at the ready. All wore paint. One brave, only one, had a rifle. There was a suggestion of indifferent carelessness in the way he lazed the weapon across his arm, a certain scorn for Paul, a hated white man. Blue and yellow paint streaked his face.

A chill passed through Paul as they checked their horses, close enough that he saw the loose-lipped expression of an Indian abruptly heeling his mount to the front. Another brave shook his lance at Paul; something dangled from its metal tip. Something black and long and greasy-looking: black hair, pieces of brownish string braided into the ends.

Paul stared in sickening recognition. The brown strings were beaver skin and the hair was Shadler's.

He spoke on impulse. "Do any of you speak English?" His voice sounded unfamiliar, tight and far away. His words seemed to hang on the wind, meaningless, lost. He had to make them under-stand, if not by words, by gestures or signs, and he said, "I am a friend. Do you understand? Friend—friend." And he tapped his hand over his heart.

Now they slid down and moved toward him, their moccasin soles husking through the grass, their alert eyes sweeping over his Morgan saddle horse and mule and pack, before settling upon him. And he heard a word that sounded like *"Tejano"*—pronounced *Te-ha-no*—spoken loathingly, a harsh, explosive sound, like spitting, said over and over with remembering hate. One man waved a stone-headed war club.

Closer, he saw the long knives in hide sheaths at their waists, their black hair long and braided, wrapped in pieces of skin, and feathered scalp locks hanging to the side, and fringed buckskin leggings, moccasins trailing beaded leather flaps on which metal stringers tinkled. These Indians were dark and heavily built. Kiowas, he thought, recalling those so pointed out to him at the agency.

When he repeated the word "Friend," the heavy-lipped Indian, stalking ahead of the others, snarled at him, "*Tejano*, no *bueno*! *Tejano*, no *bueno*!"

Paul smiled his relief. Only why did they call him a Texan? And he said, "Good—you speak some English. What do you want? Food? I have food." He pointed to his mouth.

The Indian stopped short away, in sullen silence, and Paul breathed grease and sweat and buckskin and the musk of woodsmoke that seemed to cling to every Indian he had come across. He was conscious of them all scowling at him, and he guessed they puzzled over why he didn't fight them, or why he didn't run. So their umber-hued faces told him. But he had no weapon. His useless revolver hung from his saddle horn.

And swiftly, with shock, he realized they were going to kill him as they had killed poor Shadler, simply because he was a white man. He must try to grab a knife. He must dash for his horse. Anything was better than dying like this, waiting, waiting.

"Food," he said, pushing the meaning at them. "I will give you food." He pointed to the pack, then to his mouth. Before they could interfere, he crossed to the mule; in moments he was laying his sacked supplies on the grass—bacon, sugar, flour, dried apples, coffee beans.

He stepped back, the brassy taste of fear acrid on his tongue, his chest tight. Some vague sense whispered to him that he must not show fear, and deliberately he faced them and swept a hand in invitation to the supplies.

At once they swarmed in, exclaiming, a language that was nasal and choking, knifing open the sacks and scooping the sugar and flour to their mouths; now scattering the flour on the ground because they didn't like it; now licking the sugar from their fingers. An Indian seized the mule's halter. The heavy-lipped one claimed the gelding.

Paul watched, silent, dismayed. Another Indian ripped into his pack and began digging out Paul's extra clothing and dangling it for all to see, highly amused. The one holding the mule said something. He snatched a pair of gray trousers. There was a brief scuffle and the mule-holder won. By this time another brave had discovered Paul's painting equipment and supplies and was pawing at the case of airtight small-animal bladders that contained his precious oil colors.

As the case came open, Paul felt protest surge to his throat. He held it there like gall, and like gall he forced it down, swallowing hard, knowing it was useless to speak, watching numbly as prodding brown fingers punctured the fragile bladders, one by one, and the irreplaceable oils spurted out, as other Indians, joining the fun, smeared the paint over their greasy chests and broad faces; oils he had hoarded, ironically, for portraits of Plains Indians, perhaps for this very same tribe.

Sick at heart, he watched as they slashed his roll of canvas into strips and festooned themselves and strutted about as hideous, paint-streaked actors performing an aboriginal scene of grotesque savagery, as they peered at the varidaubed face of his palette and tramped it and smashed it, likewise his easel, likewise his portfolio, and his brushes, breaking each one. Everything ruined, his months of planning and expense and expectation destroyed during these few dreadful moments.

A short pause, and they turned toward him and he had nothing left with which to appease them.

"You have it all," he said, the dike of his sick rage breaking. "Now leave—go on—damn you—you senseless heathens!" feeling he had to speak, whether they understood him or not.

The heavy-lipped brave stirred, his right hand caressing the handle of his sheathed knife. He stepped nearer, a turkey-cock strut to his walk, his head thrown back. He turned and spoke to the others, his chest swelling, his tone bragging. "I am going to kill this miserable white man," he seemed to be telling them. "Watch me." Paul caught an impression, fleeting yet incisive, which even the weirdly daubed faces couldn't mask: The braggart's show did not impress them. In his left hand he had the gelding's rawhide hobbles and he rattled them at Paul, crying, accusing, "*Tejano*, no *bueno*!"

So it was the damned hobbles, Paul saw, the ones Shadler had called "Texas hobbles" and insisted he use and which had hung around the Morgan's neck.

"No," Paul said, shaking his head, "no *Tejano*," and he pointed east. "No *Tejano*—no *Tejano* me." Again he pointed; he laid his hand over his heart. "Friend me—friend, friend."

"*Tejano*! *Tejano*!" The man was working himself into a frenzy.

Paul shot a swift look around for something he could grab for a weapon. His glance fell on the folding camp chair, on it his sketchbook and the pencil stuck inside, hurriedly left, forgotten until now; there was nothing else near. It was unbearable to die in such fashion, at the hands of a savage braggart. He faced his opponent again, opening and closing his sweat-slick hands.

And as if he were an apprentice drawing from the human model, he scrutinized the scornful face before him, the bulbous nose, the hate-glittering eyes, the paint-smeared scowl, the broad forehead, the plucked eyebrows—a pompous showoff whose stomach lapped over his buckskin breech-clout.

Suddenly Paul heard himself saying, "Look," and he pointed to the sketchbook. The Indian turned his head and Paul went to the chair and picked up the book.

It wasn't until he swung around, in the grip of an unreal compulsion, that he realized what he was about to do. He held the book open to the deer scene for the Indian to see, and he made a halting sign and to his surprise the Indian obeyed.

Tense, standing, Paul found a clean page and began sketching, resting the book on his left palm, his left elbow against him for support. Rapid strokes, sure strokes. After a span of time, his sullen subject strutted over. Paul continued to work, shifting to keep the man in front of him.

A sweat started to Paul's forehead. Under his hand the savage likeness continued to form. Would his creation delay his death or only speed it? He saw the other Indians watching, likewise curious, amused by this strange white man.

Finished, Paul held the sketch from him and saw that he had captured the face rather well, despite his hurry. And, in sinking awareness, he saw much more. Indeed he had caught the likeness! Swayed by his frustration and suppressed anger, he had brought out all the man's gross ugliness: the over-size nose, the loose-lipped arrogance, the haughty, back-canted head, the great slope of the paunch. He had, he saw, exaggerated the worst features. He would do another sketch quickly, something flattering, even noble.

Before he could turn the page a thrusting hand tore the sketchbook from his grasp. Paul's pencil fell.

Stepping clear, Paul watched the braggart stare down at the sketch, his dark glance gathering suspicion, his thick lips compressing. Paul couldn't be certain, but after several moments the harsh mouth seemed to relax.

The other Indians were crowding around, looking. Paul heard a grunted laugh that flung the sting of ridicule.

That single laugh did it. In a flash Paul saw the braggart rip out the sketch and draw his knife and charge him, eyes blazing, the long blade flashing. There was a shrieked *"Tejano!"*

He had the powerful but clumsy movements of a cow. Paul, dodging instinctively, felt the brushing swish of the other's rush as he sprang aside, startled to see the Indian with the rifle step between them. He spoke sharply. Paul's attacker stopped, glaring murderously at Paul.

Paul could hear himself breathing. A succession of tiny sounds reached him, of moccasined feet stirring the tall grass, of horses stamping, farther back. A bluejay's scolding squawk.

The Indian's eyes brightened. Suddenly, using his forefinger, he traced figures in the air. Paul nodded, impelled by a vague yet hopeful sense. Still, he wasn't sure until the Indian bent to pick up the sketchbook in the grass. One by one he turned the pages of the finished sketches, pausing at times, then pushed the book at Paul and motioned toward himself. Paul took it. The Indian folded his arms around his rifle and struck a proud pose.

Paul caught on at once. He retrieved his pencil, brought over the camp chair, sat, and eyed his subject, beating down his haste, struggling to appear calm and unafraid. At last, he had hold of himself. Only then did he draw the first line. He roughed in the high, broad forehead, the strong, hawklike nose, handsome despite its broadness— a Roman nose.

As the moments passed, the others grouped around to watch. Paul ignored them.

An increasing tension gripped him. He had to force himself to the task, to concentrate, to banish his fear to the background of his mind. This Indian was taller than his companions. His body slim and graceful, his limbs smooth and round, somewhat small and symmetrical, strongly muscled but not knotted, for example, like a blacksmith's or a prize fighter's. His features well-formed. Intelligent dark eyes that mirrored the far-seeing depths of a nomad accustomed to vast distances and deep-running silences. A young man of about twenty-five years, Paul's age, but not so tall as Paul, and whose proud face showed a young man's understandable vanity of his person.

21

As Paul worked, it was as if only one-half of himself labored, while the other half fought to shut out his pressing fear. Unconsciously he had delayed over each stroke; that was why the sketch had taken so long. It was finished now.

He sat up straighter, conscious of his shallow breathing, dropped the pencil in his shirt pocket, and viewed the sketch with a critical eye. It was the best he could do under the circumstances, and it pleased him after a fashion. That fine, wild face, proud without arrogance, without the unpredictable violence of the first Indian. A face deserving of a portrait, a portrait he would never paint.

Paul knew he could stall no longer. His subject had quit posing and was eyeing him, waiting. Paul stood, which signified the sketch was done, and as he did he seemed to hear that obscure, inner voice guiding him again. So he did not rush forth and offer the drawing, not humbly, not pleading, not begging for his life, not fawning, by God; instead, he waited for the Indian to give to his eager vanity, for the Indian to come to him, which he did, in quick, long strides, and Paul handed him the sketchbook much as he would bestow a gift of great value.

Paul watched his eyes, watched them fix on the page, as expressionless as rock, watched and felt the level of his fear soar suddenly, suspended, rising higher as the Indian turned. During that one instant the dark gaze was divided between Paul and the sketch, and then it shifted, wholly on the sketch, and Paul saw pleasure spread over the savage features.

Paul took a half-turn away, his heart racing faster. In the noisy confusion he might reach his horse. He started a drifting step.

Cries rooted him there. Was this the end? He pulled back when he saw the Indians crowding toward him, except they raised no menacing weapons. Merciful God! They were pointing to themselves and making the signs for drawing.

His tautness went out of him all at once, leaving him weak and shaken. He still had some time.

Thereafter, he drew at a creeping pace, pausing often, pretending to study his model, or to ponder a while, or he would get up and go slowly forward and scrutinize his praiseworthy subject at close range, or retreat for a more appraising view, fore and middle fingers meditatively on his chin, always, always, heeding a cool and desperate cunning he hadn't known was in him.

By the time he had completed two drawings, the afternoon sun was waning and the unsketched Indians became impatient. He took the last sketch from the book and gave it to the awed Indian and waited for his next subject.

No one stepped out to pose. One man gestured to the west and moved his wrist, making rapid, rotating motions. *Go,* Paul thought, *he means go.*

His temples throbbed like mad. Pressure smashed at the back of his head. Were they going to kill him now?

Someone snatched the sketchbook and pencil and he felt his arms seized and pulled behind him, and rawhide thongs wrapped around his wrists and drawn into his flesh. A noose fell over his neck. The Indians laughed when he tried to shake free of it and could not.

Seconds later he was jogging west between two files of riders, at the end of a horsehair rope tied to the high-pommeled, Spanish-type saddle of his captor, the rifleholder, who by some savage priority, it appeared, had become Paul's owner or guard or special tormentor. For when Paul lagged, the young man rode faster and jerked the loop tighter, often sending Paul to his knees, or hurling him crashing to the rocky footing of the gap; or when Paul was trotting downslope, the Indian would hold his mount back deliberately and force Paul to slow down or choke.

Paul soon understood. They were using him to amuse themselves, enjoying a kind of primitive game of cat and mouse. When it was over, or when they became bored, or perhaps after he had sketched them all, they would certainly kill him because he was a white man—and more certainly because they thought he was a Texan. Either was reason enough.

Chapter 2

Even before they reached the end of the long gap and dropped down to the flats, his booted feet were soring up from the rock-rubbled trail—and it was a trail, he saw, likely an ancient one, which for ages had led bronze rovers to lush hunting grounds—and his chafed neck was raw and his bound wrists were numb.

Once below the craggy mountains, the coolness vanished and the hot wind came purring and sobbing like a chanting chorus, and the short grass reminded him of a light-green sea of gentle swells, seeming so, deceiving the eye, because of the wind rippling the grass, and the solitary peaks out there made him think, despite his growing misery, of uncharted islands by the endless sea.

A brutal jerk on the horsehair rope flung him headlong, sprawling on his face. Sun-blinded, he glared up at his captor, unable to see the proud face, as if that made any difference, as if he didn't know. They were going to kill him soon— he knew that; it was just a matter of when the impulse struck them. Now? Within the hour? Tomorrow?

He staggered up, spitting dirt and grass. Be damned if he'd grovel before them as long as he could stand, and that might not be possible by the end of the day the way his strength was going and the way he already thirsted.

He could feel his fear balling up, drying his throat, shortening his breath, and his mind played with alternatives. Would they free his hands or strike him down bound?

Somebody spoke a guttural word that sounded like *gadal*, and pointed to the grazing buffalo, and Paul's captor tossed the end of the rope to a teen-aged boy; the war party, likewise leaving the Morgan and the mule in the boy's charge, swung away on the run, clapping heels to their mounts' flanks.

The hunters were more than two hundred yards from the buffalo when the leader on the edge of the bunch threw up its massive head and lumbered off. Instantly the other animals followed, tiny spring calves trailing their mothers. A yellowish fog of dust rose above the flat.

Even faster, the hunters raced in pursuit. Paul heard their wolfish yells carried by the wind, saw their fleet ponies stretching out. A rapid drumming sounded. Apart as he was, those faint voices and the racket of hoofs conveyed the pounding excitement of the chase. He saw a hunter dash at a buffalo, along its right side, bow and arrow raised for a downward shot. The hunter's arm hinged back as the arrow was released and the wounded buffalo wheeled to charge, but the trained horse seemed to expect the attack and swerved away and the shaggy beast, after a brief run, broke down.

At that moment a vivid scene flew into Paul's mind: the tremendous, humped beast, wounded, enraged, small black eyes furious, whirling to gore its tormentor, and the wonderfully alert, blood-red, buffalo-running horse, nostrils flaring from the hard run, eyes walled, springing out of danger on legs of fire, smooth muscles rippling, and the half-naked centaur low in the saddle.

Paul's right hand itched for pencil and sketch-book as the figures filled his brain, etched there, and then, like an extinguished flame, the scene went out and he returned to his misery.

A savage yank on the rope cut short his looking. His boy captor took off for the hunting ground, forcing Paul to run or be choked and dragged.

Two Indians were heaving the first buffalo carcass over on its great furry belly; that done, they spread all the beast's fours, cut across the thick neck, and sliced the hide down the spine and peeled it back on both sides and began removing the front and hind quarters.

Left alone, Paul noticed how the Indians' horses stood like sentinels on lookout, looking off between nibbles at the short grass, fox ears twitching, standing though untethered, the raw-hide reins dropped. From time to time the busy hunters glanced up at their mounts for signs of alarm.

Paul, unobserved, strained on his rawhide bonds. Meanwhile, the butchers worked fast and expertly. He saw his captor straighten up and hold a hunk of dripping liver skyward and bring it to his mouth, blood streaming down his chin, relishing the raw meat as a small boy would a hunk of watermelon. And he saw the second hunter take what resembled a piece of tallow and over it pour the contents of the buffalo's gallbladder and consume it with the greedy heartiness of a gourmand.

Paul's stomach quivered. Yet, not having eaten since morning, he thought how good the meat would be if cooked.

Before dark they came to a spring below a cedar-studded bluff and here they watered and picketed their horses and, using flint and steel, started a fire. Evidently they had overlooked the matches in Paul's pack or, not knowing their use, had discarded them. If so, he reasoned, the war party belonged to a wild band that never came to the agency for rations.

He sat cross-legged, his arms tied from behind above the elbows, which forced his shoulders back and left his hands free but limited his reach. He could feed himself by bowing his head.

He sat there while his hunger gnawed at his vitals and the Indians consumed a fantastic amount of meat, most times focusing his gaze on the low fire, just enduring.

Something plopped into the dust before Paul. His eyes jerked. It was a hunk of raw meat, reddish and succulent in the yellow light. He looked across and met the harsh stare of his captor, and that high-bridged face said, in effect: *White man, you are nothing but a dog. White man, I know you are hungry. White man, there is meat. I am your enemy, but I am generous. So take it from the dirt and eat it like the dog you are, white man.*

Paul continued to meet the despising gaze, feeling the snake of his hunger coiling around his middle, knowing he was doomed.

He had just one hope, one strength, to hold to. If he ever let his fear flicker into his face, if he ever quailed, if he ever became less than outwardly brave, they would kill him just that much sooner.

Hence, he didn't so much as dare glance at the meat, even while it seemed that he knew, through the extra keenness of his senses, how it would taste, dark and wild and sweet, and that he could smell its richness. No. And, with the toe of his boot, he kicked dust upon the meat and glared back at his captor.

The Indian's chin lifted, a sign of surprise. His smoky eyes narrowed slightly. His even lips moved on a single, hating word, "*Tejano!*" and he spat into the fire.

"No—*Tejano*," Paul insisted, adding a stubborn shake of his head.

Finally, the Indians had had their fill, the fire died to a dim eye, one brave went soundlessly to the bluff, and the rest rolled in their buffalo robes.

Paul waited. Were they going to leave him like this all night? A sliver of anger touched him. He got up to look for a place to lie down, farther out on the short grass. Hardly had he stood when his captor sprang upon him, and a second figure, and together they threw him on his back to the ground, with a force that knocked the wind from him, untied him and spread-eagled him, tying each wrist and staking it, and the same to each ankle, leaving him tethered like an animal. Like a dog.

The camp fell still. A cool wind moaned down through the cedars on the bluff like a voice in pain. Paul shivered and longed for a blanket. Over there, recognizable through the dimness by his height and size, his stout Morgan grazed. Paul felt sorry for the horse. The Indians would ride him unmercifully.

Strange images beat in and out of his head, unreal bits and flashes and throbbings that whirled through his consciousness. He had the sensation of having wandered from the body and mind of one Paul Latimer Benedict, the promising young Baltimore illustrator and portraitist, the some-what pampered scion of an honored early family, in the month of April 1873, west of Fort Sill, Indian Territory, and assuming the identity of a nameless being in another world. A golden, blue-crusted world, swept by unending wind, and inhabited by bronze centaurs and enormous, shaggy beasts, where a pitiless sun ruled the infinite sky.

He strained against the thongs, hearing the wailing shrillness of coyotes, and it occurred to him how human their plaintive voices sounded, suggestive of a serenade.

His weariness was dragging him under again, into the fitful flashes of sleep. It seemed only a short time afterward when he heard movement and then someone was untying his bonds and hauling him staggering to his feet. His captor, it was, and he pointed toward the spring, and Paul, blinking, saw the slate-gray tide of morning sweeping across the stony bluff, the stubby cedars, the grazing stock, and the implacable faces of the war party.

His rigid body ached from chill and he felt permanently bent. Humped over, he rubbed his hands and wrists, furrowed by the rawhide, and his arms and shoulders and neck and stamped his swollen feet. With the Indian alongside him, he went to the spring and drank the ambrosia of sweet water and scrubbed to the waist. Shortly, bound again, he walked back to where the taper of a small fire burned orange-yellow against the soluble murk of the changing prairie world, and he wondered what would happen to him next.

He pretended to ignore the Indians, half-cooking their breakfasts, and as he inhaled the juicy smells the keen edge of his hunger pressed like the point of a knife. Yesterday the nine of them had killed two fat buffalo. This morning the mounds of meat looked half gone.

He sat and crossed his legs, feeling the now-familiar uncertainty settling over him again. They would kill him today.

He looked away while they gorged, wishing he could shut out their smacking and the contented noises they made sucking the marrow from bones and the last particles of meat from rib bones. His captor flung him a piece of meat. Paul had expected that. It fell closer this time, at the toe of his right boot, though still in the dirt. He feigned indiffer-ence, and he thought: *Today will be the worst.*

The Indians ate all they had cooked, and then they cooked some more. After they had ceased stuffing, Paul saw that the rest of the meat was gone; only the hides remained.

He now sensed a waiting, a breathless pause, such as the moments before the curtains went up on a play, except all eyes were upon him.

Even so, Paul wasn't expecting it to happen so fast. The braggart wiped greasy hands on greasy chest and, lunging across, grabbed Paul by the hair and yanked it downward over Paul's face until he saw its yellowness.

Paul said no word. He did not struggle. To do so would be to please his tormentor.

Next, the Indian dragged Paul to his feet and held Paul's head back so far, pulling, that for several moments he feared his hair would tear loose at the roots.

"*Tejano*! *Tejano*!" the wild voice howled at Paul.

When the Indian eased up at last and Paul could straighten, he spoke and not before. "No *Tejano*—no *Tejano*," and he did not shout. He replied with what dignity he could muster, and it gave him satisfaction to see bewilderment knot the broad slab of the coppery face.

Whereupon, the Indian threw Paul to the ground and stomped back to his companions, and they all sat down, their feet drawn up under them. Paul could tell they were discussing his fate. They would look at him and gesture and talk and gesture some more. The braggart pointed south, his manner emphatic, which meant Texas.

Before long they jumped up and brought in their horses and the Morgan and the mule, and it turned over in Paul's mind how they appeared to act by fits and starts. Had they decided to kill him now, then ride on?

But his captor was fashioning a loop with his horsehair rope. He whirled it twice over his head and threw and as the hissing thing coiled around Paul's neck, a kind of grim relief settled over him also.

The war party swung southwest. Paul obeyed doggedly, at trot or walk as the mood of the Indians changed. Around midday they jumped buffalo and killed two fat cows and a young bull and camped along the slim shine of a wooded creek winding crookedly between two rows of knuckled hills.

Paul swayed like a used-up horse, head down, pulling wind from the farthest depths of his chest, eyes half-shuttered to seal out the sun glare. His fair skin burned as though from fever, and his hands, bound more tightly than yesterday, ached from the cruel rawhide.

Stupor was still upon him when his captor, roughly, quickly, untied his hands. For a frozen moment, Paul was too surprised to move.

The Indian pointed toward two tongues of fire beginning to lick the noon heat. Paul searched the wide-set eyes for an explanation, some hint of humaneness—found none whatever—and, stiffly, went to the first fire and sat.

Before long his captor handed him a stick and indicated chunks of buffalo cut and heaped on the flesh side of a robe. Paul attached a long slice and held it over the fire in imitation of the Indians. His meal wasn't half-cooked when he took it in his fingers and began gorging like an Indian. He couldn't eat fast enough of the dark meat, which was coarser and fatter than beef, and more delicious; just as soon, he had to stop. His stomach revolted and could accept no more. He waited and began again, eating slowly, savoring each morsel, feeling a flood of strength flowing into him and routing his state of weary stupefaction. He ceased eating when the Indians still gorged. In that, he guessed he understood them a little. They glutted when there was plenty; they endured when there was little or nothing.

Content, sitting in the dappled shade of a stunted elm, lulled by the unbroken wolfish chomping and marrow-sucking, Paul dozed.

Nearby movement roused him. He opened his eyes to see that the Indians had their fill at last. One was standing and holding Paul's sketchbook and pencil and motioning for him to take it. He took them blankly. In his constant weariness he had forgotten the sketches, long past having decided the capricious Indians had also. To live a little longer, he must play the game. That was why they had fed him, why he had discerned no humanity in their feeding of him.

He rose and took a seat against the trunk of an elm and signed for the Indian to sit across from him. His subject did so and Paul noticed new objects. The Indian had donned extra regalia and brought his weapons. Silver pendants dangled down his chest. Also a necklace of shells distinguished by a single bear's claw. He held a long wooden lance, on it a string of three scalps, one of silky yellowness, a woman's, the long hair as blond as Paul's. Paul sickened, but kept his face expressionless. A special scalp, carefully combed and oiled, groomed so it shone like a golden mane.

All at once the Indian jabbed the head of the lance at Paul, gesturing for him to get busy, then laid the lance across his lap and strung an arrow to his bow string and aimed the shaft in Paul's direction.

Paul let more time pass. Had he not eaten, he knew that his hands would be trembling. But they were steady enough, though commencing to sweat.

Scowling, the Indian was drawing the arrow against the sinew string and sighting along the shaft. Paul continued to dawdle, to pretend occupation of his subject. A deeper frown furrowed the Indian's brow, and he put aside his bow and arrow and drew his knife and picked up a piece of flat rock and went to whetting the blade against it.

Paul set his face, determined to outlast the other yet a bit longer.

A scowl of perplexity roiling his savage brow, the Indian sheathed his knife and stepped over to Paul and pressed his hand over Paul's heart and held it there.

Paul, deliberately, dropped his hands to his lap, feeling the sweat coming again.

And the Indian stepped back. Gazing down at

Paul, he appeared to search each feature for a sign of weakness. Briefly, he said, with a trace of surprise, "*Tejano*, no scare," and turned back to his place and arranged his weapons about himself.

Only then did Paul ready himself to sketch. After his near-disastrous experience with the braggart, he had learned what to do. This Indian was likewise ugly, if not quite so much: hog-fat around the belly and smallpox scars pitting his irregular features. It could be dangerous, depending on the degree of the man's vanity, to stress those lineaments. Accordingly, taking his pencil, he gave prominence to the scalp-decorated lance and the harsh uplight of the cruel face, hiding the great stomach behind the bow and arrow and the hands and forearms. With a sure deftness, he exaggerated the bold warrior mien, adding a touch of nobility to the scowling brow, and exaggerated the breadth of the shoulders and the deep chest.

When Paul signed that he was finished and removed the page and the Indian saw his own likeness, a childish wonder softened his dark gaze. He seemed chastened, he really did, Paul thought, as he feasted his eyes over the sketch, his pleasure pure and awed, and when he swept his liking at Paul, he conveyed it violently, with nods, and the insight went through Paul that these Stone Age savages must use violence even to express pleasure.

Paul leaned back, allowing a semblance of arrogance to swell his face, and gazed across the creek, as overbearing and haughty as they. They had taught him that, and he sensed that he portrayed it rather well.

He maintained that aloofness until his next subject was seated. Turning, quite slowly, making certain they saw his indifference, he brought his disdain to bear upon the Indian and set to work.

After a long while, he completed the sketch and he made it brave and the Indian liked it, and he did another just as brave. He was truly sweating now, his mind leaping ahead, his body a coil of tension. He couldn't think beyond the sketches. What then, when he no longer amused them?

Finally, he was lingering over the final drawing and when he had finished it, to the Indian's delight, he took deliberate steps to the creek, ostensibly for a drink, impelled to think, a panic hounding him. If he waded the creek and ran, they would ride him down in moments. If he managed to mount the Morgan, they would come swarming like hornets on their swift ponies.

As he began to tremble and his breath shortened, a hasty plan formed. Illogical and foredoomed in advance, he realized, for he had no real choice; that or wait for them to kill him on their own terms. He was going to slip down the creek to his horse.

First, the drink to deceive them.

He was on hands and knees when he caught a rapid scuffing behind him. He straightened, not too fast, hoping to appear casual, and turned and froze.

When he saw the braggart, his right hand over his knife sheath, a knowing crashed through Paul. The game was over.

Chapter 3

Paul's rigidity lasted only for a drumbeat. He spread his feet, knees bent, waiting, and when the Indian charged, as Paul knew he would, Paul broke for the low bank. He was scrambling up it, the Indian wheeling in his rush to cut him off, when Paul felt his boot slip on tree roots.

He was falling backward, off balance. Out of the tail of his eye he saw the greasy smear of the brown body bearing down upon him. He toppled backward, powerless to stop, arms flailing, the Indian somewhere above him. He hit the shallow water, floundering and splashing, the Indian after him, knife out. Paul twisted around, feeling rocks under him. He sprang up, then stooped and fumbled and felt his right hand close around an egg-shaped rock. Teeth bared, he threw it with all his might.

His aim was hurried, and the rock skipped off the Indian's ribs. In that space Paul splashed to the bank, grabbed a tree root, and swung up running. Behind him he could hear the sloshing, now the pounding hard after him.

The camp was straight ahead. His impulse was to dash on through to the horses. But there wasn't time. The Indians stood in a semicircle barring

40

his way, hands on their weapons to halt him or kill him.

He whirled to face his pursuer and found himself near a smoldering fire. Still moving, Paul felt his boot kick a piece of firewood. He snatched it up, feeling its lightness, its punky softness. When the Indian rushed him, Paul struck at the contorted face. He missed and spun about crouched, primed for another charge.

Instead, the Indian started a careful maneuvering, and sprang suddenly, swiping at Paul, who dodged, narrowly, striking at the knife arm and missing again.

Wild to finish him, the braggart pressed closer, faster, yipping a scornful hooting, forcing Paul to give ground too fast. He lashed out and Paul felt a ripping pain along his left forearm. The Indian whooped. That infuriated him and he forgot his fear and strode in, swinging the wood.

Sensing that he lost even if he won, Paul gave in to his hot and thunderous rage, uncaring so long as he smashed the face. He charged faster, overeager, took a fierce swing, and felt the spongy wood snap in two, inches from his grip.

For an unnerving moment, Paul stood flat-footed. He saw the thick arm arching back to start the downward plunge of the knife, saw the glittery intent to murder him. Dropping the wooden stub, Paul crouched lower, near the fire again. Desperation stirred him and he scooped up a handful of ashes and threw it at the face.

Most of the showering ashes missed, though they caused the Indian to pause and brush at his eyes with his left hand. As he did, Paul made a two-handed grab for the knife hand and connected. Only a second or two of that and Paul felt the other's left hand yanking him by the hair, hauling him backward. Paul held on.

But the long stretch without food and the cruel hours on the rope, trotting like a captured horse, told on him now. He couldn't hold off the knife much longer, and his neck seemed about to snap. Therefore, he drove his right knee into the overlapping belly, and heard the startled gasp of pain, at the same time twisting the knife arm.

The knife fell free. With a groan, the Indian dropped to the ground.

Paul clutched it up, seeing his foe roll over and try to rise. Paul kicked. It was a full-swinging blow. The toe of his boot took the Indian in the chest and sprawled him on his back, hands pressed to his bowels.

Paul, gripping the knife, stood over him. Suddenly it seemed wrong to be holding the knife thusly, to kill, and the heat of his rage dulled, seeing that the Indian expected to die, seeing the dark eyes waiting, resigned, helpless, bewildered because Paul did not plunge the knife.

Nausea swamped him, weakened him. He let the knife fall to his side.

And then he did an impulsive thing, unexplainable even to him, unless it was to show them his absolute contempt for their damnable, senseless, heedless, savage violence. He regarded the knife with loathing—a trader's cheap item, a thin-bladed butcher knife—and, crouching, he snapped the blade over his right knee and threw the pieces to the ground and, weaving, near exhaustion, staggered to the creek to rest against a tree.

He was trembling, sick, and he gagged once, twice, while he fought to control his quivering insides.

He stumbled to the creek and washed. After vigorous rubbings, he could still smell the smoky musk of the greasy body on him. Before long, if he lived, he would smell the same.

When he moved up the creek bank and entered the timber, no one as much as grunted or gave him a glance. He sat down and rested in the shade, conscious of the old, dull stupor of uncertainty harassing him again, denying him even a moment's peace of mind.

A figure was limping toward him—the braggart. He wore a sickish look on his meaty face. Paul searched it for at least one remote expression of human feeling, just one grain of gratitude for having spared his life.

His expectancy vanished when, instead, he read the same sullen hatred of himself, possibly a deeper hatred. Chilled, Paul watched him scuff on to the creek, and as he followed him with his eyes a perception spread through Paul. He had humbled the Indian before his tribesmen and destroyed his status as a warrior. In this primitive society of Plains warriors, where obviously self-glorification was the main pursuit, loss of face could be ruinous.

When evening came, Paul's captor gave him tallow to rub on his slashed arm and invited him to eat again at the fire. Paul speculated while he gorged. Why? Why did they let him live? Him, a hated *Tejano*?

Afterward, by signs, his captor ordered him to lead his war horse to the creek. Paul's pulse jumped. He started to obey, feeling the quickening desperation to gamble one wild attempt at escape while he could still find the settlements.

He halted on a guttural command and faced his captor, seeing the open contempt creasing the hawkish features, and the added trace of ridicule. The Indian had caught his intention at once.

Paul held fast, his fear building. Had they fed him just to torture him into thinking he might live?

But, no, he saw. The Indian was patting his rifle and he pointed again to the horses and toward the creek. Paul shrugged. Striding to the horses, he pulled the picket pin and watered the animal and led it back and staked it. When he returned to the fire, his captor signed for Paul to fetch more wood. The fluent hands formed a derisive postscript, *Heap wood, white man!*

Paul understood at last. The signs could be no clearer: He was a slave.

Chapter 4

Next morning the rope stayed on his captor's Spanish saddle and Paul trotted like a loose horse between the files of warriors.

By watching the sun he could tell that the war party was bearing northwest. More times than not he was forced to jog. He trudged along on swollen feet, through a dusty pall of pain and weariness and thirst, astonished at his endurance, trying to pace himself and asking why he bothered. Why not just lie down and die? What would they do if he balked—kill him or leave him?

To see, he came to a stumbling halt and let his arms hang. When his captor swung back, Paul indicated that he needed rest and slumped down in the short grass on one knee.

A slashing across his shoulders shocked him upward and away, arms lifted protectively. The Indian commenced quirting him, cutting, methodical blows that enraged and humiliated Paul. He grabbed for the quirt and missed, grabbed again and missed again, and fell back and the painful rain of snapping leather drove him into line again.

So he learned they wouldn't leave him here on the clean prairie to die in dignity; they would punish him mercilessly before they killed him.

Nevertheless, he ached to live, whatever happened, and because he was young he had the hope that some way he would live past all this, no matter. Walking, jogging, trotting, he jerked along like a puppet without strings, aware that the land ahead was flattening, long, broad swells replacing the humped figurines of the hazy Wichitas; and when he could see their last dim outline no more, it seemed that he had lost his final tie with civilization.

He became suddenly bitter and overrunning with self-pity. He wasn't Paul Latimer Benedict anymore. He was nothing, scarcely human. He turned to plod forward, in time to see his captor drop his lifted quirt.

Paul learned anew that there was no predicting the whims of the Indians. They relished forcing him to the brink of his endurance, and beyond it. After a long stint of driving him, they would halt and waste time for no logical reason. Out of the sun-blasted emptiness a band of antelope appeared, slim, dun-colored phantoms, like fanciful beasts out of a child's book, their bobbing white rumps flickering signals that even he, a mere white man, understood: *Catch me. Catch me, if you can.*

And the fool savages gave chase. Relieved to sink down and rest, he watched them pursue the fleet creatures and fail to ride close enough for a kill, for of course it was only a lark, and return on horses foaming sweat. For them, he decided, time was forever, to be spent with the prodigality of a savage.

The day wasn't yet over, the sun a glowering red eye, when the party camped for the night. Paul, after a grunting, two-handed tug-of-war, got off his boots and was dismayed to see the condition of his swollen feet. Come morning, he couldn't pull on the boots. As he bit his lip, he heard a slap beside him and was dumfounded to find a pair of old moccasins, beadless, too large for him, but durable, thrown him by his captor.

Paul bared a humorless smile. A sound slave was valuable property. A sorefooted one was useless. He put on the moccasins and wore them the next day, gladly. Inasmuch as the boots were symbols of his past, he could not bring himself to discard them.

They came to the strangest river of Paul's experience. Wide and shallow and as red as dust, a lazy snake gliding between low, broken bluffs on this side and sprawling flats on the other. His mind retraced the map left in his pack and which the Indians had discarded. Fabled Red River. Over there lay Texas, broad and endless, an infinitude of humming silence and smoky-white heat waves.

The days passed like wind and smoke, with

little meaning or form. All he felt was weariness, which never ended, and sometimes hunger, for they let him eat when they killed game. He stumbled through an unreal, vaporous world. Now he carried the boots around his neck on a rawhide strip tied to the straps. His swollen feet in the moccasins had healed. He ate when ordered, he watered his captor's war pony when told, he gathered mesquite for the fires.

On the fifth day after crossing Red River, he saw the undulating face of the land rising to the choppy brows of hills and breaks. Cleaving that brokenness spilled a narrow stream like a splash of silver.

Excitement swept the war party. The youngest member galloped ahead and disappeared. Paul noted how they painted themselves, hideous streaks of yellow and red and blue, and donned their best clothing.

Finished, impatient, they mounted and Paul rose to fall in line, caught unawares at the reminding hiss of the horsehair rope whipping down around his neck. Paul lurched into a fast trot that wasn't fast enough. Cruelly his captor yanked him running. Paul saw the canyon widening and the red walls rising around him, in the distance conical, light-tan hide lodges. A camp. A village. From it people streamed on foot to greet the war party. Paul caught voices, women's welcoming voices, shrill and joyful, and realized he hadn't expected these heathens to possess such human feelings.

The warrior who had taken poor Shadler's scalp and the warrior on whose lance dangled the woman's blond hair rushed to the head of the war party, evidently the position of honor. Behind them paraded Paul's captor, proudly exhibiting his white captive.

An elderly, dignified woman walked before the procession. She carried a long lance, and now the honored scalp-takers tied their trophies to the lance. The woman flourished the lance. Everybody whooped.

Paul's captor, not to be overlooked, pointed to him and called in a loud voice, "*Tejano! Tejano!*"

At that, a hag as wrinkled as a prune, her worn teeth ground down to brown stubs, ran up snarling and spat into Paul's face. He swiped it off, his movement furious, and strode on, head up, while she flitted at his side, enraged, witchlike, howling indignities.

Another woman, just as ancient and hideously ugly and vindictive, brandished a long-bladed butcher knife and barred his way.

Paul's captor waved her off.

She paused, her shrilling voice accusing, and tremblingly exhibited her mutilated left hand.

Paul felt a flinch of horror, a reach of sympathy. All her fingers were off to the first joint. Scars slashed her forearms. He had read, somewhere, how grieving Plains Indian women hacked off fingers and slashed and disfigured themselves when mourning family warriors lost in battle and other departed loved ones. It mattered not that Paul hadn't harmed her family. Her vengeance included any enemy. Any white man would do. Especially the most hated of all whites, a *Tejano.*

Squalling piteously, she lurched toward Paul. His captor quickly swung in front of her and drummed his painted chest and shouted.

It was Paul's turn to be amused. He gathered that if there was any killing this contemptible white captive, that his captor would do it, no one else.

She shrank away, still shrieking, and the parade continued on to the village. To Paul's nostrils rose the hungering smells of meat and grease, the heavy warmth of many horses, the pungency of leather, of woodsmoke and trampled dust. Wolfish-looking dogs sniffed their suspicion of him. Children stared at him, behind their large, gentle eyes the budding of the hate that he had learned to accept and expect.

He could sense it everywhere, as palpable as the rope choking his neck, as he was hurled to the ground and bound and dragged and tied to the pole where the scalps now hung.

Horror wrung him. They were going to torture him to death; that was why the war party hadn't killed him.

He sat with the back of his head against the pole, his eyes swelling, his jaws clamped, held by a stupor of helpless resignation. And slowly the drums began to throb and the dancers trailed forth and he heard a low chanting and the piercing notes of a flute. Around and around him the dancers, men and women, circled, their moccasins tinkling, their beads and porcupine quills and necklaces rustling like dry leaves.

A bedecked warrior whirled out of the revolving mass. The drumming quit. Pointing to the scalps on the pole, he addressed the dancers with a high, recounting voice. Now and then he drew his knife and described scalping motions.

Paul recognized him. Shadler's killer. He was reciting his deed before his people. He finished, and the vibrant drums struck the slow cadence and the dancers formed the shuffling circle again.

Some of Paul's dread receded, but he had learned to expect the startling, the unforeseen, from these wild people. Sweat began to bead his forehead. He pushed against the pole when a warrior leaped from the chanting ring, knife out, and seized Paul by the hair. It was the braggart.

Paul closed his eyes, set his teeth, prepared for the pain of death. Several moments. Yet he felt no pain except the yanking at the roots of his hair. Opening his eyes, he felt the braggart release him and start howling over him and waving the knife, making slashing passes at Paul's face and body, a pantomime of killing and scalping.

Stomping, chanting, he paused before Paul, glaring his hate, and strutted back to his position in the circle.

Not till then did Paul feel his breath return. Of a sudden he was quite weary, and the drums, throbbing again, slowly, were as a pulse inside his head. He saw that it was evening. Beyond the circle of dancers, across the little stream, the shadows swam in pools of plum purple along the foot of the canyon wall, and he thought how strange that he should still take note of details. Was it because his tortured mind sought release, else it would snap?

The canyon wall drowned in blackness and the night grew old, and yet there seemed no end to the energy of the dancers or the whirling pantomimists or the spectral figures crouched over the pulsing hide drums.

At some vague point he realized the drums had ceased, for he could hear a tethered horse stamping behind him, and the dancers had vanished to their pole lodges, for he saw no motion and heard no voices, and the ashes of the dead feast fires lay like gray puddles in the tallow sea of moonlight.

He dared sleep then. His dulled senses let him slip beneath the restful waters of a dark-green pool of forgetfulness.

He came to himself again in mealy darkness, groaning, in bound pain, stiff, wolf hungry. Something had waked him. A sound. A quavering. A far-off crying. He turned his head, listening, and placed it upcanyon from the camp, probably near the rim. The voice of an old man. Probably a wise elder, once a war leader.

The voice went on and after a time Paul experienced a deepening consciousness, vague though clear somehow, as if he could understand that high, prayer-like voice. A crying for good times, for good hunting, for good health, for protection from enemies. The timeless cry of an elder praying for his people, to whatever god these barbarians prayed.

He slept again.

Waking, he strained to catch the shrill pitch of the old voice. It was silent, fled like a night bird before daylight. And he saw the day approaching, its pink fingers parting the changing eastern sky. With it, the horror of his nightmare passed, and through his pain, true and strong, an unbelievable sense of peace reached him.

He was going to live.

Chapter 5

Although they allowed him to live, he had no status as a slave. He ate what his captor flung him, sometimes much, sometimes little. To occupy his time, he fashioned a crude hut, more wickiup than tipi in form, of brush and a worn hide formerly used on his owner's comfortable tipi; and because erecting shelter was women's work, he drew looks of blended contempt and amusement.

The shy, near-naked children were kinder—they merely watched him as an object of interest, careful to keep a safe distance, though in their solemn, round faces he saw a curious fascination, a possible liking, inasmuch as they were too young to know the extent of real hate. The first time he smiled at them, they bolted like colts; resuming his work, he pretended not to notice when they crept back, somewhat nearer this time. He had no wish to frighten them and so he turned and said, "Hello, there," speaking gently, and the strangeness of hearing his own voice made it sound unlike him.

They fled in a giggling rush, but soon stopped and cast backward glances at Paul. Before they could begin another stealthy approach, a woman ran up and her scolding voice drove them toward the village. Scolding and no more. Paul had yet to see the Indians spank or switch their children.

After that, the children stayed away and his loneliness grew. He found a broken knife blade and fashioned a crude cedar bow and two willow arrows to which he affixed turkey feathers as guides. There were flocks of turkeys upcanyon, a meat supply that he noticed the Indians did not touch and that he learned in time they considered taboo.

But the new bow bent too readily to the sinew string for much distance and his awkward arrows, neither straight nor balanced, flew like crooked sticks, and he killed not a single rabbit or turkey. The Indians broke into rare smiles at his ridiculous hunting attempts. It seemed he was always entertaining; furthermore, he saw, they regarded him as harmless. And always their dark faces reminded him: *White man, you are nothing. Remember that.*

He fetched wood and water when his captor's wife and mother so ordered, which wasn't often because they preferred that he stay away from the lodge.

And, until he could escape, he resolved to improve on his meager comforts. He cut a breech-clout from a piece of castoff buckskin. A simple, comfortable contraption, he found, and adaptable for this hard life. He drew it up between his legs and passed it under his belt, front and behind, letting the ends flap loosely almost to his knees. His boots had disappeared the day of his ordeal at the stake; in time, using sinew for thread and a bone sliver for a needle, he made a pair of rawhide-soled moccasins and buckskin leggings that extended from foot to hip and looped to his belt, and a long-sleeved buckskin shirt, crudely sewn, but serviceable. Now his blond hair hung to his shoulders and his beard covered his face like gold-colored moss.

His isolation troubled him most, his wordless existence, like a muzzled dog. Sometimes he would comment aloud on what he saw and felt, or try to recall recitations unspoken since he was a schoolboy; anything to hear the sound of his stranger's voice. And the Indians, hearing him, would make the whirling sign close to their heads, which meant Crazy or Foolish.

He used up much idle time observing these people, noting their dress and decorations and customs, and he drew figures in the sand and thereby inscribed them on his mind, storing them away for that hopeful day when he could create them on canvas. But his muteness, his inability to communicate, left him stranded under a sky of silence. He decided, therefore, to learn their bewildering tongue, full of nasal and guttural sounds, choking to the ear, harsh. And since they would not speak to him, he would speak to them in signs, hoping to catch words to remember.

He tried hard, but the Indians wouldn't reply to him except by brief signs and, rarely, a few grudging words, and as time passed and they wearied of his insistence, they accorded him even less attention. The words he did glean came through alertness and careful listening when the men conversed among themselves. He picked up such simple words as *gadal*—buffalo and *tsen*—horse and *tsenhi*—dog and *do*—tipi and *pia*—fire and *ton*—water; beyond common terms he was helpless.

He thought up scheme after scheme of escape, none of which he found feasible. It wasn't only the constant surveillance of the Indians—not the way a white man would stand guard, right over you; rather a kind of loose-reining watch, of which Paul was aware everywhere he went—it was that he hadn't the faintest idea where he was in north Texas, what stream, what canyon, or where to flee if he did escape.

At night he stalked the horse herds to steal a mount, and always the alert boys spotted him before he could reach an animal, or the horses, not used to his white-man scent, would snort alarm.

He lost all sense of days and weeks. Time became measureless. He was experiencing his heaviest discouragement since his capture, which, now, seemed so long ago, when he was that other person, that impetuous and idealistic

Paul Latimer Benedict, the artist. Yet, rested and free of fear for his life, at least for the present, he found his mind returning irresistibly to his work, longing to record the flood of vivid impressions around him.

On a lazy afternoon, he saw his captor spread a huge buffalo robe on the ground and over it, carefully, reverently, lay a decorated white hide, and take up a slim stick, dip the chewed end into a small wooden mortar, and draw on the hide.

Surrendering to a joyful excitement, Paul forgot all else. He slipped quietly over and stood still, not too close, straining to see. His gaze fell on flat, naturalistic figures painted in profile. Figures of horses and men, red and yellow and blue, the sun and moon above the small scenes. Did the hide represent a sort of tribal calendar? Not of days and months, instead of events to mark the seasons?

Suddenly the Indian discovered him and waved him away and Paul, disappointed, moved away.

One morning early he walked upstream to wash. Below him two Indians boys were driving the family pony herd to water. Paul scrubbed to his waist and hand-dried himself, his rubbed body tingling to the breeze fanning through the canyon. He had noticed the cooler mornings and nights, and he guessed September had come.

The racket of the driven animals reached him as a muffled drumming, and of hoofs clacking on loose rocks and crunching gravel as the bunch swept in to drink. He pulled on his buckskin shirt and idly watched these wild-born creatures, affected as always by their vivid, natural colors, watching the vaulting sun rays catch a mélange of reds and browns and whites and blacks and roans.

The Indian boys were talking back and forth, their young voices light and clear.

"They say Straight Lance wants to lead a raid against the Utes. I wish we could go."

"We're too young. Straight Lance won't take us."

Paul stood entranced, his lips parting, unable to believe his ears, too startled to move. Why, he understood them! Every word! He did! He knew exactly what they had said. It was as if a golden tide of light were dispelling the darkness of his fettered mind.

Suddenly, joyfully, he went shouting downstream, unmindful of heads emerging from tipis, of old women pausing from wood-gathering to stare at the amusing white captive acting foolish so early in the morning.

Now able to understand, he chattered like a magpie whenever an Indian would listen to him, hungry to learn all things. And he would sit around the village just to listen to the cackling, scolding women, and the family wrangles, the joys, the prayers, the smoke talks of the men.

These unforgiving savages were Kiowas, he learned, an autonomous and loosely organized band, and they called themselves the Whirlwind People, or Those-Who-Live-Far-Away, and they spoke in derision of their tribesmen living on the reservation near the Soldier House on Medicine Bluff, which Paul understood meant Fort Sill, Indian Territory. The Whirlwind People. He liked the appellation. It fit them. It excited him. It evoked images of dust devils and horses as red as blood and black torrents of buffalo and boundless grass swells.

He learned names. His captor was Straight Lance and his childless wife was Star Woman. Paul's old enemy, the braggart, was Bear Neck, the spoiled son of a prominent man.

Where he had supposed none existed, Paul discerned strict lines of caste based chiefly on war exploits and wealth in horses. Bravery and generosity were the most important qualities of a Kiowa's life; how much better to perish in battle while feeling the full vigor of life than to become an old man, unable to hunt or fight, ailing, one's eyesight dim, one's teeth gone, unable to enjoy buffalo meat, and finally "thrown away to die on the prairie."

The highest warrior society was the Koitsenko, The Ten Bravest; to be leader of the band meant becoming an important chief or band leader, a *topadok'i*.

He heard Bear Neck's mother, spiteful, sharp-tongued, taunt Star Woman:

"Your husband is not a great warrior. He is only a minor chief."

Star Woman had a smooth, broad face and a large, well-shaped mouth. And wide eyes closer to black than brown, her aquiline nose flaring proudly at the nostrils, her hair so black it looked blue, parted in the center and combed straight down, loose, falling across her shoulders. Another face to paint, Paul thought.

He saw her lay down her hide-fleshing tool, a piece of iron attached to a curved bone handle. "He will be an important chief someday, one of The Ten Bravest. He led the last big war party. They took scalps. Everybody came back. He is wise as well."

"Your husband"—the older voice shrilled—"kept my son from taking his first scalp."

Star Woman slumped in laughter. "That miserable *Tejano*'s—when he had no weapon to defend himself?"

The older woman slunk away.

When Paul could converse with ease, he sought Straight Lance and told him, "I want you to free me. I have never fought your people. I am not a *Tejano*. I come from where the sun rises."

"You had *Tejano* hobbles on your horse. You are blue-eyed and light-haired like many *Tejanos* we fight."

"The hobbles belonged to my guide, the man

whose long black hair your war party took in the mountains."

"A coward's hair. He fought like a calf, bleating all the time."

Carefully, Paul said, "Just the same, you had no right to kill him. He had never hurt you."

"A dog white man and you ask why we killed him?" The indignant ring of the voice made Paul suck in his breath. "Yellow Horse took the scalp. A white man killed his father on the Arrowhead River. We gave him the honor to make things even."

"Just any white man's scalp?" Paul said, with weariness. "Even though my guide did not kill Yellow Horse's father?"

"Why not?" Straight Lance flung up a hand and brought it down, a chopping gesture of finality. "*Tejanos* kill all Kiowas on sight."

Paul didn't doubt it. Eye for an eye—that was the way both sides played the senseless game, piling hate on hate. And his mind reached out as it did so often these days, questioning, "Why have you let me live?"

"I'm the only warrior in the band with a *Tejano* slave. Could I let Bear Neck, who has no standing as a warrior, kill what was mine? I am proud." And, upon that, quickly, Paul heard the special scoffing tone Straight Lance seemed to employ whenever he mentioned the white race:

"Your tongue flaps like a crow's wing. All

white men talk too much, just as all white men are cowards." He started to go.

"Listen to me," Paul said, aware that he must speak further if he played on his captor's ambition. "Your village is small. You are poor in trade goods. Back where my home is, where the sun rises, I have money, much money," and he crooked his thumb and forefinger to form the sign for metal or money. "I will pay you much money if you let me go back to my people. That, or I will pay you much trade goods."

Paul received a smoky glare in rebuttal, with a dash of haughty pride, and he thought again how abruptly these savages could swing from one extreme to another, from joy to anger, from generosity to cruelty, from stoic mien to self-mutilating grief.

"Let you go—so you can tell the *Tejanos* and the pony soldiers where we camp? This is our best place. The hardest to find. Here the women and children are happiest. There is plenty to eat. Buffalo on all sides of us. Plenty water. Plenty grass. No white-eyes around."

"I won't tell where the village is," Paul swore, summoning all his earnestness. "I give you my word," he promised.

"All white men are liars."

"My word is from the heart," Paul said and swept his hand out from his left breast. "I will buy heap trade goods. Have them brought where you say. Someplace the white-eyes don't know about. We can use Indian guides."

A pause. An intensity swept out of the dark eyes, a calculation, a new and bright hunger running all through the lean face. "Rifles? New rifles?"

Paul was caught. "No rifles," he said, after a moment. "I don't want you to go on killing people."

Before he could say more, the Kiowa was striding off.

"Wait," Paul called. "There's something else. If you're going to hold me here like a mule, I want you to call me by my name. It's Paul."

The Indian turned and Paul saw the high amusement that he resented, the belittling eyes, the way the Kiowa's lips thinned as he turned up one corner of his mouth.

"Your name," he said, "is *Tejan—Tejan* it will be."

From that time on Paul set about planning his escape on foot; first, caching a supply of dried buffalo meat. He scrounged a long-necked water gourd, on it geometric designs, affixed a rawhide string to the neck, and thus he could carry it like a canteen. He fashioned an extra pair of moccasins, rawhide for the sole, buckskin for the upper parts, sewing them together with sinew.

By listening to the men, he gained a clearer picture of the country. According to his reckonings and his memory of the long-ago map, the nearest settlements lay southward where the hated white hunters were slaughtering buffalo for their hides alone, probably along the Clear Fork of the Brazos, or far northward into Kansas, across the Arkansas River, which the Kiowas called the Arrowhead River.

But the vast distances in between discouraged him, and he doubted that he could find either destination. Gradually a much simpler logic took over his thinking. Why not leave the canyon as he had entered it, but instead of traveling due south, which the Indians might expect, take the longer route and make southeast, roughly retracing the war party's trail? By holding a southeasterly course, he could reach Red River and follow it on down to the first settlement on the Texas side bordering the Indian Territory.

He began to taste a restless excitement. He had imagined alternatives before. This was different. He could make it—once he got away, and if he hoarded his water, if he found more water, if he kept his head. The Indians themselves had conditioned him for the attempt, hardened him and forced him to learn the necessity of endurance to survive in a land as cruel as the Whirlwinds.

However, boys were grazing pony herds down the canyon, and his captor, seeming to sense Paul's intention, watched him and so did the other Indians. Sometimes at night Paul heard movements in the brush around his hut. His impatience gnawed. Feeling the cooler nights, he wondered when the first snow came to the Plains. If he dallied many weeks longer, he would have to winter with the Kiowas.

He woke in darkness, hearing a light rustling. His first thought was of his night-prowling watchers, except the noise was too gentle and it came from overhead, more like a caressing patter —rain. He'd almost forgotten what it sounded like out here. He lay back and burrowed deeper into the old buffalo robe, content, sleepily listening to the first salvo of thunder and the wind rising, the rain whipping faster.

His drowsy brain seemed to spin and spring awake the instant he flattened out. *Now,* it shook him, *now.* He could escape while the Indians were closing tipi flaps and staying under cover.

As he started down the canyon, the howling wind flung rain shot against the back of his neck and head and the flanks of his bearded cheeks. Drawing the buffalo robe over his head like a hood, he let the tailing storm boost him along, aware of an unmatched exhilaration. Lightning blazed and he flinched and saw the ghostly triangles of lodges and dark figures scurrying there, hearing the hurried blows of wooden pegs being pounded tighter to secure the hide coverings. When no figure ran toward him, he stole past and the shapes dissolved behind the sheeny curtain of blackness spangled with slanting rain.

After some distance, unable to distinguish ahead of him, he realized he was facing the unoccupied side of the canyon. But there was a way, the shallow stream; tentatively, he moved on until he felt water rising around his moccasins, and he turned downstream, using it as his guide.

Lightning tore the murk apart. Jerked taut, he caught the panicky racket of frightened horses; through the searing glare of another flash his searching eyes found them like a gaudy print splashed against the rough canyon wall. A glistening, churning mass of nervous horseflesh, loosely held there by the herd boys. As the sky went black again, he waded to the opposite bank and hurried on.

After what seemed a long spell, his senses told him that the canyon wall no longer towered above him on his left. Minutes ago, he had lost the little stream. Turning to find his bearings, he made out the wall's faint outline, high and ragged, against the calming sky. That meant the canyon was widening, that he had reached its mouth and ahead lay open country. The storm still rumbled back there, but it was breaking up and the wind had dropped.

A feeling started up, reaching higher and higher: He was free. He couldn't believe it, but he was free at last.

Chapter 6

He swung into a dog trot. Beyond him the moonlight was as water and the dim folds of land as the swells of an enormous sea. Behind him, grumbling, he could hear the hollow voice of the storm passing eastward.

Thought of the Indian camp stirring sent him plunging into the murk, his little hoard of dried meat and his few belongings wrapped in the buffalo robe, his gourd canteen on the rawhide strap slapping at his side.

Shortly, he was stumbling up and down, over rocky footing, through brush, traveling blindly. Slackening pace, he reasoned that he would be in the breaks several hours more, possibly until morning. He foresaw one slim consolation in that. This choppy country, with its vicious stretches of red clay badlands, afforded a plenitude of cover should he sight pursuers. He remembered also from having come afoot through here with the war party: water as bitter as gall, distressful to the stomach. The Kiowas, letting him drink some, unwarned, then laughing at the face he made.

He legged up an uneven slope and started down it, stumbling, groping, just half-seeing through the deceptive dimness. There was no warning. He felt his right foot slip and come down on emptiness, and then he was falling and clutching.

He struck flatly on loose rock, at the last moment managing to keep his head up. Pain gouged through his right rib cage and he heard a squashed popping. He lay there stunned, straining to regain his breathing. Under him he heard a gurgling, gone almost at once. With a twist of his body, he came frantically out of his daze and groped for his canteen, dreading, knowing, and picked up its wreckage, each wet piece like life itself slipping through his fingers.

A cold panic seized him by the throat. Looking upward, he saw the side of the rocky wash down which he had fallen.

Shaken, he got up and took an accounting of himself. His right hip hurt and his ribs ached where the gourd had crushed against him. Otherwise, the thick buffalo robe had cushioned his fall. All his precious water was gone, every drop.

Daylight found him free of the breaks, upon land that pitched and tossed, his eyes meeting flexings of short-grass prairie dotted with spiny yuccas and clumps of prickly pear. Feeling thirst, he put a pebble in his mouth and kept going.

Often he looked back and always he saw no pursuit. From time to time he eyed the sun to keep himself heading southeast, walking and jogging. He rested and ate a piece of the dried meat, and when he struck ahead he felt stronger, goaded by the hopeful expectation of finding a branch or creek or pool of water; but the reddish earth was as dry as powder. The storm hadn't passed this way. He made on.

He came to a place where the prairie seemed to be a trembling brown mass—buffalo. Approaching closer, he saw the solemn beasts plodding south-west into the steady wind; he noted their peculiar, nodding gait. Bulls and cows mixed together, for the Kiowas said this was still the moon when the cows were in season, begun in midsummer. He studied them, half-submerged in thought, not a little fascinated, thinking it odd how hell-bent they seemed, guided by instinct to some mysterious destination. And he experienced the terribly important impulse to sketch them, to re-create them on paper before they passed from mother earth for all time, and because Paul Latimer Benedict might not see them again.

Another thought crowded in. Couldn't the buffalo be going to water? Why not? It seemed logical.

He waited until they had passed—a thousand or more, he guessed—and swung in behind them, following their spreading banner of yellow dust. He had gone but a short distance when a large bull dropped out and turned toward Paul with lowered head, suspicious, belligerent, building up to charge.

Paul felt like laughing, and he knew what a Kiowa would say: "Go on—I won't steal your women," and, by that, he realized for the first time that he was beginning to think like an Indian.

He stayed back. When the bull rejoined the herd, Paul trailed them for more than an hour. By then he was tiring and the buffalo were rumbling down onto a huge flat, raising a high veil of dust, and Paul, taking his look from the backbone of a ridge above the flat, hopefully raised his eyes to catch the shine of water.

Suddenly he slumped to his knees, his breath let out. There was no stream down there. The buffalo were plodding on southwest, never pausing, and he couldn't chance following them any longer. He needed rest. His throat felt on fire.

That evening he ate another piece of dried meat, which increased his thirst. Trying not to think of water, he rolled up in the buffalo robe and fell into a tossing sleep, and dreamed of the cool spring under the oaks near his childhood Maryland home.

Hours later, it seemed, he roused to a powerful, constant sound. A *roo-roo-ooo*. A low rumbling carrying from far away across the clear, star-speckled night. A bellowing. He recognized it, he'd heard it at night in his canyon hut, though never so close. The voices of hundreds, maybe thousands, of buffalo bulls calling, mating, challenging.

Although his robe felt snug against the prairie

chill, his thirst kept pestering him to wakeful-ness, and when daylight broke he ate sparingly and set out southeast.

In no time at all the dreadful dryness took him again. He placed the round pebble in his mouth, conscious that he was weaker this morning than yesterday. He recognized none of his surroundings; everything had a glazed monotony—the far swells of grass, the occa-sional draws and gullies exposing the raw flesh of the reddish earth. So much grass, he thought, and yet no water. Even the soft blue sky had changed to a pitiless dome of whitish light, and the sun wasn't really a sun but a smoky gun barrel holding its searing bead on him as he struggled across this infinite prairie world.

When the sun punished him from straight over-head, he was toiling up the long slope of another grassy rise. By the time he gained the crest he was swaying, leg muscles twitching, his throat like straw. As he squinted for signs of water, a glassy haze threw back a weird unreality, a hellish glare.

Intently, he trailed his gaze from left to right, and shook his head and dropped to the grass, facing southeast, while a puzzlement pecked at his weary mind. What had the Kiowas done for water last spring while driving him like a tamed horse? A detached and logical part of him seemed to answer: *Why, that was the rainy season, Paul, and don't you remember the pools of fresh water and the little springs the Indians knew just where to find? And how they carried water in the buffalo paunches?*

Trouble was there could be a seep spring within fifty yards of him and he'd never see it, the way the heat distorted objects.

He stumbled up and sagged down the slope at a stiff-legged walk, his right arm hanging loosely, his left cuddling the old buffalo robe. As hot and burdensome as it was, he couldn't leave it. A robe meant a bed at night and shade during the day.

He was beginning to doubt his vision and judgment; at times he seemed to see double. Or was that the heat waves again? Did those specks he sighted way off there raising dust mean anything? Were they real? Yet, when he turned toward them a second time, the specks were not only still visible, but more distinct.

Suspicious, Paul stopped to hand-shade his eyes for a longer scrutiny. Not buffalo. He knew buffalo; they ran in bigger bunches. Going forward, he covered about a mile to a rise and looked from there. The specks were streaming toward him from the southwest, strung out, creating long tails of dust.

He felt a start. Horses? Horsemen? He hunkered down, hastened by the fear of being outlined here on this high place. Awhile and he huffed out his relief between clenched teeth, for the horses were riderless. Besides, the Kiowas would come from the northwest, if they came. By now the horses were dipping down into a grassy draw. They disappeared suddenly. Wild horses. Mustangs.

He had all the patience of an Indian while he waited for them to come out. Minutes; long minutes. One by one, he saw them straggle out and begin grazing.

A dead certainty plunged through him. They'd come for water.

He sprang with the thought, keeping the draw in sight, marking the location by a knoll on the left. His exhaustion fell away from him and he hurried into a trot, downslope and up, never mind the easiest way, taking the harder shortcut, jumping gullies, climbing gravelly slopes.

Approaching above the draw, making a racket in his haste, he saw the mustangs throw up their heads and eye him curiously. He ran to the edge of the draw and the moment he looked down and caught the gleam of water, a dizzy weakness seized him. A strangled shout, and he went sliding and pawing to the bottom and rushed staggering to the pool at the base of the reddish-white rocks.

On his knees, he buried his face in the cool water and gulped. One swallow and he shrank back, spitting. It tasted like gall, like brine. And as that meaning flashed over him he could feel something breaking up inside him, his face crumbling, his chest choking, and he bowed his head in his hands and wept, great fat drops of tears gliding off his bearded cheeks. Even very little of the water would make him ill.

When he lifted his head the mustangs had vanished. Ever so slowly his mind took charge. There was, after all, something he could do for his deprived body, and, stripping, he waded into the pool and sat, splashing himself, soaking his hair and beard, sipping water from his cupped hand and holding it in his mouth, letting just a few drops trickle down his begging throat, willing himself not to drink more. Without warning, the dam of his resolve broke and he gulped a big swallow, another and another, before he could control his craving.

Feeling refreshed when he left the pool, he used up the dying afternoon alternately resting in the shade of the high bank and soaking his body; now and then, when his thirst became unbearable, he allowed himself a tiny sip of water. Toward evening he ate a strip of meat. A vague unease warned him away from even another tiny swallow. Just before he dozed off he heard the bulls commence their bold *rooing*. Later he began to toss uneasily, dreaming of the sweet water at the cool spring under the old oaks at home and drinking his fill.

Afterward, as the night advanced, he stiffened to the first painful onrush of stomach cramps, and thereafter he slept no more, his body bathed with sweat. By daylight he was too weak and upset to stand for long, and his feverish body cried for sweet water. A piece of buffalo meat, carefully consumed, gave him strength. On that will, around nine o'clock sun, he lurched up and reeled away, ever southeast, in his left arm the robe, his right pressed to his aching bowels.

All that morning he straggled through a nauseous haze that worsened with his thirst. By noon his mouth and throat were afire again. That was when he noticed his tongue was swelling, when he tried to shout and his voice came out a hoarse croak. A panicky fear, close to terror, clutched him and squeezed his brain into a tight ball.

About then he caught sight of a strange lake shimmering off there, so cool-looking and near. *Just out there yonder on the flat, Paul. Not far, Paul.* He ran toward it, ran and ran until he sank strengthless to the grass; and when he raised up and squinted through the dancing heat waves, he saw the lake still the same distance from him, as vast and strange and cool as before, and the shivering waters seemed to beckon him onward.

He staggered up, affected by a nameless desire to laugh. How absurd that he couldn't reach the lake. Wasn't he a fast walker? He was. Hadn't he legged it all the way from the Wichita Mountains to the canyon? He had. *Just yonder there on the flat, Paul. Not far.*

He made off, fiercely determined to get there this time, striding, striding. But when he dropped again, winded, one hand outstretched toward it, the lake was still no closer, and the flat lay freckled with the drifting shadows of passing clouds, and the prairie seemed to stir and shift, as if alive, and the heat waves rained showers of splintered glass, jeweled in flickering, quicksilver images.

That was when he knew he never could reach the lake, and then he saw the images no more, because he was falling backward. The last Paul remembered was the molten eye of the sun glaring down at him from the reddish whirlpool of the merciless sky . . .

His next sensation was of a wonderful coolness on his face, faint but real. He touched his cheek and felt a wetness.

He opened his eyes. Through the sun glare above him towered a blurred figure. A coppery, naked torso. A hawkish face like a copper plate.

"*Tejan*," he heard a deep voice say. At the sound Paul struggled toward a dim and elusive recognition. "*Tejan*," the voice repeated.

The strangest of joys passed through Paul, a kind of irony as well. The voice was his captor's, though he had no fear. For he was past fear. He felt the shock of water sprinkling his face, felt a hard-muscled arm lifting him to a sitting position, and he tasted water and felt it running wasted down his beard, and desperately he cupped his hands to save it. That single taste set off a wild and uncontrollable craving. He snatched for the buffalo paunch with both hands. Straight Lance jerked the water paunch away.

"You want to die?"

That enraged Paul. He summoned the strength to rise, to grope wildly for the paunch. The sudden exertion left him powerless. He flopped to the ground, too weak to lift his head.

Afterward, he was conscious of the swaying motion of a horse, of hands holding him fast. He did not recall when the horse stopped. When his mind cleared he saw that he lay within the latticed shade of a mesquite.

Straight Lance rationed him another sip, and presently another, and he said, "*Tejan*, only a fool would come the way you did—on foot, through the bad-water country." He shook his head. "All white men are fools."

"The water made me sick," Paul groaned and discovered that he could speak with some ease now. He eyed the paunch. "I see you found some sweet water."

"I brought water. We Kiowas are not fools, and we know where the springs are."

"I fell and broke my water gourd," Paul said, annoyed at the savage show of superiority. "And don't tell me that all white men are clumsy. It happened in the dark, the night I escaped. I couldn't see."

"One gourdful of water wasn't enough." The

black eyes glinted ridicule. "There was water all around you, *Tejan*." Paul frowned as the Indian crossed to a prickly pear and drew his knife, slashed and cut off stickers and peeling, sliced two pieces and held them out to Paul, who, not moving, just eyed them with suspicion.

"Take one," the other told him, amused. "Not poison. Put it in your mouth. Had you known you could have escaped." When Paul still didn't accept, the Kiowa took a piece and began chewing it. Paul, hesitating, tried the other piece then. It tasted surprisingly good, tart like an apple.

"One piece of pear will keep a man's mouth from getting dry for a long time," the assured voice said.

"Why tell me?" Paul mocked him, inviting contempt. "I'm just a fool white man." It rankled him to remember the many prickly pear clumps he had passed when he was foolishly chasing the mirage. "Why did you come after me? Why didn't you let me die?"

"In one way that would be good. Because white men made sorrow come to our camp. They killed my father, my two brothers. My mother has only the stubs of her fingers left." He made a violent gesture. "I hate all white men—everywhere." His eyes flashed. "But you, *Tejan*, you have brought me power, and power comes in many ways. In vision quests, when a man starves his body to free the spirit; sometimes when a man is alone on the prairie or in the mountains; sometimes when he is hurt. Yes, *Tejan*, you have given me much power."

"Power?" Paul felt like sneering. "That's impossible." He saw anger swell the harsh features.

"Ever since I captured you my power has been strong. I feel it here." And the Kiowa touched his naked chest over the heart. "And I know it here." And he touched his forehead.

"A white man would say I bring you luck," Paul said, half-mocking. "Still you hate me and I have never harmed you or your people. How can you hate me when you say I bring you power?"

He couldn't see his captor's face. He was fumbling inside the rawhide saddlebag tied on his horse, and behind him the sun was lowering itself into a bed of flames. No more was said.

They camped there that night. Next morning Paul was too weak to walk and Straight Lance helped him mount, then took the reins to lead the horse.

"I see you don't trust me," Paul said, pretending dismay, "else you would let me hold the reins."

"You are a white man."

That afternoon the paunch was down to a few sloshes of murky water when the Kiowa entered the neck of a rocky wash. The horse threw up its head, scenting the wind, and quickened gait. Paul saw they traveled a dim trail. It wasn't very long until the Indian paused, and Paul saw the oval pool of a spring seeping beneath reddish rocks and the sparkling thread of water trickling down another arm of the wash.

Side by side, the three of them drank the sweet water, the horse in between. The Indian raised up first, then Paul, then the horse. Paul, dipping with his hands, deluged his body, over and over. Already he was feeling stronger.

"This is the sweetest water that ever fell upon earth," he said, gratified.

An unusual admission of pleasure changed the dark face. "No white man could find it," the Kiowa vowed, his expression turning harsh again.

"True," Paul conceded, and impulsively: "Since you say I'm your power, that I make you strong, can't we be friends—even if I am your captive?"

"You are a white man."

"You saved my life. I was just about gone. I am grateful."

"What I saved was my power."

"We can be friends," Paul insisted.

The Kiowa's response was to turn away and sink the paunch in the pool; when it filled, he tied it on the Spanish saddle, stabbed Paul his contempt, and mounted.

Paul caught the shift immediately. They were back in the captor-captive relationship that he resented so much as a man, and once again he was totally dependent on the other for water and food. Sighing, he rose and swung into a weak-legged walk, ahead of the horse.

Near the close of the second day, when they approached the mouth of the canyon leading to the village, he set himself for the feel of the hissing rope about his neck, for the savage yank to remind him of his captivity. Nothing occurred. He turned to see why and the Kiowa inclined his head for Paul to go on.

The second morning after Paul's return, Straight Lance, wearing only breechclout and moccasins, took a buffalo robe, a white soapstone pipe, tobacco, flint and steel for fire-making, and vanished upcanyon on a vision quest.

On the morning of the fourth day, his captor had not returned and Paul was gloomily mending a wall of his miserable hut. His mind kept wandering, dreading the late fall and long winter to be spent among the Kiowas. An alternative suggested itself. If the band moved west or northwest, soon, he might escape to the New Mexican settlements.

The excitement of voices rising above the camp's indolent murmur broke his preoccupation. He could hear the scuff and slap of hurrying moccasined feet. Dropping the slender cedar branch he was about to begin weaving through the stakes supporting the side of the hut, he went outside and crossed to the camp. Everybody was staring upcanyon.

Paul saw a reeling figure. Crying, the people streamed out of the village, and Paul, following, scarcely recognized his captor, his black hair hanging loose and dusty, his face haggard, his body drawn to a wolfish thinness. But the brilliance lighting up the dark caverns of the eyes was not a sickness.

No one spoke a word to him.

Paul in that moment thought as a Whirlwind Kiowa and understood: To speak to a man returning from fasting and praying might destroy his power.

Neither did Straight Lance speak or show recognition. He reeled on toward his tipi, past Star Woman and his mother, the latter's grief-scarred face a mirror of the dread Indian women felt for their men preparing to ride into danger.

Shortly, men began going to Straight Lance's tipi. Paul, having seen the order of events before, idled back to his hut. By these primitive rules you organized a war party for scalps or a raiding party for plunder or a vengeance party for the sole purpose of "getting even," killing as many of the enemy as the enemy had killed of the band in its last attack. At this very moment the ceremony-doting Indians were discussing his captor's power, in short the guidance or omen he had received through a vision or dream. After eating, they would smoke the pipe. Paul sat in the sun and fell into a deep dejection, thinking again of escape.

Toward the middle of the afternoon he heard the camp crier, an elder named Heap-of-Bulls, calling, "Straight Lance's power is strong. He will lead a raiding party against the Utes. All of you who want to go get ready."

Paul saw warriors stirring, among them Red Calf and Wolf-Appearing, both experienced raiders, and the spoiled and boastful Bear Neck. It was common talk that Bear Neck, having no power of his own, though he had prayed for it, must follow well-known warriors to build his own lack of reputation.

Old Heap-of-Bulls continued to stroll about the lodges as he called. Paul turned sharply, a new intentness to his listening. The Utes? Where was their country? He had only a vague idea. When the old crier finished and rested, Paul crossed over to him. "The Ute country—where is it?"

Not recently had he met such raw scorn. The old man was a noted warrior and buffalo slayer; it was said that he had killed his captives with a hatchet when they delayed the march, hence he had none to assist him or his aging wife about the lodge, and his sons were dead, killed in raids.

Paul had no sympathy for him. He asked again.

Northwest, the drawn and veined hand pointed. That was all. The coals of the black stare dismissed the white man.

"North of the *Comanchero* country?" Paul kept on, receiving an indifferent nod, and the eroded old face signified that even a stupid *Tejano* should know. Paul left, gripped with excitement. That was all he needed to know. It meant northern New Mexico or southern Colorado, in the mountains.

He could hear Straight Lance drumming and singing. Warriors were ducking in and out of the big lodge. His captor had his hide shield on a scaffold beside the doorway to absorb the sun's medicine rays.

Paul was gravitating that way before he was quite certain of his purpose, falling in behind a young Indian. He entered the spacious lodge and sat cross-legged on a robe. His captor was resting at the moment, his head bowed. As the lodge filled with new callers, Straight Lance roused himself and lighted his soapstone pipe, gingerly taking a coal from the fire, and passed the pipe to his left. The first man accepted it with ceremony, and blew smoke to the sky, next the four directions, and passed it. The next man declined to smoke, as did the next one. Paul knew why: They did not care to go. Fighting was an individual choice. No man had to go.

Not until the pipe reached Paul did his captor discover him. Through the gloom it was curious to see his pure surprise, then astonishment, to see emotion affect the harsh features, now painted, and alter their savagery to a somewhat civilized look.

Solemnly, Paul drew the kinnikinnick tobacco smoke from the long wooden stem and expelled it upward; now a southward puff over his shoulder, and one to the west, the north, the east, as he had observed the others doing. Done, he passed the pipe. As it left his hand an odd tremor of excitement crept over him.

Onward the pipe moved, ceremoniously, and after a time, when it reached Straight Lance, the men rose quietly to leave. Paul stayed. Only he remained when he saw his captor, impassive and as unmoving as a painted idol, turn to him:

"You can't go." An incredulous tone. "You—a white man."

"Not just *a* white man. I am your power. Remember? You need me."

"Why do you want to go?" A tremendous scowl furrowed the broad forehead. He seemed at loss. "I don't understand, even though I know about your power."

"I am tired of the camp. There is nothing for me to do."

"You're a captive. You have to do as you're told."

"I will need to borrow a horse. You have plenty." And when the Kiowa leaned back, dumfounded, Paul said, almost gaily, "Make it a good, gentle horse. I haven't ridden in a long time."

"We will take plenty horses," the Indian boasted. "We Kiowas are great horse-takers. But what if the Utes discover us? There may be a big fight. What then? Would you help fight them?"

"I wouldn't kill a man in order to steal his horses," Paul said, not hesitating, and saw the other's immediate disgust.

"I don't understand you white-eyes. At times you kill for no reason at all. My father was riding along on the prairie. Soldiers rode up and killed him."

"We whites are not all alike."

"It is good to kill your enemies. It makes you feel good." A pause of sudden alarm. "No white man has ever ridden with us Whirlwinds. You could spoil the medicine."

"How could I do that," Paul contradicted, "when I have made your power stronger? You said so yourself. I bring you luck—remember? You may need me along to make certain everybody comes home and there is no mourning in the lodges." He was talking big, like a Whirlwind. He had learned that well from observation, puffing out his chest, holding his head back, curling his lips for arrogance, making them heavy. He was standing as he finished, before he could be denied again; but as he ducked through the flap opening, he wondered if his captor had suspected his intent.

Restless, he roamed downcanyon to watch boys racing ponies and playing war, yipping like coyotes, cavorting like acrobats all over the bareback ponies, hanging like black-haired burrs on first one side, then the other, using the sweaty ponies as shields between themselves and the imaginary enemy. The trick, Paul saw, besides hooking one leg over the pony's backbone, was the rope plaited into the mane, and slipped over the youth's head and his outside arm, thus freeing both hands for shooting or picking up objects while the pony ran full speed.

One slim boy got down and sprawled, assuming the role of a wounded warrior. At once two riders bore down on him. Racing neck and neck, sweeping low, arms outstretched, they picked up their fallen comrade between them and swung him to safety in front of one of the riders. Over and over they practiced the stunt.

The afternoon was waning when he started back, darkly discouraged. He passed the scattering of lodges and came in sight of his wretched hut. He held his glance there and stopped dead, struck by astonishment.

A brown horse stood tied by the hut.

Paul ran over, as excited as any boy, visualizing a swift and clean-limbed steed eventually bearing him back to civilization. One close look and his excitement dulled. To be sure, a gentle horse, as he had asked for. Likewise, an old horse, heavy-footed and sluggish, standing hipshot. A gentle gelding he recalled seeing Star Woman riding. A gentle horse to drag the long cedar *travois* poles. A gentle horse for children to ride, too slow for Paul to outrace anyone on. Still, he couldn't help grinning over his own comeuppance. His captor had both granted his wish and seen through his ruse. Even so, Paul was going. He was.

Mounting the bare back and riding off, he felt his spirits lift a little. The old fellow was slow, but he reined nicely, had an easy trot, and he seemed sturdy.

Returning to the hut, he fashioned a crude saddle pad of buffalo hide and strapped it on the horse. Straight Lance's singing and drumming reached Paul again, and he remembered it was customary for warriors to leave during the night after they had held their dance—daytime was bad medicine. Because he did not intend to come back here, Paul gathered up his possessions and supplies. The cherished buffalo robe he would need in the high country, an extra pair of moccasins, his supply of dried meat and mesquite meal. Long ago he had discarded the crude bow and arrows. He hadn't even a dull knife.

At twilight he heard the singing and drumming cease. Paul ate, waiting for the first drumthrobs calling the warrior-dancers. Then camp became unusually still. As darkness crept in, and the eroded walls of the canyon closed shutters on the scarlet and yellow world beyond, he heard the single stroke on a rawhide drumskin. Other drummers joined at once; suddenly all the drummers were singing, their voices high and piercing, somehow sad.

It was time to leave. Paul led the gelding into the village and tied up near the lighted dance circle. The gentle old horse sagged on the spot, content to rest again.

And as Paul stood there, listening to the rise and fall of the drumming, seeing the bounding dancers, some concealed emotion within him seemed to respond, a wild tingling.

His captor wore new buckskins and new moccasins, no war bonnet, and his streaked face displayed his medicine colors of blue and yellow. He was singing as he danced, a simple song, yet solemn and moving, deep and strong:

Riding tonight,
  Going a long way.
Think of us,
  Far in the mountains.

He was singing the Going-Away Song. He sang it four times, and other men sang.

An old warrior—it was Heap-of-Bulls—came out and signed that he wished to tell a story. While the dancers rested, he recounted a successful raid against the Utes many years ago in which he had struck two coups and taken many horses.

Paul hadn't moved. He felt strange as the drumming picked up and the dancers returned. He was not conscious of motion. He had watched like a spectator, absorbed, observing, and only now could he feel himself advancing on the circle. At once, quite close, he saw the leaping fire and the weaving figures, and just then did he sense that he was going to dance with them.

He stamped his moccasined feet, bobbing and twisting and crouching, yet aware of no clumsiness, no sense of intrusion, and no one signed for him to leave. Everything was so strange and somehow exalting, even though he sang no song.

He danced, then rested, and a knowing told him that he had circled four times, the medicine number. It was strange that he knew.

Now Straight Lance was leaving the circle, the volunteers following on that signal. The drums became still. The only sound Paul heard was the soft scuffing of rawhide soles as the departing warriors went to their horses. Paul did likewise, mounted, and followed them.

When the warriors had assembled, Straight Lance motioned Paul to a place beside him. No word was said. And Paul understood: The leader's power must be protected. And, once again, he thought how extraordinary that, at times, his mind traveled like a Kiowa's.

As the raiding party swung upcanyon, Paul heard a prayer-song rise like a following wind. A high-pitched voice crying for them, crying for their safe return. It sounded like the same quavering voice he had heard the night of his torture at the stake.

Chapter 7

Around midnight, following the pale snake of an ancient buffalo trail winding northward up the canyon floor, Paul saw his captor turn off and prepare to sleep. No one had spoken since leaving the village. Beneath the great wash of moonlight the sagebrush seemed dipped with silver. The *hoom—hoom* of a hoot owl sounded startlingly near. High up on a canyon wall Paul heard a mourning dove utter its haunting call.

A warrior murmured in fear, in superstition.

"Go to sleep," Straight Lance broke the silence. "This will be a good raid."

For some time afterward, Paul lay awake, feeling the high-plains coolness on his bearded face as he watched the star glitter. He had no fear of the night, nor of the long journey to the *latakop*, or Ute Mountains, nor of what might happen on the raid. He was content, and his contentment puzzled him.

At dawn Bear Neck took a place behind Straight Lance, who promptly pointed for him to ride at the rear and motioned Paul to take the forward position again.

"Why do you let the white man ride up here?" Bear Neck protested. "He's never counted coup."

"Neither have you," Straight Lance said. "Get back there."

"And why did you bring no buffalo doctor with power to heal wounds, and no owl doctor with power to tell us what's going to happen?"

"I have all the power we need. Ride where I tell you or go back to the village and stay with the women."

Bear Neck turned to obey, for a leader ruled all volunteers as long as they remained with the party, but not before the young Kiowa showed Paul the knife-edge of his glittery jealousy.

The sun appeared like a golden shield, and Paul, seeing the painted canyon walls rising higher and higher, had the sensation of invading a deep and primitive solitude, a sheltering place, mysterious and brooding with age. Here and there side canyons gashed the rocky brows of the escarpments, flashing vivid clay yellows and sandstone browns, coppery reds and rich purples, and occasionally, like relics left stranded by time, shaped by the gnawing winds and sudden torrents, rose crested turrets and stout battlements, peculiar-looking peaks and solitary towers standing like solemn totems and grotesque effigies.

Paul kept turning to observe the passing hues, the fantastic shapes, the cedar-studded slopes.

On the afternoon of the next day Paul saw his captor halt and search the brokenness, that searching that Paul knew well by now. He was looking for a landmark. Not far on, when an eminence resembling a lofty lighthouse jutted up, Straight Lance took an eyebrow trail that lifted them out of the massive chasm, which the Kiowas called the *Palo Duro*, the "Canyon of the Hard Wood," and upon a great plateau where the short grass rolled before them like a foaming yellow wave, rippled by the constant wind. Paul, impressed, guessed that they had reached the Staked Plains. The Kiowas called it "The Prairie."

In the days that followed, Paul had no complaint. Save for his forward place, which Straight Lance ordered him to take each morning, the Kiowas ignored him.

Once, when they rode abreast, Paul asked his captor, "Why do you fight the Utes?"

"We have fought them ever since we left the north country," came the reply. "They are our enemies. We kill them, we steal from them. They do the same to us when we are camped farther north."

"If you want to stop the Utes from raiding you," Paul reasoned, "why don't all you Kiowas band together and wipe them out?"

He received a startled stare. "That would leave only the white-eye *Tejanos* and the pony soldiers to fight. They don't fight like Indians. They don't raid just for horses sometimes. It is always to kill us or to drive us in. Make us live in a wooden tipi. Make us put leather straps on our horses and work them like mules and pull the iron things that tear up the grass."

"Farming," Paul said, nodding approval.

"The Caddos and Wichitas are farmers, and look at them. They're going downhill."

"Someday the buffalo may be gone," Paul said thoughtfully. "Then—if your people have any-thing to eat—they will have to make things grow in the ground."

"There will be buffalo forever," Straight Lance vowed. "If the Kiowas did any farming, the women would have to do it, and they're too busy in camp."

They watered at a shallow, fresh-water lake, filled the buffalo paunches, and rode on in silence, across land as flat and treeless as a tabletop, a land of no echoes, with the solitude of a benign sea. Paul felt dwarfed to insignificance.

"You're going a long way just to steal horses," he said as they toiled away from the lake.

"And the Utes are strong and live in big villages." The dark eyes glided over Paul's face. "But my power is strong, *Tejan.* When we get there, you will see."

The Indian's belief bewildered Paul, linked, he sensed, to the mysticism and fatalism the arid plains seemed to instill in these wild people.

"This power you say I give you," Paul said. "There is no such thing. Whatever has caused you to think this . . . just happened. That's all."

The Indian rebuked him with a look. "Only a white man would say that. My power *is* strong. I feel it here." And, for emphasis, he laid his hand over his heart in the familiar gesture.

Paul scarcely noticed as the days slipped by, passing like the transient winds sucking red dust into the blue void of the sky. By now his yellow hair, a source of admiration among the vain, scalp-conscious Kiowas, hung below his shoulders. Since he had no wish to braid it as they did, he let it hang like a horse's mane, and in the eternal wind he could feel its roots plucking at his scalp as it streamed out. His gold-colored beard, growing thicker, and untouched, often drew the eyes of the smooth-faced Indians, who, using tweezers made of bone, plucked all hair from their faces and eyebrows. He rode naked to the waist, clothed only in breechclout and moccasins, drawn down to the lean of his body, thin to emaciation, though he had never felt stronger or quicker, nor had his senses felt keener.

He had learned to humor his durable old horse, which could become as obstinate as a mule when tired or exercising temperament, resisting every kick or ruse Paul could devise to stir him faster than a listless trot, a gait that he could hold for hours, neither faster nor slower, bumping along in the dusty wake of the party like the tail of a dragging kite.

There was the usual punishment of midday and afternoon sun, when the short grass actually crackled under hoofs, when mirages glittered and flickered, never still, always drifting away, always beckoning, remindful of the siren lake that had nearly enticed him to his death. But the mornings and evenings were glorious. And by dusk the breezes sprang up, and Paul, ever obsessed by colors, sat on his robe and watched the florid horizon. It was then that he became Paul Latimer Benedict again, and thoughts of his work filled his mind and the other world he had left that seemed so unreal from here, never lived.

The day Paul saw the mountains for the first time, lying like the disjointed parts of an enormous beast, Straight Lance was leading the raiders west. He then turned northwest, taking them into sear, up-and-down country that the Whirlwinds called the Bad Place, distorted and weird to the eye of a stranger like Paul, gashed with dry washes, forsaken of all life and sustenance, it seemed, until the Indians, never failing, found water before the paunches hung empty. Cold at night, a glaring desolation by day, stretches that only an Indian or Mexican could traverse, where the white heat parched dry the body's juices and shriveled the mind. A smoking hell swimming before Paul's burning eyes, a sterile wilderness of stone and sand and brush, awakening images of lurking reptilian monsters, all of which left Paul longing for the Kiowas' wind-swept prairies.

Just when he felt they were doomed forever to ride this cheerless waste, Straight Lance brought them out of a cluttered canyon and upon an expanse of prairie, level to rolling, thinly grassed, which the Kiowas called the High Grass. On the third morning Paul, hearing muttering excitement, looked north and saw the lofty crests of snow-crowned mountains.

His captor sent Red Calf and Wolf-Appearing ahead as scouts. Later, when the party came to a rushing stream, the scouts rode out of the timber, and everyone dismounted to talk. The Utes, Red Calf reported, were camped in a valley. As expected, they had many good horses; as expected, the horses were closely guarded. Then Red Calf took a stick and drew a map on the ground and described the best route to the village and marked where the village stood and where the horses grazed.

Paul got the impression of a carefully conducted game: the Utes there in their mountain valley just where the Kiowas figured to find their village, the Kiowas slipping in to steal their horses. As if both sides observed a strict set of rules, each more interested in the zest of the game than eliminating the other.

The likeness to a game recurred to Paul the next morning while riding slowly northward through drenching mountain sunshine as the scouts fanned out and reported at regular intervals, and still no sign of Ute lookouts.

Evening found the Whirlwinds hidden amid timber, conversing in the hushed tones of prairie-born people uneasy in the mountains, near enough to the village to hear dogs barking. At Paul's questioning look, his captor shrugged and said, "When a Ute dog barks, we throw it a piece of meat and go on."

Paul closed his eyes, dozing off and on, the old false sense of unreality hounding him once again. At length a floating cry invaded his consciousness, a wolf's howl up the valley. A cry that wasn't a wolfs because it echoed too much. He had learned that of all voices the human voice echoes more than any animal's in broken country; up close like this, though still some distance from the village, the difference was distinct. It was a scout's signal to come. He peeled back the robe and got up, aware of the others stirring.

Assuming his role was to remain behind with the horses and another guard or two, he did not step forward when the raiders bunched to leave. At the same moment his captor spoke into his ear:

"*Tejan*, you come with us. Bear Neck will watch the horses."

"I have no weapon."

"Here is a knife. Pray you won't need it."

"I'm no horse-taker."

"You will see. Come on."

Suddenly Paul knew why. Straight Lance needed his "power" near at hand tonight, all his strength. Nothing must go wrong. Nobody must be lost. As illogical as it all was, rooted in primitive superstitions, Paul saw that this was no time to differ. Belief gave a man strength and confidence. And, last, his captor was making certain that Paul did not steal a fast horse and escape.

The voice of the night wind sighed and moaned through the pines, as real as that of a wounded warrior tossing in agony. The Kiowas shrank still. Someone muttered uneasily, "Bad sign—bad sign."

"Are you women—afraid of every little sound?" Straight Lance belittled them, and stepped ahead, Paul alongside him.

They passed from the dark timber into moonlight so bright Paul could see his captor's stern brow and mouth banked with concentration; onward, the scouts joined them. No one asked questions. All seemed to know what to do as in an often-played game. They filed through more timber and halted on the other side.

Before many minutes Paul heard a dog bark, and now he could pick out the pale peaks of huddled lodges, like so many small sugar loaves, and, off from the village where the valley widened, a dark, unmoving mass that he knew was the grazing horse herd.

"*Tejan*, you stay here. A white man's smell scares Indian horses."

The Kiowas slipped away in pairs, angling toward the horse herd, like ghosts on the pallid night sea of the mountain grass. Every warrior carried horsehair ropes. The plan, Paul knew, wasn't to run off the entire herd, which numbered hundreds, and stir up a hard fight, but to take only as many horses as each man could lead out.

Paul watched the Kiowas melt into the farther murk of the valley. Although alone, hearing no sound except the mewing wind, even the querulous voices of the camp dogs stilled, he realized that he was more intrigued than afraid. And he wanted the Kiowas to come back. He wanted them to succeed.

Time dragged. He fidgeted and began to shiver despite his warm buckskin shirt, shoulders hunched, arms hugged to his chest. He could see no change in the dark blot of the horse herd, and he heard no outcry.

Finally, he saw slow-moving blurs bobbing across the valley floor toward him. Little by little they acquired the high-headed, long-backed shapes of led horses, and dimly, in front, the figures of their new Indian masters.

Straight Lance came in leading four horses. Paul sensed his elation as he hurried them into the timber and turned to watch the others, caressing the slim noses of his captives and holding his buckskin sleeve to their quivering nostrils for them to learn his odor.

When the last horse-taker trailed in, everyone hastened through the gloom of the hiding pines and out into the moonlight on the other side and on presently where Bear Neck stood guard. Mounting, the Kiowas led the stolen horses at a muffled walk down the valley.

Beyond earshot of the village, they trotted the horses. That for some time, no faster. And then Paul saw his captor sweep his string into a gallop.

To Paul, trailing on his old horse, which soon fell behind, the knots of headlong horses ahead of him seemed as low, wind-driven clouds racing the great golden eye of the mountain moon, and he felt the wild excitement of the Kiowas coursing through him.

Toward morning they crossed the brawling stream and halted to water and graze the horses and eat dried meat. The Ute horses, Paul observed, looked heavier than their prairie brothers; if perhaps not so fleet, just as durable and more sure-footed, accustomed to rocks and up-and-down country. Not once had he seen a Ute horse stumble.

After a short rest, his captor had the party streaming south for the High Grass, still leading the Ute horses. There was no visible pursuit. They rested again at midmorning; as they started off,

Paul heard grumbling. Several warriors urged bunching the horses now.

"We're still in Ute country," Straight Lance reminded them. "We can't handle loose horses if there's a fight. Come on. Ride hard." Paul saw the hard impatience go out of his face, saw the eyes, raking over the Kiowas, one by one, impart confidence. "All of you will live to ride into our village. I know this is true. All of you will take back some good horses."

And right there he gave Bear Neck a fine mouse-colored horse for standing guard near the Ute village. No *topadok'i*, Paul saw, could have been more generous. The Whirlwinds liked that. They forgot their complaint. Generosity was always the sign of a great man.

Paul dropped behind on the old brown nag, forced to let the poor beast idle along in his slow, jolting trot. As the hours passed, Paul even lost sight of the Kiowas at times. Now he recognized the High Grass, that broad track of treeless plain running north and south, deeply gullied on the west, whose high-desert brightness somehow suggested a tropical savanna.

Paul's pity rose for his mount. He slipped to the ground to lead him, and stood, in sympathy, considering the punished animal that had carried him these hundreds of miles. Clumsy and stubborn, but truly a gentle and brave old horse.

Dulled by the monotony of his creeping ride,

and the glittering sameness of his surroundings, and the dazzling afternoon heat, he hadn't looked behind him for some minutes. Turning now, he froze on the instant.

Dots were moving back there, looming larger by the moment, raking up long ribbons of dust. Antelope? That was his hope, but he knew he was wrong. Antelope never run toward a man. And now the dots became shapes and those shapes became horsemen, a large knot of them, and out in front flew a single rider.

A drawn breath, and Paul grasped mane and swung up like a Kiowa, clapping heels and quirting the ends of the reins across the gelding's shoulders. The old brown horse snorted and gave a startled jump, and for a moment Paul thought he was on the brink of a decent run. A few lunges, however, and he fell back into his vexatious trot, with all the resolved stubbornness of a goat.

Paul, in a tension of near-panic, waved at the Kiowas, who looked far, far away. He kept quirting and heel-digging and glancing back and waving, and although, finally, indeed, he saw the Kiowas slowing, he also saw they couldn't race back in time to help him.

Over him crashed the closing racket of hoofs, and when he turned his head again, time seemed to stand still, and for one split instant his whole life seemed to rise up before his eyes in quick, bold strokes, an unreality shattered by the deadly earnestness of the one rider tearing toward him on a powerful blue roan horse, feathered lance raised.

Paul tugged on the right-hand rein to haul the stubborn beast about. Maddeningly, the brown head inched around, the eyes walling, and then the rest of him followed, stiff-legged, crow-hopping, and then, sulking, obstinate, the old horse stopped dead.

Paul, grabbing his knife, looked up in time to see the Ute, not prepared for the other horse to halt, overrunning his target and rushing past. He made a flashing turn, whooping for courage, the blue horse pivoting and cutting back, a practiced, skillful maneuver that made Paul's heart sink.

A trained Kiowa war horse would have danced away from the Ute's charge. Instead, Paul's old plug stood his ground like the stolid, unimaginative *travois* animal he was.

There was no more time for Paul. Through a telescoping blur he caught the bobbing head of the blue horse, the perfect white star on the forehead, the painted face of the whooping young Ute, the metal-tipped lance—just before he threw up a shielding arm, before he heard horseflesh thudding together and a horse's scream and the lance swishing past his face and he felt the impact tossing him backward.

Paul crashed on his back in the grass, and the spinning immensity of the blue sky turned black, shot through with splinters of light, and he had no breath. He was gasping. He rolled over. Something glittered. His knife. He took it and pushed up and looked around. His poor old horse was down and kicking, and the handsome blue war horse, though standing, stood shaken with dragging reins. His young Ute master lay still.

A curious fascination drew Paul across; tentatively, he touched the Ute and flinched, startled, when the young man stirred and groaned, struggling to rise, gazing up at Paul, pain sliding beneath his ocher-streaked face.

Paul was repelled. It was the dark eyes. In them he read resignation and death. The young man expected Paul to take his life and his hair, for he was powerless to resist. But because he was brave he would not beg for mercy.

A drumming reached Paul. Horses coming furiously from the north. He saw two Utes, their horses neck and neck as one, and he recognized their purpose: the running pickup. Why interfere?

Backing out of the way, he found himself near the blue roan. It was beginning to perk up its fine head; in moments it would stray away. He took the rawhide reins and watched the Ute pair, hanging low, draw slightly apart and sweep in and scoop up their injured comrade without slowing the horses, and go wheeling off, racing back to the north.

The game, Paul saw, struck with admiration. A

perfect pickup. He was glad, because the young Ute looked badly hurt. Then Paul sobered. Something was wrong. Why didn't the other Utes (and there appeared to be ten or fifteen or more off there) rush in and finish him and take his hair? That was part of the deadly game as well.

That was when he remembered the Ute's lance. As he picked it up, a fresh horse racket rolled over him, this time from the west. He recoiled at the sight of more Indians fanning out of the eroded gullies, and gripping the lance tighter, he gave a gasp of relief—Kiowas.

Straight Lance, dusting up on the run, glanced from Paul, holding the reins of the blue horse, to the Utes and back to Paul, who had never seen his captor show such approval.

"*Tejan*," the Kiowa called, "you struck the Ute. You took his war horse and his lance. He rode in front. He was their chief. You've turned them into a bunch of women, afraid to fight. Look!" And he pointed north. "They're leaving. *Tejan*, you are brave!"

"Brave?" Paul blinked, agape at being praised after the farcical fight. For the first time, he saw the broad faces show him a grudging respect.

"It was my horse," he began to explain, and turned regretfully to his old beast, out of its misery now. "That is, I was trying to turn my horse . . . when the Ute's horse—"

"We all saw it," his captor cut him off. "You

fought the Ute chief in close. He had a lance—
you had just the knife. But you didn't run like a
rabbit. You met his charge. It was a great deed.
You are brave, *Tejan*!"

"I tell you I didn't do anything."

"You white-eyes," the Kiowa said, dumfounded.

"It just happened," Paul insisted, "when the
horses ran together."

"We saw you raise your arm to strike the Ute.
We saw that, *Tejan*, just before the horses ran
together. We saw the Ute fall. How did you avoid
his lance?"

Paul saw it was futile—they wouldn't believe
him. He was about to turn away when a feeling
closed in upon him. Why not let them believe
he was brave? It might lead to his freedom. He
pretended to reconsider, and after a moment he
canted back his head like a Kiowa, not too much,
and let just a trace of arrogance swell his face.
"Maybe my power was strong today, for the Ute
was brave." And they nodded, wanting him to
speak thusly, as they would have.

They were riding south, Paul on the blue
gelding, now rightfully his, when he spoke to his
captor:

"You used me as a decoy to draw the Utes into
an ambush. If they had killed me or captured
me, you'd have lost your power. Did you think of
that?"

"Would I let the Utes take my power? But

you surprised us. You turned and fought." He became thoughtful and did not speak for a while. "Your power is very strong, *Tejan*. It would not be right for me to use it all for myself—that is selfish. I remember what my father said happened to the Cheyennes after the Pawnees captured their medicine arrows years ago. Ever since, the Cheyennes have had bad times."

"I don't understand."

"I will tell you. I was wrong to use you as a decoy."

"I still don't understand," Paul said, frowning at him.

"From now on your power will be used for all the Whirlwind People. Your power belongs to the band, not to me alone. So we must guard you closer."

Chapter 8

And so that evening even Bear Neck, who had
never shown Paul any face other than scorn or
jealousy, treated him with the utmost Kiowa
deference for a man who had fought in close
and counted coup by striking the enemy and taken
a fine horse. And Paul, wisely prudent while
thinking of escape, gave up explaining what had
really happened.

But one aspect did not change and that, he soon
saw, was their careful vigil over him. After the
horse-takers had crossed the Bad Place and were
bound southeast, grass under their horses' feet
and water no longer a worry, Paul made some
rough calculations. Albuquerque should lie southwest. He decided to attempt escape that night; if
nothing more, he could ride until he came to a
river and simply follow it south. He would have
to leave without water. The Kiowas kept the
water paunches.

The night was old when at last he sat up and
observed the sleeping forms around him. As he
rose, Red Calf mumbled, turned on his side, and
returned to sleep. Paul breathed easy again.
Picking up his robe, he strayed toward the
hobbled horses. The light was just right, a film of
clouds over the face of the raiders' moon.

His pulse jumped at sight of the horses so near. Not far now. He marked the outline of his horse, the blue gelding he called Star, and stepped faster, making no sound.

He flinched back when a figure appeared to rise out of the grass at his feet, between Paul and his horse. "*Tejan*, you are restless tonight." It was his captor.

Paul found his voice. "I thought I heard something among the horses."

"To do that you brought your robe along?"

"The night is cold."

The Kiowa closed in a step, lowering his voice. "We'll wake up the camp. Let's go out a way and talk. I want you to listen to me, *Tejan*." Paul followed him. Then: "This is bad. You have performed a brave deed and we treat you like a child, watching you night and day."

"You mean like a captive," Paul said bitterly.

"Yes—a captive. I don't like that anymore."

"Then let me go. You know I wouldn't lead the soldiers to the village. Anyway, I couldn't find it."

"I'm not sure about that. You are learning fast. You would make a good Kiowa." He paused. "There is no way we can let you go back to live with the white-eyes."

"It's this absurd power belief you have," Paul said, weary of it. "It means nothing."

"Nothing—when I feel it? When I know it

works? *Tejan*, you make me feel good and strong."

Paul could see the Kiowas' harmony with nature, the way they considered all animals as beings, particularly the buffalo, their fatalism, their mysticism, their heathenish notions, their veneration of the sun—yes. But this utterly nonsensical belief in his power. He must squelch it right now.

"There's nothing to it," he said, his impulsiveness causing him to fall into English. So he repeated it in Kiowa.

"*Tejan*," the Kiowa said, before Paul could go on, "I see now what we must do for you. I will take you on a war party and you will kill a *Tejano*, and we Kiowas will adopt you into the tribe. You will find a young wife. You will be one of us."

Paul was too surprised to reply, and voices were filtering into his consciousness. The two of them had waked the camp. His chance was gone. Hereafter the Indians would watch him like brown hawks because he had a good horse.

Without another word, he made his way back and lay down. At dawn when the Kiowas stirred, he was still awake . . .

The whole camp ran out when the raiders, who had waited until daylight, rode in leading their good Ute horses, and when the Whirlwinds saw that all the raiders had returned, there was shouting and suddenly much singing, and that evening they built a big fire for the Victory Dance, and four old men, the drummers, set the great drum close to the flames so the heat would tighten the hides and make them sound full and hard.

Watching, Paul asked himself why he had come when the stone of his discouragement bore him down so heavily. He was, he sensed, at his lowest ebb since the early days of his captivity, on the edge of self-pity.

Before the drummers began, Straight Lance came out and stood in the center of the dance circle. He described the long journey across The Prairie, how they had ridden across the Bad Place and saved their water, how welcome the High Grass looked. How they had crept up to the Ute horse herd, how many horses each man had led out, and that Wolf-Appearing had taken the most, five good horses, and how Bear Neck had stood guard and done as he was told.

At each man's feat the women raised tremolo war whoops.

"There was a brave fight later," Straight Lance continued. "Just before we reached the Bad Place. This man rode an old horse, but he turned and fought. He counted coup on a Ute chief and took his war horse. We all saw him do it and the Ute had a lance and this man only an old knife." Paul went stiff, aware of a sensation both hot and cold on his face. Around him the people murmured approvingly and looked at the participants in the raid to single out the unnamed hero. Then Straight Lance said: "I want all Whirlwind People to know I honor *Tejan* tonight. He was the one. He's only a white man, but he is brave and I respect him. I want everybody to know that. *Tejan*, come out here."

It seemed natural for Paul to move out there, to stand in the circle, to see the light playing on the taut faces like fingers of fire, and everybody singing to him now, and all at once a mist obscured his vision and blurred the faces. Something was filling his throat. It was his voice, uncertain, now deep and strong, rising stronger and stronger, joining the others. He had never felt like this before, and when the drums pulsed and the horse-takers started the Victory Dance, his body responded in unison without hesitation, and his estrangement from the world was gone and the smoke rose straight up to the sky . . .

Some days after the raiding party had rested well, Paul saw his captor outside his lodge, bent over the hide calendar. Remembering his earlier experience, when waved off, Paul turned aside. But the Kiowa motioned him over and pointed to freshly painted figures of running horses and armed warriors.

"I have named this 'The Fall They Took the Utes' Horses,' " he said, giving Paul a satisfied look.

The front legs of the horses extended forward

and the rear legs backward, which wasn't correct, Paul saw at once, though the flat horse figures were pleasing to the aesthetic eye, nevertheless.

"Soon we will smoke the pipe for another raiding party."

"To take more horses?"

The Indian nodded.

Paul couldn't curb his surprise. "You have many horses. Why more?"

"Raiding keeps the young men brave."

"It also helps a man become a great *topadok'i*, does it not?"

The other appeared to condone the remark as one might that of an old friend. "*Tejan*," he said earnestly, "I want you to smoke the pipe again."

"Why?"

"You know why."

Paul did, with a sweep of feeling. And the familiar weariness of his captivity, like old melancholy, held him fast and the lightness of spirit he had experienced since the Victory Dance deserted him entirely.

"So you still believe that foolish thing?"

"We have rubbed out that no-power talk." The dark eyes flashed and the Kiowa chopped his fist downward as he would swing a stone war club. As swiftly, his voice softened. "Since you are a white man I can't expect you to understand."

The Kiowa arrogance, the barbarous superstition and blind faith in signs and fetishes, the savage emotions, always given to extremes—everything got to Paul at once and refusal formed in his throat. He opened his mouth to speak and stopped himself, his mind steadying. He must try again. Once again he must go with the hope of freeing himself. He had no chance here, always watched as a white captive, and now as a respected oddity, a brave white man who had brought power to the band.

"Where," he heard himself asking, "will you raid this time?"

"Against the *Tejanos*." The black eyes were like coals.

Paul thought that over, seeing the dangerous complications, and, with a rush of hope, that he would be that much nearer the settlements. "I will smoke the pipe," he said, almost indifferently. "But I won't kill anybody. I won't kill a white man."

This time Straight Lance headed an even larger raiding party, the success of the Ute raid having attracted new followers eager for self-glorification. For three days the Kiowas rode south, passing through great scatterings of buffalo. On the morning of the fourth day the Indians veered southeast, and that night when they camped, Paul decided they were in the vicinity of the Clear Fork of the Brazos or on the Salt Fork.

Next afternoon, coming upon Longhorn cattle, Bear Neck notched an arrow and killed a cow to demonstrate his contempt for the white-eyes.

"That was not a wise thing to do," Straight Lance rebuked him. "*Tejanos* will find the carcass and know we are around."

No fires that night. The raiders ate the tasteless but strength-giving mesquite meal and dried meat, hobbled the horses nearby, and Straight Lance picked the men to stand guard. Paul wasn't included. He never was. Before dawn the scouts slipped away, to return after several hours. Paul could tell they were excited the way they quirted their horses. His captor went out to meet them and rode back.

"The *Tejanos* are close," he explained. "They have built houses along a creek. Some of the houses are like small forts, with poles stuck into the ground and cut sharp on top and only one way to get inside." He kept fixing his attention on the young men, already restless. "There are many white-eyes in this place. We would be foolish to rush the forts. There are plenty of horses to take."

Bear Neck spoke up, disagreement roughing his voice. "Do we take prisoners?"

"We came for horses. This is not a vengeance raid or a war party." Paul sensed a deeper issue here, behind Bear Neck's manner and in the raid leader's hardening speech: "My power works best in taking horses. It's a horse power, mainly. You know that. You know how strong my power is. You know how many good horses we took from the Utes. So we won't take any women or children prisoners."

Paul saw Bear Neck scowl, although as an apprentice warrior he dared not disobey, and he saw Bear Neck glance at his young friends, who likewise looked disgruntled.

"Listen to me," Straight Lance warned. "White women would only slow us down and cry all the time, and after we take the *Tejanos'* horses they will organize a party and chase us hard." He drove his meaning at Bear Neck. "I will whip any man out of camp who spoils my power and brings a white woman back. But kill all the white-eye men you can when you go after the horses. Burn some houses. Every year the whites push farther out on the prairie. Every year they kill more buffalo and the hunting gets harder."

About dusk Paul mounted with the others and rode several miles to a conical sandstone hill, shaggy with oak trees, which offered an unbroken view to the east.

"There," Red Calf said, pointing to indicate a line of trees, "is the place."

Paul saw a creek and some scattered houses and sheds and corrals massing darkly in the twilight. Ringlets of light began to glow; their sight thrust an awakening homesickness through him, and a wild compulsion grasped him to rush to his horse somehow, to tear down there and warn the settlement. But when he looked he saw Indians too close to the blue horse. A moment later Straight Lance was calling the raiders together. Still, Paul hoped. By chance, perhaps, he would be left with a few boys to guard the horses.

"In the morning, Kills-Something and Hawk Above will stay here with the horses," he heard the heavy voice order, and he wondered, in bitterness, why he could have thought otherwise. "Come back here as fast as you can. Everybody be brave. *Tejan*, you will go with me. Now let's sleep."

Paul couldn't rest for dreading the coming of morning. Men would die. This was a big raiding party. He turned from side to side, gazing up at the night glitter through the branches, hearing the breeze off the prairie rustling the dark oak leaves.

"Go to sleep, *Tejan*."

"I keep thinking of the white men who will be killed in the morning. Why don't you just take the horses?"

"The whites always try to kill us."

"I'm glad you told the young men not to take any women and children. Why?"

He heard Straight Lance stir. "You heard what I said. Captives make trouble, and we will be chased. The *Tejanos* always chase us until their horses play out."

"Was that your real reason?"

"Go back to sleep."

"You didn't answer me."

"Listen to me, *Tejan*. My heart is hard. I was on

the Tipi-Pole Timber River five winters ago when the pony soldiers rode through the snow from the north and surprised Black Kettle's camp and killed the Cheyenne women and children. The Kiowa camp was downriver. We painted our faces and came out like the buffalo bulls when the cows are attacked. The Arapahoes and the Apaches got there, too. We cut off a bunch of soldiers. They did a foolish thing—they turned loose their horses and lay down in the grass to shoot. We charged them, we killed them all. I felt good when I killed those pony soldiers who had been shooting and hacking the women and children. My heart is like stone, *Tejan*."

"Even against me?"

"Go to sleep."

Paul let the talk die. It was enough, for now, that his captor had told the young men to take no prisoners. He heard the Kiowa settle down, and for a long interval he heard the wind chanting in the treetops.

In no time at all, it seemed, he felt a touch on his forehead and he opened his eyes, his mind yet swimming through the murky depths of sleep. Roughly a rude clarity flung him fully awake— the raid, and the Kiowas and the unawares settlement rose before him accusingly. He groaned and sat up.

Like a sleepwalker, he fell in beside his captor and went down to the base of the hill where the raiders were assembling. No one spoke. Straight Lance, moving out, strode into the mealy, weblike darkness, the horse-stealing darkness, the false darkness just before dawn, when light seems to wait like a tense runner, poised to dash upon the slack earth.

About Paul fell the almost inaudible brush of moccasined feet. When the smudge of a corral loomed ahead, everybody moved faster. Paul saw forms go ahead and vanish, leaving Paul with Straight Lance and two others.

Paul felt himself straining. *Don't run. Not yet. Not yet. Wait.* He walked on a way.

Somewhere ahead a rifle cracked, and a great weight of relief lifted from Paul's chest. *They know now, in time.* Then he heard a white man shouting and horses running free from the corral and the Kiowas' curdling whoops. These horse sounds hammered closer. Paul recognized the meaning: loose horses flying like the wind, terrified by the howling voices behind them.

He froze, feeling fear low in his bowels, and out of the muddy light he picked up the dark mass of horses surging wildly toward him, almost upon him. As he darted to his left, he heard the Kiowas scattering out of the way. He kept running until he heard the horses thudding past, behind him, and when he looked back, an unbelievable sensation tore at him: He was alone. God Almighty, he was free at last. Straight Lance and the other two

Kiowas had rushed one way and he the other, the horses between them. A long string of them and still coming. Light was breaking stronger every moment. Over there he saw a house. He ran for it.

By the time he ran up to the house he was sobbing for breath. There was no one around and the door stood open. He had no fear as he ducked inside, just an oddness, as if he were returning from the dead, the impact of seeing familiar objects again, the chairs and the table, all rough-hewn, and the fireplace where someone had started a little fire and left it hurriedly, and the dishes on the table and the slept-in beds, hastily vacated, and the strange smells of white cooking and living—these he absorbed into his being in one sweeping of all his senses.

He stepped to the center of the room and paused, his eyes on men's clothing hanging on the wall, coat and trousers, a hat beside it.

He swung toward a sliding and scraping sound, instinctively drawing his knife.

A shriveled old man, his thin, white beard shaped like a spade, his back against the log wall, was rising behind a crude box used to hold fire-wood, his veined hands trembling, the small, dark cave of his mouth frozen open, his eyes bugging as he stared fearfully at Paul.

Paul, controlling his surprise, held out his right hand to reassure him, but it was the hand holding the knife, and the old man flattened against the wall and Paul drew back his hand. The old man was staring in the wildest, leering, accusing way.

"Cuss your heart—" he spat, his white-crusted face working. "Them eyes—that hair. Why, you're white!"

Paul hesitated, groping for the awkward, calming words. "Listen . . . don't be afraid." He edged in to pacify him. However, he yet held the knife and his motion merely sent fear spurting into the taut old face, and the old voice, strangling with fear, flung out hate as bitter as gall:

"White . . . white renegade!"

Stooping swiftly, he snapped up with a hatchet from the wood box, scrambling, cursing, and he lunged for Paul just as Paul was sheathing the knife. He was agile for one so old, and his rage made him quick. Paul shot out a hand, catching the sour sweat of the other's fear, and easily wrenched the hatchet free. The old man fell to the floor.

"Listen—" Paul said, helpless to convince him.

That was all he had time to say before the old fellow, as lean and wiry as a tomcat, sprang up and fled through the doorway.

"Come back here," Paul yelled and followed. Outside, he saw him tearing for the creek where a picket house stood, fashioned like a stockade, hollering and waving his arms.

A figure stepped out of the stockade. Paul, still running, slacked up when he saw the man raise his rifle, then lower it to wait for the old one to run past him inside, then raise it again. Paul braced to a flat-footed stop, conscious that he gripped the hatchet in his right hand. He tried to stop the rifleman with a raised shout—"No! I'm white! No!"—but the words had no meaning, dwarfed by the thudding of running horses and the steady banging downcreek. He kept shouting and waving, even after he saw the rifle swinging level.

Something died within Paul then, something seemed to shrivel and wither away, as he shrank back and dropped the hatchet and whirled and ran dodging the way the Kiowas did when under fire.

Short ahead loomed the corner of the house. At the same straining moment, he felt a hot blow smashing high into his back and he heard the crack of a rifle. He staggered. He caught himself and ran on and on, though he was beginning to feel strangely weak.

His strength deserted him all at once, in a sudden gush. Ahead he glimpsed Kiowas, indistinct figures weaving there. Or were those flat, naturalistic figures on a hide? Or bronze dancers in the failing light? Behind him he thought he heard horses sweeping up like the wind.

He couldn't see so well now, and abruptly the earth heaved up like a great brown wave and rolled over him, sucking him under, and as he went down he heard the shrill voices of the Kiowas coming closer. But, strangely, he couldn't see their faces.

Chapter 9

Paul opened his eyes to blue sky and the sensation of fire burning high across his back and chest. And the sky wasn't right; it was bobbing and shifting up and down and film covered it. A noisy clopping jarred his ears. He was moving. It required all his strength and will to turn his head and he saw that he lay on a slant, to his surprise on a *travois* or drag, pulled by his blue horse, Star. He could hear the ends of the poles scraping and slithering through the grass.

He let his eyelids drop, exhausted. Some time later, noticing the sky again, he realized the film was across his eyes. There was something lumpy under his shirt. He touched the pulp of a prickly pear poultice, and he could feel another against his back. Even that small effort stripped away his puny strength.

The next he knew he was no longer moving, and he heard horses and choppy Kiowa voices. As through a whitish mist he recognized Straight Lance and Red Calf and Kills-Something.

"You bled a lot," his captor said. "The bullet went through you. That is good. The *Tejanos* are chasing us. But we have split up and they are confused. I have sent the young men ahead with the horses." The Kiowa voice, full of clicks and

126

nasals, seemed to reach Paul from a great distance, and the broad faces seemed to diminish, then grow larger than before, shivery images that were shrinking again.

He felt himself moving again, too weak to watch the sky, transported lightly; motionless sometimes, he caught snatches of droning voices. Once, hearing horses running, an instinctive alarm caused him to raise up. He was alone, his blue horse tied to a chinaberry tree. His exertion left him trembling weak, his heart thumping, and set off his hurting again. He touched his chest. His hand came away with blood.

And once he heard shots and yells and horses racketing hard. He was powerless to move. Voices. Kiowa voices. His face contorted with relief, for if the *Tejanos* found him they would kill him as if he were a Kiowa. Through the long hours he drifted off and on the edge of consciousness. He blinked when someone touched him and gave him water.

"Why don't you let me die?" he pleaded, opening his eyes on Straight Lance's face.

"When the *Tejanos* quit chasing us—and their horses are played out—we will kill a buffalo. Some raw meat will make your juices strong again."

Paul had no desire for food; the mere thought of raw buffalo sickened him. He dropped down into a nightmarish sleep, punctuated with images flashing and passing, faces and places, nothing that made sense.

When he woke, it was evening and he lay on his *travois* bed on the ground. A figure bent over him and he heard his captor say, "Eat," and he tasted the nauseating, bloody richness of raw liver. Somehow he swallowed, too weak to resist.

"*Tejan*," the Kiowa said, solemn and impressed, "that was a brave deed."

"Deed?" Paul repeated, too weary to comprehend. He longed for sleep, deep sleep. "What deed?"

"When you chased the white man and charged the fort with only a hatchet."

Slowly the mist cleared from Paul's mind. Everything stood out, equally clear-cut and impossible. Understanding clutched him. "I was shot," he breathed; speaking was difficult. "Was that brave? Anybody can get shot."

"*Tejan*, you always pretend you don't perform these brave deeds, such as when you fought the Ute chief, armed with just a knife. We saw you chase the white man. You kept on even when the white man at the fort aimed his rifle at you. That was brave."

"Did you see me turn and run? Was that brave?"

"You made your charge first, in close. That's always the sign of a brave man."

Paul grimaced and fell back as a stab of pain quivered through him. He thought he could feel blood leaking down his chest. He labored for breath. "The white man that ran . . . was frightened. I wanted to talk to him."

"Talk? If so, why did you chase him with a hatchet? Why did you charge the fort?"

"I didn't," Paul said. "I didn't . . ." It pained him too much to talk further and he realized that he could not conceivably convince the Indian.

"It was a brave deed," the Kiowa said. "Red Calf and Kills-Something and Wolf-Appearing also saw you. We will all vouch for you at the Victory Dance."

Hearing that, the same old sense of frustration and weariness and discouragement, so akin to despair, fastened upon him and mocked him and he wondered if he would live to try again.

In his childlike weakness, he was conscious of only a vague awareness of time passing. He knew when night fell and when daylight arrived because he could feel the dark coolness and the harshness of the high-plains sun. He sensed the tedious passage of days, that they traveled carefully, often pausing for him to rest. Why? Why hadn't they left him to die, which he was going to do, anyway?

He lay in his crude brush hut, closer to dying than living, covered by his buffalo robe, too weak to walk, staring up at the low ceiling; when the afternoons warmed up, he turned his head to gaze through the doorway at the blue sky, as if it were a pain-free Elysium where he longed to go. At intervals his captor brought him food and fed the blaze in the floor's fire-hole and helped him outside and back, and once Paul heard him exclaim, "*Tejan*, you are too brave to die!" But the high-up pain never left him, and sometimes he coughed up little puddles of blood.

And the buffalo doctor came, because the buffalo had the power to heal wounds. His name was Walks-the-Clouds, taller than any other Whirlwind, and he had sunken, staring eyes and the longest, slimmest fingers Paul had ever seen, like yellow tapers, with the nails curving under like claws. An obvious charlatan given to flourishes and making portentous claims as to his magical powers, such as belching up bullets and bringing down the sun from the sky—if he so desired. Nevertheless, he practiced hard at his self-proclaimed curative skills, rattling a gourd over Paul for hours while he prayed and chanted, attired in a buffalo-horn headdress and buffalo tails dangling from each bony wrist. When Paul did not improve after some days, Walks-the-Clouds suddenly circled the fire and out the door, where he loudly informed Straight Lance, "My medicine won't work on a dog of a white man," and, to Paul's relief, he did not return.

Autumn passed slowly and painfully, like a

wounded thing, crippling on toward winter, spreading a clammy chill through his thin body at night.

Paul guessed it was late December—for first snow had come to the red-hued canyon, gentle flakes as fragile as a child's dream gliding down out of a wolf-gray sky, as light and feathery as cottonwood seed, vanishing the instant they touched the brown earth—when he began to notice that he seldom coughed.

On a mild winter afternoon, he was sunning outside his hut, observing the somnolent life of the village, his eyes following the ravels of smoke drifting above the tipis like tattered shawls, the burdened women bringing firewood from upcanyon, hearing the idling hum of voices. The Kiowa tongue was not melodious like that of the Caddos, whom he had heard around Fort Sill; forcible and vigorous, like the Whirlwinds themselves, every vowel and syllable distinctly enunciated, which, to his ears, conveyed the effect of a chant, and coupled with the rising inflection of the Whirlwinds, lent a querulous tone even to ordinary conversation.

He felt stronger. The exhaustion of depthless sleep had passed, leaving an aftermath of languid contentment, as if he waited for the well of his drawn body to fill up and renew his strength, and a dreamlike state in which he hovered over the village, bodiless, hearing all, seeing all, observing these wild nomads living their simple and remote lives under the sun.

From down the canyon Paul heard a yell; on the heels of that the drumming rush of a running horse. He sat up. An Indian youth raced in and called out something that across the distance sounded to Paul like "Wrinkled Hide."

After a few minutes, Paul heard bells and a procession of riders and pack mules came stringing up the canyon. Traders, Paul thought. *Comancheros*? A white man wearing buckskins and a broad-brimmed hat rode foremost, his silver-mounted saddle glittering, his blooded bay horse constantly tossing its proud head, behind him a straggle of Mexican riders. The white man wore the bold and assured bearing of having been here before, and he disregarded the chattering villagers, all save Straight Lance, to whom he waved a greeting. His host stood unmoving, without expression, without welcome, Paul saw, then gestured the traders to a camping place beyond the village.

Later that afternoon, Paul strolled over to watch the trading, drawn, like the Kiowas, toward the broad, dominant figure of the white man displaying his goods on blankets under a giant cotton-wood tree: twists of tobacco, butcher knives polished bright to mask their cheap metal, bolts of gaudy blue and scarlet cloth, little baskets containing glass beads, blue and white and red; silver trinkets, some brass cooking pots, and an assortment of old rifles and revolvers and cartridges.

Mostly junk, Paul judged, with suspicion. The short walk had tired him. Sitting down, he saw why the Kiowas, given to literal names, called the trader Wrinkled Hide. A virtual oak-trunk of a middle-aged man gone to loose flesh, the strong column of the neck creased with folds of fat, the wide slope of the paunch, the soft-looking, pawlike hands. Still, underneath that spongy softness, the suggestion of physical strength, and in the slant of the bearded mouth, in the piercing gray eyes, now fixed on Paul, a shrewdness equally calculating and bland, so evident that Paul wondered why the Kiowas, despite the gullibility of primitive people, couldn't see it.

A Kiowa spoke, drawing the trader's attention, and Wrinkled Hide's fleshy features did a bland switch and he gestured grandly toward the clutter of trade goods, and when he spoke it was with perfect, unctuous Kiowa:

"I have brought many fine things."

The Kiowas continued to stare, their eyes bright with anticipation. A woman edged nearer the blankets. She considered the glossy beads, her dark eyes revealing a shy longing, and looked toward her husband, who said to the white man, "How much?"

Wrinkled Hide pointed to one of the little

baskets. "Two robes," he said. His tone shed generosity.

The Kiowa shook his head and folded his arms, whereupon the trader shrugged and looked away, indicating the talk was finished. The Indian's arms dropped. He glanced toward his wife, and after a moment he went back to a small mound of robes and brought two. Soft and silky-looking robes, dark and rich, taken in the late fall or winter, beautifully tanned as only a woman of the prairie tribes could, hand-rubbing a tanning mixture of buffalo brains, grease, basswood bark, soapweed, and water into the flesh side of the robe, stretching and drying it, a process that required days.

The white man held up each robe for inspection, his manner critical, indicating each was just acceptable, no more, after which he laid them behind him and signed for the woman to take one basket of beads.

An expression of delight broke her dark impassivity. She chose blue beads; cuddling her purchase, she backed out to her husband's robe pile and sat down to inspect the beads.

Indignation knotted Paul's face. The baskets held about three handfuls of beads whose value totaled a few cents at most. At the trading store south of Fort Sill, he remembered seeing visitors from the East paying fifty dollars for comparable robes.

Yet he controlled his impulse to interfere, sensing that the Kiowas, hungering for these white-man objects, would consider any interference bad manners. Therefore, he watched while the trader swapped his cheap articles for more robes and for deerskins of beautiful, muted lemon yellow. The old weapons went for horses. That the horses bore brands made no difference. An old handgun brought five good mounts, an old rifle ten.

When all the trade items were sold off the blankets, the white man made the sign for Finished, bringing his closed hands together in front, right to right, left to left. Tomorrow, his hands said, the trading would resume. Smiling at the Kiowas, he gathered up his blankets and disappeared inside his A-shaped tent.

Strolling toward his hut, Paul saw Straight Lance alone. He looked troubled. It was then that Paul recalled that the Kiowa hadn't taken part in the trading.

"The white man is asking too many robes and horses for his trade goods," Paul told him.

"I know."

"Why didn't you stop the trading? He's cheating everyone."

"We all know Wrinkled Hide cheats. But we need the things he brings here."

"His guns are old and worn out."

"They will still kill *Tejanos*."

Paul shook his head. Killing Texans. Sometimes that purpose alone seemed to drive the Whirlwind People.

"Tomorrow," he said, "why not tell your people to make harder trades? Tell them not to take the white man's first or second offer. If Wrinkled Hide refuses, tell them to walk away. He'll trade. He doesn't want to haul that junk
  back to the settlements."

"You say that about a white man?"

"He's just a thief." Paul went past him, the weariness dropping over him like a cloak. Coming to his hut, he ducked inside and lay down, groaning softly, grateful for the luxury of the buffalo robe, sinking into a warm exhaustion. For a moment more, dim light hovered at the outskirts of his consciousness, and a recognition wound through his head like a daydream, yet real and true: He didn't feel like a captive anymore.

Next day, when the trading began, Paul saw Red Calf motion his wife to stay behind as he came forward. He was skinny for a Kiowa, more inclined to length than width, his pipestem legs overly bowed from riding, with the moon face of an actor sitting like a bronze pumpkin on his narrow shoulders. Picking up a butcher knife, he ran his thumb back and forth along the cutting edge. As he did, his expectation ebbed.

"Wrinkled Hide," he said, puckering his lips, "the blade is dull."

"You can sharpen it to your liking."

Red Calf, kneeling, tested the blade again and slanted an eye at the trader. "How much?"

The ropy lips formed a twisting smile. "Three robes."

Red Calf smiled back, a wiveled grimace that sent waves of wrinkles across his smooth face and drew his eyes down into slits. "Too much," he said.

Suddenly the white man's smile washed out. "Wrinkled Hide is a great friend of the Whirlwinds. He has brought these fine things a long way. He rode many sleeps to come here," and he pointed westward, toward New Mexico.

"Too many robes," Red Calf said, still smiling. He put down the knife and stood to leave.

The white man hesitated. "You are a great warrior. A great horse-taker. A great friend. You may have the knife for two robes."

Red Calf continued on. Several steps and he turned deliberately about, drifting back. Paul, knowing the Kiowas, saw something underlying the moonish features. Red Calf bent down and picked up the knife and took the tip of the blade between his left thumb and forefinger, springing and flexing it, ignoring the trader's grunt of protest. There was a sharp *ping* as the thin blade snapped. The white man let go a nervous, slack-jawed start. His face changed swiftly, on the tip of anger; in time he caught himself and

137

recovered the beginning of a beaten smile. "My friends," he called out, waving an arm, "no knife could withstand the great strength of Red Calf, but because I am generous, I will sell all the knives today for one good robe each."

As the Kiowas swarmed forward, chattering, Paul saw the white man cut him an accusing look, then turn to his trade, his manner as effusive as ever. In a short time the blankets were swept clear, and although the hour was early and the Indians lingered, the white man brought out no more trade items.

Paul left, pleased over the turnabout. The winter sun was like a light warm blanket thrown over his thin shoulders as he made his way back to the hut, and there he reclined in a crude lounge chair fashioned of cedar and chinaberry wood that he had lashed together with strips of rawhide and padded the seat with pieces of an old robe, an ugly but rather comfortable contraption that, during the laborious making, had amused the Indians at great length; for in their tipis they lounged on robes and grass-stuffed pillows made of small-animal skins.

He hadn't rested long when he heard heavy bootsteps. It was the trader. Paul, sitting up, saw the print of his accusation.

"Reckon I can thank you for what happened," the white man blurted, affecting a hurt mien.

Paul came to his feet, aware of the trader

138

towering over him, thick, slothful, knavish, dirt rimming the corners of the shrewd, light-colored eyes, grease stains streaking the front of his buckskin shirt, dispelling the last illusion of the glittering figure Paul had seen riding into the village like a great white god. The quarrelsome face had a long spit of a nose and the veins stood out like worms at the temples. His buckskins exuded a stale odor, a sourness of body and grease and soil and whiskey. Paul, wanting to avert his nose, realized his response was not unlike a Kiowa's sniffing the strange, armpit rankness of a dirty white man who imprisoned his body in clothing.

"Yes—I told them you were cheating them," Paul said. "But credit them with intelligence— some of them already knew."

"Took me years of risky chances to build up my trade, bringin' in the things they need."

"Such as glass beads and cheap butcher knives and worn-out guns a white man wouldn't have?"

"Better than nothin'. Nobody else's got the nerve to come in here." He was commencing to bluster. "Texans'd hang me in a minute if they caught me with branded horses." He concentrated a prying, curious look on Paul. "I smelled trouble when I spotted you yesterday. First time they ever let a white man live amongst 'em. Who the hell are you, anyway?"

"They call me *Tejan*."

An eddy of contempt swirled into the heavy mouth and eyes. "I mean your real name, white man."

"That's enough here. Who are you?"

The bearded mouth closed, then parted, imitative of Paul's evasion. "They call me Wrinkled Hide." And into the cagey eyes there crept a slyness. "You wouldn't be on the dodge, now, would you? Maybe killed somebody? Maybe deserted from the Army?"

Paul smiled in spite of himself. "Nothing like that. I'm a captive. Haven't they told you?"

He wasn't expecting the sudden switch of manner. Nor the backward glance at the village, nor the confidential air. "Listen," the man said, "I can guide you out of here. Dodge City. Fort Sill. We can make it."

The cocksure, promising voice could be that of the late and garrulous Shadler in the Wichita Mountains. "To hear you," Paul scoffed, "all you have to do is ride out. Believe me, it isn't that easy."

"I'll figure out a way. Leave it to me. I know these here Whirlwinds. It's gonna cost you some money, though."

"I was wondering when you'd get around to money. How much?"

The trader squinched up one bloodshot eye, measuring out a sly appraisal. "Have to study on that a bit. Man wants to be fair." He straightened his face and the familiar blandness flowed across the roguish features like oil. "Five thousand," he said. "Uh-huh. It's gonna cost you five thousand."

It was a struggle for Paul not to laugh at his open avarice. "What makes you think I'd pay that if I could?"

The canny gaze was boring into Paul, behind it the flare of some guarded knowledge. "I figure you'd better pay whatever it costs you."

Paul was puzzled. He said, "I'm in no real danger here. They treat me well. In fact, I owe Straight Lance my life. Not once—but twice."

The white man all but sneered. "I'll tell you why you'd best hightail it out of here, my young friend—you're a wanted man in Texas."

"Wanted? I don't believe you. There's no reason."

"Maybe you'll believe this," the white man said. His voice had a pouncing quality. Reaching inside his shirt, he drew out a folded sheet of paper, yellowed and creased, which he shoved at Paul.

Paul, baffled, opened it with unsure fingers. A reward notice, he saw, such as one would see posted in a public place. Shocked, disbelieving, lips tight, he began reading the heading, set in heavy black type, and the incredible words:

ATROCITY IN YOUNG COUNTY . . .
$1,000 REWARD . . . DEAD OR ALIVE . . .
For the white renegade seen with the band of

Indians, believed to be Kiowas, that attacked the settlement on Elm Creek, near the Salt Fork of the Brazos River, upstream from Fort Belknap, November 8 last. . . . Three white male citizens were murdered in the wanton attack. Some hundred-odd horses, mostly prime riding stock, were taken by the treacherous red devils. . . . A Mr. Kutch, an aged and respected citizen, saw the renegade firsthand. His description of the murderous arch fiend follows: about twenty-five or -six years old, blond hair and beard; blue eyes; slender build, regular features. Frontier authorities are of the opinion this white man, believed to be an Army deserter or an outlaw, is leading most of the raids against the North Texas settlements and ranches. . . . Any person having reliable information should notify the sheriff of Young County, Graham, Texas, or the Texas Rangers. Reward is offered by the State of Texas, payable in gold.

Renegade. White renegade. He read it through again and again, unable to believe his senses, while seeing in the cabin's gloom the old man's fear-glazed eyes memorizing his features.

Against his ear, the shrewd voice was murmuring, "I knew it was the Whirlwinds. Had to be. No Indian—not even the Comanch' or them Kiowas around Fort Sill—can steal horses

like a Whirlwind Kiowa. That was a big raid."
The relishing voice went on: "An' that description fits you like a glove, don't it, Mr. Renegade?"

Paul stepped away, sickened of the man. "You came here because of this?" he demanded, shaking the paper.

"Naw. My main game is guns for horses. I figured if there was a white man here that might put a little extra frostin' on the cake—such as guidin' him to safety."

"What makes you think I have money?"

The worldly eyes, assessing him again, became mocking. "You give yourself away. Way you talk. Way you act." The facsimile of a sneer formed. "Like you was used to more genteel livin'. Now you ready to talk business?"

"There is no business," Paul said, feeling the acid burn of loathing.

The cagey eyes blinked. "You'd stay with these dirty red heathens? I'll make it fair an' square, man to man. How about four thousand?" Paul was silent. "Might even go a mite lower. I tell you I'd be takin' some chances, besides the ruination of my trade."

Paul was bursting with feeling, a wildness. Before he knew it his hand rested on the handle of his knife. Like a Kiowa, primed for violence, he realized for a moment, and was shaken at his impulse.

"Go on," he said. "Don't come back."

"Wait'll them Rangers get a-holt o' you. They'll hang you sure."

"Go on. I don't like your smell, white man."

He watched the trader turn and heard the heavy crunch of the fading bootsteps, his mind at grips with the black-lined sheet of paper he still held in his left hand, with the strange but distinct feeling he had of the destiny that seemed to exile him among the Whirlwind People, and also to bind him to them somehow, at a very time when he might be able to escape, a destiny that he sensed held him here with invisible bonds.

Chapter 10

Winter's brown residue still hugged the reaches of the great canyon, and the Whirlwind People, weary of the long nights and the endless wood-gathering, turned suppliant faces to the fugitive sun struggling to break through the gray sky, eager for *Son-pata*, or "grass-springing," known to be near when the mares foaled and the breasts of the eagles began to turn white and the panther whelps were born in dens high up among the rocky ledges on the painted walls.

It was 1874, Paul was aware, probably March. Not that knowing so was important to him. Time had come to hold no value except to mark the change of seasons; all through the winter he had kept time at a distance, like an unwelcome and persistent visitor whom he chose to ignore, while he rested or entertained himself painting on the small-animal skins, since he was too poor to own a buffalo hide other than his precious robe. Slender, sharp bones for outlining, a chewed willow stick to apply the paint, and a mordant or sizing brewed from skin scrapings boiled in water to go over the paint to set it. Charcoal for black, iron oxides and colored clays for pigment, the latter baked to powder over a fire, ground in a stone mortar mixed with tallow.

He experimented with geometric designs and the flat figures of warriors and war horses as the Indian men painted them, in profile and without background, painting whatever struck his fancy, or a scene of the village in depth, or the bold symmetry of a Kiowa face, capturing the strong prominence of the cheekbones. He was lean and sometimes he soon tired, like a winter-poor horse, but he was well and growing stronger and he felt neither self-pity nor discontent, only a vague haste, impelled by that prickling inner voice, continually after him, hurrying him: *Observe, listen, smell, put down, remember. Detail! Detail!* No small feat on the crude surfaces.

It was late in the Leaf Moon, and the lithe young men were becoming restless as the horses fattened up on the new grass, when his captor came to the hut.

"*Tejan,*" he said, with enthusiasm, his eyes glowing, "it is time to go to the Great River"—gesturing far, more south than west—"to ride across for many good Mexican horses."

Paul laid the willow stick aside. "Mexico?"

"We call it the Waterless Mexican Country. Below the mountains by the river."

Paul, becoming thoughtful, decided that meant the states of Chihuahua and Coahuila. "I thought you raided those places only during the Moon-of-Deer-Horns-Dropping-Off?"

"We didn't go when the moon came last season.

Our village is too small to keep a war party out as long as that takes. Sometimes a man will in the Mexican country two winters. The Leaf Moon is a good time to go. The grass is up for our ponies, and the Mexicans won't be expecting us early in the raiding season."

"About how many sleeps is it to the river?" Paul realized he was stalling his captor. It was hundreds of miles to the Rio Grande, the stretches long and hard between infrequent water holes and springs.

"The good horse you took from the Ute chief will make the journey seem short. Get ready, my friend."

Paul shrugged. The Kiowa wasn't above artful flattery to get his way.

A note of tribal pride stiffened the nasal voice. "The white-eyes call the trail the Great Comanche War Trail. They forget we Kiowas also have taken many horses over it and brought back many captives."

Paul nodded. He had observed a scattering of Mexicans in the village. Some as servants. Some as wives. Some as adopted children, loved as Kiowas. Some as warriors, young and old. The raiding had been going on many years. Behind these captives, and the reflection had crossed his mind many times, untold death and terror, devastated towns and *haciendas*.

"A long way to bring sorrow to those poor

people—farther than the Ute country," Paul said critically, knowing in advance the Kiowa's reasoning; now hearing it as if spoken almost by rote:

"A young man who hasn't made one of these big raids into Mexico will never be a famous man, no matter how strong and brave he is. You forget our old people, *Tejan*. It's great comfort to a father in his old age to know his son stole horses from the Mexicans." The dark eyes smoldered. "If I had a son, I would want him to be the greatest horse-taker of all."

Paul, smiling faintly, shook his head. "Raiding in Mexico—stealing horses—killing people—taking captives—burning houses—I don't like it. It's bad."

"What am I to do? Me, a Kiowa? Live like a white man in a wooden tipi? Hunt no more? Scrape the grass away and plant seeds? Do women's work?"

"I don't mean stop hunting. Just stop killing people and stealing."

Straight Lance's response was humorless laughter. "When the *Tejanos* stop, we Kiowas will, too. Listen to me. The *Tejanos* want to drive us out of Texas. All the whites want to put us on a reservation. I won't have that. I was born free. When we Kiowas go raiding over the prairies, we feel happy. But when we settle down we grow pale and die."

Paul folded his arms, opposing, yet understanding. Raiding was the one way Straight Lance could become a great *topadok'i.*

"Are you going with me, *Tejan?*"

The question took Paul by surprise, shattering his preoccupied state. Sweat stood out on his forehead. The glistening broad face swam before his eyes, upon him again the baffling instinct or compulsion, paradoxical and loose, contrary to all common sense, that he must go because it was somehow preordained, for a reason that evaded his faculties.

His head was aching, and he pressed the fingers of both hands to his temples.

"What is it, *Tejan?*"

"Nothing," Paul said, running his hands through his hair and looking up.

"Will you go?"

"Yes."

Two days later the tireless blue horse was bearing him steadily away from the broken escarpments of the Staked Plains, away from the scowling brow of the caprock, riding amidst a big war party of Whirlwinds, passing like red dust whorls across the florid face of the boundless land, the lead rider, Red Calf, pointed like the tip of an ash lance for the Rio Grande country.

Straight Lance had composed a new War Journey Song, and now and then he sang or chanted:

Going on a long ride,
That's a young man's way.
To be brave,
To do great things.

Sometimes they covered sixty to eighty miles a day. One morning they watered their horses and filled the buffalo paunches and swung off and Straight Lance started singing, his strong voice carrying high and true, rich with a warrior's confidence. His voice echoed back, hollow and ghostly sounding, apparently from the tops of the twisted cedar trees in the short canyon where the war party had camped.

At once the Kiowas reined still, as timorous as children hearing a strange noise, frozen by superstitious fear of the unknown. Even Straight Lance was motionless. Everyone kept watching the place, as if the stubby cedars might speak again.

"Spirits," Red Calf murmured uneasily, not certain.

Paul dared not smile. "It's an echo," he said. "His voice bounced back from that high bluff over there."

Straight Lance seized on that. The cloud over his face vanished. "Good sign! This will be another successful raid." Afterward, when he sang again and the terrain was too flat to create an echo, he said, compromising, "Most good signs come just one time. That's the way with strong medicine."

Paul found Kiowa superstitions no more absurd than when a white man turned back after a black cat crossed his path, or when a white man carried a rabbit's foot or nailed a horseshoe over the doorway for good luck. Every Kiowa had his own personal "medicine," just as some white men had guardian angels or patron saints. So far the omens for the raid were propitious, if you believed in power and medicine and taboos, of which his captor was an ardent devotee.

"*Tejan*, I hope you see that we Kiowas believe in our medicine. We aren't like our brothers the Comanches, who hunt and kill bears and eat them. That led to Heap-of-Bears' death when the Kiowas and Comanches joined to fight the Utes."

The day before leaving camp Straight Lance had taken Paul into the woods where a buckskin-covered shield hung on poles, in the manner of a painter's easel.

"Take off the covering," Paul was told.

Doing so, he saw a decorated medicine shield, painted upon it a sun and lance, his captor's favorite weapon, and an attached eagle-bone whistle and four raven feathers tied in a tuft.

"Now touch all these things. Handle them."

Wondering, Paul ran his hand over the shield, pausing over the sun and the lance, and took the whistle and the feathers in his fingers. The shield was like a magnet to his eyes; being a white man, he had not been allowed to touch one or even come close. It was made from buffalo hide, probably from the shoulder hide of an old bull, the toughest part, and stretched over a circular wooden hoop and sewn with rawhide thongs passed through eyelets. When he stood back, he heard the Kiowa's explosive relief:

"Good! You looked the shield in the face, you touched the sacred things, and the spirit wasn't angry. You are protected now. I want to make certain nothing happens to you this time. I failed to do this before we took the *Tejanos'* horses. It will work. My medicine is strong."

Paul, searching his face, felt unexpectedly touched. The man was wholly sincere. He believed in these ornaments and he was sharing their occult strength. Maybe that was what counted most after all, believing. Paul heard himself replying, "I know your medicine is strong, my friend. If it weren't, I would be dead."

At times the Kiowas appeared to be rushing blindly south and west without reason, sometimes astride a dim trail, sometimes not even that; but after some days Paul saw a beaten trace slanting in from the north, and the Kiowas swept upon it like charging Huns. From their remarks Paul gathered that the trail was an ancient one, used by their fathers and grandfathers. Broad and well-traveled, it resembled a thoroughfare, its often erratic course determined by nature's whimsical placement of water and grass.

As the country became more arid, Paul noticed the gaps widening between springs. Once late in the day they heeled their horses up the steep face of a mesa, and soon Paul saw a trail and on top a fine spring flowing out of a round hole. It was "Sun Mountain Spring," Straight Lance confided, and the *Tejanos* didn't know about it. A secretive smile brushed his face. "Only Kiowas and eagles come here."

Although the undulating plains and low hills had a sameness, broken by solitary landmark peaks, their prodigal dawn lavished all the wonderful colors of a rose garden, and teasing cloud shadows freckled the great, hoof-hammered trail, and often bands of buffalo and antelope grazed the greening distances, splashed blue and red and white with erect clusters of bonnet-shaped flowers.

And as grudgingly as the arid land released its precious water, Paul discovered it also could show generosity in one unexpected gesture of liberality. Here the deep-cut trail swung sharply into shouldering hills, and as he descended them he saw a broad smear of running water. The Kiowas had a name for the oasis: "The Big Spring." Discarded lodge poles and bleached fire-holes littered the site.

Spurning a branch of the main trail forking south and east toward more benign-appearing country, the Kiowas clattered southwest at daybreak. Paul entered a forbidding emptiness; to his concern the Kiowas drank freely from the paunch waterbags, even though the sun had become a glowing red core and the horses suffered, a condition that the Indians ignored with usual indifference.

It was late when a low line of tawny hills humped ahead, lying northwest by southeast. Hills, Paul reasoned, should mean water. However, these were as glass gleaming in the sun, enveloped by a shimmering pall. He squinted to make certain, then sat back—sand dunes. Surely the Kiowas would go around that arid hell.

As the trail bent back to the southeast, Paul watched for Straight Lance to turn off. Instead, the Kiowa held to the same bleak course, on into the desert sand, not so much as hesitating as the pale humps of the hills rose around them and the horses sank to their shanks. Yet, Paul saw, there was a trail twisting and turning, which the Kiowas followed.

Of a sudden Paul spotted water, a large, clear pool, willows rimming it, and beyond them dwarf oak trees raised shinnery faces, and scraggly mesquites and patches of waist-high grass. Straight Lance threw him a "we-Kiowas" look of satisfaction and slid down to let his horse drink. Afterward he explained:

"The foolish *Tejanos* don't know there is plenty of sweet water in here. They think it is all desert, a bad place. Comanches and Apaches also come here. It's a good place to hide when the *Tejanos* or the pony soldiers are chasing you."

Before dark several Kiowas took bows and arrows and slipped off and returned, bearing the carcasses of small, reddish deer.

"Tomorrow," Straight Lance told Paul after supper, "we cross the Little Great River."

Next morning they took the war trail down into an arid purgatory of alkali flats and naked ridges where Paul could see no living thing except rattlesnakes. Hours, and a distant gleam caught his eye. A sinuous river off below, glittering and squirming across the hot plain as a greasy snake travels. With the sight, the prankish Whirlwinds went yipping down the gravelly slope, and Paul gave the blue horse its head. On the flat the horses raised a white veil of dust whose acrid smoke burned Paul's eyes and throat. He passed an alkali pond rimmed with the skeletons of horses and cattle, and swam Star across the narrow, high-banked, brackish river, which, according to his vague calculations, he placed as the Pecos. More skeletons, especially horses, whitened the range south of the river.

It was late in the day when he and the warriors, lips cracked from the heat and dust, drew up to a spring. "In the old days," the war leader said, "we could have camped at the big spring." He jabbed a resentful finger toward the east. "Then the whites put their soldier house on the main trail to deny us the good water. Only a white man would do a mean thing like that."

"Was it the water—or did the soldiers build a fort there to try to stop you from raiding Mexico?" Paul queried, his tone casting a kind of judgment.

The Kiowa laid the point of a stare on him, disagreement balanced with mockery. "*Tejan*, sometimes you sound like the Broadhat people on the reservation when they talk from their black Medicine Book, the Jesus book. I believe the white-eyes call it preaching about their god. Our greatest god is the sun."

Under the racketing hoofs of the blue gelding the passing country was changing to ragged mountains and wide, thin-grassed valleys, the heights wearing a thin dress of stunted cedar, greasewood on the lower slopes. On the flats, giant yuccas lifted offerings of bell-shaped blossoms of white and tender beauty, and suddenly the familiar yearning for pad and pencil overwhelmed Paul and he craved to halt and sketch before the view escaped him. No sooner did the hungering come than it passed, wasted as the choking dust of the advance horses thickened around him and dispelled the mood.

On the evening of the second day after leaving the spring west of the fort, which Paul hazily tabbed as Fort Stockton, Paul made his bed on the bank of the Rio Grande, the "Great River," west of the ghostly figures of the mountains; in the morning, following the unhesitating Kiowas, he found sound bottom, and the swift water lapped no higher than to his mount's belly. Once he had forded the river, he glanced back and traced the route they had come: the beaten war trail as livid as an old scar, as broad as a highway, winding back in among the peaks for miles.

Now a session of dread haunted him, of violence and burning.

Straight Lance guided them into a region of rocky peaks and landscape dry and barren. They ate sparingly; they drank at seep springs found along the crumbling feet of cliffs. After four days of traveling southeast, Paul sighted the first sign of habitation below the river, a scarf-shaped plume of smoke far off.

"A big *hacienda*," his captor said. "We have always taken plenty of horses there."

A short time before dark the scouts rode in. Bear Neck rushed up, dangling a dark scalp aloft on the head of his lance. "A goatherder," the young man crowed. "He died bleating."

No one appeared impressed, and the scouts showed no inclination to vouch for the deed, and as well as Paul knew the Kiowas, he was puzzled, for although the victim was just a pathetic herdsman, there was yet some honor in taking the scalp.

Bear Neck, still mounted, continued to display the scalp, playing with it. But Paul could tell something was wrong as the scouts kept silent.

"How did it happen?" Straight Lance questioned. A rawhide quirt hung from his right wrist.

Bear Neck's bluster began to fade. The leader asked him again, as only a Kiowa could speak, harshly, and the younger warrior released the halting words: "There were two of them. I couldn't kill them both. The other one ran into the brush."

"So?"

"He was quick as a panther. Strong as a buffalo bull." He was gushing with explanation, his voice still tinged with bragging. "I rushed after him. He threw a knife. I ducked. He . . ." Bear Neck faltered.

"He dodged your lance and got away?"

Bear Neck let the tip of his long weapon droop. He nodded.

"He will warn the *hacienda* and the Mexicans will send to the town for soldiers. You were foolish again, Bear Neck. I told you to scout. Not try for coups."

Anger and hurt arrogance bulged Bear Neck's face. He said nothing.

The leader reached him in one lunge, lashing the quirt across his naked shoulders. Bear Neck recoiled for another blow, but Straight Lance did not lift his arm again, and Bear Neck, chastened, rode through the circle of warriors and dismounted behind Paul. Whipping about, he vented his blazing affront: "You—white man. Ever since you came to our camp, Straight Lance has been against me. Me—a warrior!" He beat his chest.

"You young fool," Paul said, overcoming his surprise and answering him as an older warrior would. "You brought this on yourself. Now behave."

The Kiowa slapped his sheathed knife. "Someday soon we will fight again. Next time— white man—better not break your knife."

Paul stepped away from him, disgusted.

Straight Lance was saying: "Red Calf, what did you find?"

"They are herding the horses in a valley between here and the *hacienda*."

Paul's captor reflected briefly. Now: "The one who escaped will tell the herders and they will drive the horses to the *hacienda* when morning comes."

"Or sooner."

"We won't give them time. We'll take the horses tonight."

"Tonight? The moon is weak, like a buffalo calf."

"Mexican eyes are no stronger than ours."

The struggling new-born moon scattered a muddy light at best and the Chihuahua desert night was cold. Paul, hugging the buffalo robe around his shoulders, felt lost, adrift on a form-less sea, guided by horse sounds alone. Somewhere out in front Red Calf and Straight

Lance were leading the way, walking the horses. Possibly an hour passed. The Kiowas halted, and Paul heard the muted tap of two horses leaving. A pause. No one spoke. Then an owl hooted eerily, the call floating softly from afar, so real and natural-sounding that Paul was caught off guard when a Kiowa gave an answering hoot, just as true. A sheepishness crept over Paul, for he should have known. Tonight, because of his dread, he was a white man again.

Off the Kiowas went, minutes later turning and circling, the blue horse obeying whenever Paul pressed with his knees, right or left. Out of the darkness, riders loomed to rejoin them, Red Calf and Straight Lance. A whispered warning, passed back, and when Paul's turn came, he said quietly: "Get ready. The horses are near. Spread out. Wait for the signal."

Movements reached Paul: Kiowas making ready their bull-roarers or noisemakers, slats of wood attached to rawhide strings which, when twirled, created a weird, cranking sound, and preparing to drag pieces of bull hides as stiff as boards.

Paul could see nothing distinct at first. He shifted his gaze off and back, slowly, and picked out a dark mass beyond the Kiowas. A horse snuffled.

Straight Lance howled, "*Hooo—kaa-yaa!*" and the Whirlwinds whooped like a whole tribe of Kiowas and their horses, perfectly still until that instant, sprinted toward the night-grazing herd. Star needed no urging. He knew what to do, and Paul let the reins go loose and felt himself carried into a headlong run. All about fluttered the cranking bull-roarers and the crash of the stiff bull hides scrapping and rasping over the flinty earth.

Before Paul there materialized the apparition of a dark wave, and he heard the hoof-clacking and snorting of terrified horses milling faster and faster, and then the wave bent, and broke, and the specter herd tore away, chased by the hideous cries of the demon Kiowas.

Shots ripped the night to Paul's right, staccato spatters, cut short. He crouched lower. But the firing wasn't repeated, and the spooked *caballada* raced wildly on.

Paul forgot the shots and began to ride like a Kiowa, trusting to his horse, responding to the hammering rush of the excitement, thinking, relieved, that the herders had fled at the outset, else the Kiowas would have paused for their hair.

Daylight uncovered the shapes of sweat-slick horses, bunched, worn down, subdued, driving obediently, too jaded to trouble the fiends ever driving them onward; when a horse did swerve to turn back, an alert Kiowa headed the animal at once. Paul's practiced eyes told him these were indeed good horses, not so chunky and large of bone as the mountain horses of the Utes, but

161

among them, however, horses revealing the unmistakable small muzzles and broad foreheads and wide-set eyes of Arabian blood.

It wasn't until taking a second long look around that Paul realized a figure was missing from among the familiar Kiowa horsemen. He didn't see Red Calf, and there were no scouts out. Suddenly he remembered the shots.

Awhile, and he began to puzzle over the direction they were taking. Not swinging northward, not yet turning for home. But riding southwest into a collection of treeless hills, in them a remote watering that only Mexicans or Indians would find?

There was water in the naked hills, an undaunted little spring running free at the heel of a bluff, and there, with the hard-driven *caballada* filled and grazing, carefully watched, the Kiowas flung down to rest.

Straight Lance did not rest. His dejected face alone told Paul what had happened to Red Calf. Likewise, the loss of a single man reflected on the raid leader, especially losing Red Calf, who had what a white man would call judgment.

Wolf-Appearing and Kills-Something crossed over, and the latter drew air pictures and formed the signs for Gone and Bad, adding, "Red Calf was brave. He could smell like a coyote and see like an eagle," to which Straight Lance nodded without looking up.

"Since we took so many horses, the Mexicans at the *hacienda* won't be expecting us," said Wolf-Appearing, and again Straight Lance nodded. This time he looked up, a keenness coming into his face.

Paul stiffened to their meaning. They weren't going home, they were going on a revenge raid. If a Kiowa warrior was killed, tribal honor demanded that an enemy scalp be taken. One scalp was enough to accomplish the mission.

"Who will stay with the horses?" Kills-Something asked.

The leader turned his face to them then. "Young Two Tails and White Bird. They can talk any nervous horse to sleep."

"And Bear Neck? If he hadn't let the herder escape, Red Calf would be alive."

"Bear Neck will ride in front with me. That way he may prove he's a man."

Bear Neck got up and strutted forth. "You will see," he boasted, and he whirled into a rapid dance, singing:

You will see,
You will see,
How brave I am.
You will see.

repeating it over and over, a tuneless, grating monotone. Finished, he swaggered back toward his robe, the turkey-cock strut of a vainglorious young man who would never possess the judgment of a Red Calf.

Straight Lance's disapproving voice trailed him: "These Mexicans will not be herders afraid of the dark. *You will see.*" He rose and left the camp and paused beyond earshot, looking down, brooding. Paul followed. "My friend," he said, searching for the words, "you have taken many fine horses. By now the Mexicans at the *hacienda* know that. They will have sent word to the soldiers in the town and the soldiers will come."

"Why tell me things I know?"

Paul, thinking of the women and children at the *hacienda*, studied him before replying. "So you won't go. So you'll go home."

"We have to make the raid. You know why. It's our way. I have no choice." Nonetheless, he sounded weary, Paul thought.

"Bear Neck killed a goatherder," Paul said. "Doesn't that make everything even?"

"Not for a Kiowa. Red Calf must be avenged more than one miserable goatherder. Our hearts burn."

"Does your heart burn to make war on defenseless women and children?"

"Our enemies make war on Kiowa villages."

"So," Paul taunted him, "you will kill a few poor Mexicans and you will carry off some frightened women and children. Is that brave?"

"*Tejan*," said the Kiowa, unmoved, absolute, "always we have raided the Mexicans, same as we have fought the Utes and the white-eyes."

"What if I decide to stay with the horses?"

The cords in the thick, bronze neck stood out. "Your power—your white man's luck—will be with me just the same."

"Not," Paul countered, his mind quickening to dissuade, aware that he must speak as a Kiowa would, as if from a well of savage superstition, "if you misuse it. Not if you use it for the wrong purpose. To war on women and children."

The cutting edge of the dark gaze sliced into Paul's face, and the Kiowa brushed past him, hurriedly. Was that a faint though troubled look in the warrior face, at last a doubting? And why hadn't his friend shown the usual explosive Kiowa temper when Paul had baited him about his bravery, which, as everyone knew, was unquestioned?

Chapter 11

From the crest of the flat-topped peak, Paul observed the murky world filming the hulk of the *hacienda* sleeping on the silent plain. Not a ranch such as he had imagined, a sprawling house and a brood of outer sheds and corrals, everything open. Rather, from what he could piece out of the gloom, it resembled a fortified town. A high, stout wall appeared to enclose it.

That afternoon the Kiowas had recovered Red Calf's body, bathed it, painted the face with vermilion, sealed the eyes with clay, dressed the corpse in the warrior's finest and folded a blanket around it, corded with thongs of rawhide, and buried Red Calf in a stony crevice where, sitting, he could face the rising sun, and then had covered the grave with rocks.

With his eyes, Paul traced the dim line of a road struggling southward toward the town, which he understood was but a few hours' ride. Somewhere along that road roamed Crow Bonnet, another aspiring young warrior, dispatched to watch for soldiers. Wolf-Appearing and Kills-Something were out there afoot around the *hacienda*, gone an hour or more.

He, Paul realized, was here because it had

seemed cowardly not to come, because remaining behind with the horses wouldn't change what was going to happen. And so again he waited like a spectator, uninvolved, helpless, and once again he had the wearying sensation that he was someone else, not himself, not the Paul Latimer Benedict he used to know.

Before many moments they were jogging softly across the sooty plain, more phantom-like than real, drifting toward the low shape of the *hacienda*. No one but a Kiowa, Paul thought, could time a dawn raid so exactly, robed in darkness until in close, reaching the point of destination just as the sky flushed pink as at this very instant.

A light shuffling of hoofs, and the Whirlwinds, hugging the wall, passed a tower and reached the gate. It was closed.

"*Hoom-hoom . . . hoom-hoom.*"

It was Straight Lance hooting. A signal.

A creaking of hinges, and Paul's jaw fell when the wooden gate began to open, pushed from behind. As it swung wider, he saw the slumped body of a guard and Wolf-Appearing and Kills-Something. Two Kiowas tossed them reins to riderless horses.

"*Hooo—kaa—yaa!*"

Everyone whooped, everyone rushed inside.

Paul had no choice. His eager horse shot ahead, a part of the bumping, pell-mell charge that sucked Paul into a broad courtyard. And suddenly he saw the *hacienda* itself, the fawn light on the tile roof, the wide porches.

There was a narrow passageway like a little street leading to the rear, and down this the Kiowas clattered, their cries shrilling to screeches that chilled Paul's blood. Rabbit-like, a man bobbed along a wall. The Kiowas ganged toward him. He seemed to cringe. They rode him down as though he were a strawman. His figure bounced and flopped. All the Kiowas tore ahead.

Paul, forced on by the warriors pressing behind him, saw the passageway open on sheds and corrals, in there terrified horses milling wildly.

Like hornets, the Kiowas swarmed for the horses, jerking at the corral bars, and others afoot, inside, whooping the horses out. A rifle banged. The Indians ignored it. Another shot. It seemed to come from the back side of the *hacienda* as a Kiowa mount broke down. The Indians paused.

Someone shouted as Paul pulled out of the milling bedlam, and he saw four Kiowas, draped low over their horses, cut out to silence the threat. One was Bear Neck. Paul lost sight of him when a knot of loose horses flashed past. When he glanced again, Bear Neck was riding along the porch and crashing his war club against a wooden door. The three Kiowas rushed on, and again Paul heard the rifle. Across, the main body of warriors continued to open the corrals and free the horses. Now the rifleman had quit firing.

Then Paul saw the three Kiowas hurrying back. More Mexican horses scudded past him.

Inside the *hacienda* a woman was screaming, and the sounds knotted and sickened Paul's insides and cut at his breathing. There was a shouted command—Straight Lance's prodding voice—and he saw the Kiowas in motion again, for the corrals were empty, saw the Kiowas streaming for the passageway, howling as they came.

He held up, his eyes caught nearby on Bear Neck lurching from the *hacienda*, a bundle of white slung over one shoulder. A woman screaming and beating her fists against his back. He flung her like a sack across his horse and vaulted up behind her, as lithe as a fat cat, heeled his horse after the departing warriors, and raced past Paul.

A feeling of suffocation began to besiege Paul, an accusing sense of being an abettor to all this, and with it fear. Wildly, powerfully, he had to get out of here. When he galloped back to the courtyard, the Kiowas were holding up, eager, he saw, to pillage the front part of the *hacienda*, yet hesitating. Their delay puzzled Paul until he saw Crow Bonnet, on a sweat-drenched horse, waving and shouting, "Soldiers! Heap soldiers coming!"

And the Indians swept away, howling, and Paul, likewise, clapped heels to the blue horse and followed. By the time he rode outside, the Kiowas had the noses of the Mexican horses pointed north and beginning to run. It was strong daylight. Paul let Star run at will.

Onward, nearing the barren peak where he had first watched the *hacienda*, he looked over his shoulder and sighted the head of the soldiers' column just entering the place.

Sighing, he loosened reins and felt time fall into place, unlike back there, when it had seemed to stand still. The entire raid, he realized now, had required but a few minutes. No wonder the Kiowas terrified the Mexicans.

Turning north, he breathed the dust of the captured horses, his brow puckering as he saw Bear Neck and the poor girl or woman he had stolen.

When the party slanted off into the hills where the *caballada* grazed, Paul expected the Indians to rest and divide the plunder before continuing north; but after time to water the *hacienda* horses and to assign duties to the warriors, Straight Lance called for everyone to hurry.

That was when Paul had his first chance to observe Bear Neck's prize, while the Kiowa sought a horse for her to ride. A girl, though she had the full body of a woman. Sixteen or so, he judged, trembling with fear, yet struggling to mask it, shocked into understanding of her helplessness, waiting, waiting. The slim face of a girl, softly turned, childlike in the loose, white cotton nightgown. High cheekbones like an Indian's and her braided hair as black as a Kiowa's, only softer-looking, and her skin had an olive tint and her nose was high-bridged. She held her head aloof, as if they were a pack of barbarians, beneath her, mere dirt under her bare feet. Brave. Very brave.

Paul saw the large, black eyes discover him all at once, widening, startled, and rising up through them a desperate appeal. When he neither spoke nor moved, he saw her entreaty dull and go out, and she turned back to her waiting.

Pity for her filled him and overflowed. And what could he do except pity her? By the rigid rules of the Kiowa raiding code, she belonged to Bear Neck, since he had touched her first and taken her. She was his property as much as any horse or mule he might take. Just seeing her left Paul deeply touched and miserable, aware that he was powerless to help her, that, indeed, he was almost as helpless as she.

He turned his gaze away.

Yet, after the Kiowas drove the horses out upon the brown plain, it was seldom that Paul's eyes did not seek her, and he fell behind as Bear Neck, slowed by leading his captive's horse, also lagged.

Straight Lance hastened back and signaled Paul forward to his usual place. Paul, moving up alongside him, saw something shuttle over his captor's face as Straight Lance split his attention between Paul and Bear Neck and the girl, before racing back toward the point of the *caballada*. With the blue horse running, Paul looked southwest and felt a tug of surprise.

There on the plain, coming hard, roiled the dusty smoke of pursuit. A big band of riders.

The *caballada* was traveling at an easy lope. Straight Lance raised a shrill and hideous yell, more animal than human in sound, a drawn-out cry that hung above the steady clattering, and Paul recognized the chilling scream of the cougar. The other raiders took it up, crowding the spooked horses, which laid back their ears and walled their eyes, stretching out, surging, fleeing, banded in fear, haunted by the screeching fiends behind and on their flanks.

The pursuers' dust, Paul saw, was no nearer. When he looked again, the dust hung as a low, brown ball; it was beginning to fade. Long minutes later it had disappeared.

He could not recall a similar ride so relentless, not even when taking the Ute horses. This was a bigger, deadlier game. The Kiowas forced the horses to run long after they began to tire and rebel; when a weary animal cut out, the Indians yowled it back.

But even Spanish horseflesh could run out of iron, and finally Straight Lance pulled in and waved the riders to ease off the brutal pace;

and they let the horses lope a spell, then trot and running-walk. For some miles it was thus. Presently the raid leader yipped a signal, a coyote-sounding cry, urging yet unhurried. The Kiowas picked it up, the notes like singing, like a chorus, Paul thought, and the *caballada* began to stir, sweeping faster, faster, but without the previous fright, with soft rustlings; in seconds the plain erupted in dust, the band loping again, a pace it could now hold for miles.

Far later, Paul saw a hump of land jutting above the plain. Beyond it the horses reached water; by then the afternoon sun was wearing down. While the horses went to grazing the stunted grass, the Kiowas ate and rested.

The time had come, Paul was aware, for the war leader to divide the spoils. Here the man who had excelled most in the raid received first choice of the horses. A war leader, who must be liberal to maintain his status, got what was left.

As Straight Lance moved toward the *caballada*, the Kiowas rose with him. To Wolf-Appearing and Kills-Something, he gave first choices of the best mounts, for the two warriors had been the bravest, scaling the high wall of the *hacienda* and killing the guard and opening the gate—a feat the Whirlwinds would be telling over and over for years to come. Crow Bonnet, the young warrior, rated next for watching the road and sighting the soldiers, then racing back to bring the alarm. After him came Buffalo Head and Eagle Heart and Yellow Horse for killing the Mexican with the rifle, and Bear Neck for taking the captive, and others accordingly for lesser roles. Each warrior picked his animals, eyeing them carefully to memorize their markings. Thereafter, on the homeward trail, there would be no question of ownership.

"*Tejan*," Straight Lance said at the end, "there are some good horses left. Take two. You have ridden hard. You haven't complained."

"*Ah-ho*," Paul said, thanking him, his right hand out, the palm parallel to his body. "I have one good horse. That's enough."

The Kiowas laughed. Only a white man would say that. "Every rider needs more than one horse," Straight Lance said, waiting hopefully. But when Paul said no more, he took the refusal with a shrug, saying, "I will make you a good Kiowa yet. Just wait."

The division concluded, they turned for camp. Suddenly Bear Neck yelled and took off running and Paul saw the captive fleeing. Her black hair flying, her flashing brown legs slim and round, she made Paul think of a frightened child as she clutched her gown above her knees to run the faster.

Bear Neck, charging across, soon caught her and carried her back, kicking and flailing. Paul watched, mouth creased, fighting the wildness quivering his vitals. Now Bear Neck dumped her on his robe.

The girl, with dignity, righted herself and sat apart, aloof and proud, a slim, frozen white image. Bear Neck offered her some dried buffalo meat. She turned her head aside without so much as glancing at it. He offered again, as if to force her to accept. She pushed it away.

Angered, he caught her wrist and dragged her to her feet.

Paul held his arms against his thighs and felt his insides kick over.

She fought to free herself. Bear Neck, angered, took hold of her shoulders and shook her violently. She struggled harder. Out of patience, he struck her to the ground. She screamed.

It was the scream that broke through Paul's rigidity. He was almost upon Bear Neck before he realized what he was doing. He caught him by the arm and spun him about and heard his explosive grunt. The girl, sprawled, raised great startled eyes to Paul.

Paul, seeing Bear Neck's knife at the same instant, drew his own and faced him, a dead certainty ringing in his mind. This time he had to kill Bear Neck; yet if he did so the Kiowas, bound by honor, would surely kill him for taking the life of a tribesman.

"*Tejan*, I will cut out your white man's heart—

I will eat it raw," the Kiowa swore. "You will not break your knife *this* time."

He leaped forward wildly, his suddenness driving Paul back. Shuffling for footing in the sandy soil, Paul was suddenly half down and the Kiowa charging him like a buffalo bull, knife swinging.

With a violent scramble, Paul wrenched up and slashed—missing, but causing the Indian to hesitate and miss his own cut—and then they squared off, knees bent, feet wide, circling. Paul held his head and body well back, the knife blade extended before him like a sword, his left hand clenched and low for balance. Bear Neck, grip-ping his knife with the point down, made a thrust and drew back.

They started circling again at the crouch, and when Bear Neck drove in slashing, and Paul slanted out of reach, the Kiowa hooted scornfully, "Fight—white man! Fight!" He was growing bolder.

At once Paul aimed a slicing lunge at the generous belly. The stroke missed by a hair. For a moment it wiped the taunting from the heavy-lipped face. Paul began to tire. The hot sliver of the forgotten pain of his invalid months burned his chest again, but when he hawked in his throat and spat, there was no blood and he felt better.

Bear Neck seemed to sense his advantage. He

started narrowing the circle. They fell into a locking wrestle, and Paul's arms grew weaker and the hurt in his chest deepened, as if some piece of him had pulled apart.

Bear Neck was slowly forcing his knife toward Paul's heart. Paul heaved and budged the blade back a little. There it stayed. Nor could he hold it there much longer.

Swift, pounding steps. A shout. And Paul felt powerful hands tearing him and Bear Neck loose, and saw a figure wedging between them and throwing them back. And Straight Lance's furious voice lashed them:

"Fools—you have fought long enough. A Kiowa cannot kill a brother." He blocked them off, his eyes flickering from man to man, daring them to disobey him, the war journey leader.

Bear Neck, recovering from his surprise, whapped his chest and howled, "She's my captive. You saw him butt in."

"Why did you do that, *Tejan*?" the Kiowa leader asked, cutting him a curious look, puzzled rather than reprimanding.

That he had no ground to stand on, Paul was well aware. Anyway, he said, "As a friend, I ask you to return her to her people. She's just a girl. Not a woman."

"She's Bear Neck's captive. And your eyes deceive you, *Tejan*. She's old enough to make him a good wife or a slave for his mother."

Paul shook his head. "She's too young. Send her back."

"It's the Kiowa way, my friend. I can't change it."

Finality flattened his tone and Paul saw its effect freeze the girl's face. But she did not whimper or beg. He was startled, next, to hear her release a volley of Spanish at Straight Lance. What she said took him by surprise. He answered her, speaking broken Spanish, using gestures to fill in his words. She spoke faster, higher, her earnest desperation touching for Paul to see.

"I don't understand," the Kiowa said when she finished. He trailed his gaze from Bear Neck to Paul, and his voice acquired a judicial inflection, "Who touched her first? Bear Neck," he asked roughly, his old vexation with the younger warrior showing, "are you telling the truth?"

"Truth? She's mine. Everybody saw me ride out with her. Everybody saw how brave I was!"

"I didn't call you a coward," Straight Lance said, annoyed. He turned to Paul. "Are you claiming her? If you are, why didn't you speak out instead of trying to kill a brother?"

Some instinct stifled Paul's denial while his mind sorted out the blurred segments of the action at the *hacienda*. The running horses, the Kiowas either busy at the corrals or dashing for the passageway. Possibly no one, he gathered

178

suddenly, had seen Bear Neck actually take the girl. He found himself groping toward that bare chance, compelled by her child's appealing face, by the dark, importuning eyes.

"Yes," he said, equaling the arrogance of Bear Neck, "I also claim this young woman."

He saw his captor's skepticism; that—and then Paul saw what he had recognized before in times of crisis, his friend expressing what he longed to believe: the keen hope that Paul at last was truly becoming a Whirlwind Kiowa. By now Bear Neck was howling and arm-waving his claim and beating his chest.

The war leader silenced him with a single look. "We'll let the captive decide. She's the only one who knows," and he addressed her in rough Spanish, a certain ceremony about his manner.

She lifted her head, that high, proud way that Paul knew now was characteristic of her. A small, fine face, he saw, the bones softly molded. A face lined with fear, the paleness of a face that could scarcely be more than a girl's.

He heard her begin to speak, a slow distinctness to her words, and he saw her point to him, and to Bear Neck. Her lips ceased moving. Paul's eyes were still upon her when Straight Lance spoke to him in Kiowa, "She says you touched her first there on the porch of the *hacienda*. Then Bear Neck rushed up and took her away on his horse . . ." He paused, alertly eyeing Paul's face for deception, and Paul, meeting that ferreting, that warrior's shrewdness, hoped his eagerness did not betray him as he nodded.

Swiftly the Indian smiled at him. "So now you have a wife, *Tejan*," the pleased voice informed him. "A good Mexican girl. Like all Mexicans, she will soon make a good Indian and she will bear you many brave sons and you can live like a Kiowa. That is good. Take the dun mare she rode." His hand described a fluid sign for Done. The war leader had decided; no one could refute him. Bear Neck slunk off, for once voiceless.

Paul, too dazed to more than glance at her, and aware that all were waiting, went over and touched her; and, like a proud Kiowa lord, signed for her to follow him. Rising obediently, she trailed him as he led her mare where he had picketed the blue gelding and spread his robe for the night.

There he motioned for her to sit. She obeyed, though not meekly, more as if accepting his invitation. She was trembling, and in her eyes he saw shreds of the fear she had shown Bear Neck, which stabbed him to the quick, which sent anger flying through him. Her face smoothed, as if she must learn to please him.

"*Gracias*," she murmured. "*Muchas gracias, señor.*"

His ego hardly required that. He needed time, much time to think what he was going to do with her, his slave, his captive, his "wife." He became flustered. To cover his confusion, he opened a rawhide pouch containing dry buffalo meat and extended it to her. She hesitated. "Eat," he ordered her, making the sign. She took a small piece. Feeling more agitated by the moment, he led Star farther out and staked him and came back. She was nibbling hungrily on the tough, dry ration. Picking a place on the robe well away from her, he sat and started on his supper, thinking: Uncomplicated. Simple. No doubt beset by evil spirits and haunted by devils, though adroit enough to circumvent Bear Neck with a determined lie. He admired her stratagem. What white woman could have thought so quickly?

She turned toward him, and her voice startled him. "*Americano,*" the question in her eyes lying unspoken on her tongue: Why are you here?

He sat up. "You speak English?"

"*Inglés*—a little, yes. My people—we lived in Juarez two years. I attend the convent of the Sisters of Mercy. My father—the customs. My father's politico friend, he is shot, so we come home." Her voice pleasantly against his ear. Not so simple after all, soft and musical.

"How old are you?"

"Seventeen."

Motion took his eyes away from her. A figure advancing toward them. He thought immediately of Bear Neck, back to fight, though he couldn't be certain in this light. Rising, he saw that it was his captor.

"*Tejan*," he began shaking his head, puzzled. "Although you ride like a Kiowa and are brave, I wonder how you, even you, while sitting your horse, could reach many lengths of a horse and touch the captive first when another Kiowa, afoot, was already there . . . But I understand. You have unusual powers, my friend. It is good." He passed on, and Paul released his pulled-in breath, the warm, parting words lingering in his ears, "*Ghet-tai-ghe*—it is good."

"Is wrong?" she asked, alarmed.

"Nothing wrong. It's all right," he said to reassure her. As he faced her, asking what in the name of God he was going to do, it burst upon him that he forgot he had the power of life and death over her. She was *his* property. *His.* He could keep her or give her away. Also, he realized abruptly, he could return her to her people. He knelt and began to talk rapidly:

"The soldiers aren't very far behind us. When they come in sight tomorrow, you can ride back to them and they'll take you to the *hacienda*."

Dismay caught her face. "Ah, *Dios*! No—no. They're as bad as the *Indios*. No. You give me a horse. I will ride alone."

"We're many miles from your home. You'd get lost. Die of thirst. I'll take you back." His meaning startled him. He hadn't realized he meant to say that.

"You forget—no, no. You look like an *Indio*. My people would kill you on sight. No. No."

He could see why, and he dropped the matter. Feeling the sudden chill of evening, he remembered she wore only the gown and no shoes. Digging into his light pack, he brought forth moccasins and a buckskin shirt and gave them to her. Lost in the folds of the loose-fitting shirt, she reminded him more than ever of big-eyed child.

"*Gracias*," she smiled, hugging her arms.

"What is your name?"

"Bianca Chaves."

"Mine's Paul—Paul Benedict." It was strange how foreign his name sounded from his own tongue. "The Kiowas call me *Tejan*. You'd better get some sleep."

She curled up and drew one edge of the big robe over her, and he took the other side of the robe, doing likewise. Later, he opened his eyes to starlit darkness, thinking, for a moment, that he lay in his canyon hut. The air was still, yet there was a sound near him. All at once he remembered where he was. It was she, stirring in her sleep, and he drifted off again, groaning softly, troubled. What could he do about her?

Chapter 12

At dawn, he came awake to the harshness of Kiowa voices and the restless whistling and stamping of the *caballada*. And, nearby, the *chuff* of moccasined feet in the sand. Sitting up, Paul saw her returning from the spring, touching at the black gloss of her hair, her small face freshened and hopeful, unafraid and natural for the first time. As her eyes discovered him, a tiny fear penciled her forehead.

He stood, in him the acute wish to please her, to dispel what he saw. "Today," he said, "you are going home."

Her expression altered only slightly, thoughtfully. "Is long way."

In lieu of a reply, he dug into the rawhide pouch for their breakfast.

The horses were milling like nervous ghosts, the Kiowas mounted. Paul switched his saddle to the dun mare and helped Bianca Chaves up. Soon, Straight Lance led away, and the *caballada*, quite large now, went rustling by, a tide of solid colors flowing northward toward the plain.

Not far, and Paul reined out of the dusty column, apprehensive that someone would attempt to stop him. No one did. She was his, indeed. For the band swept ahead, the Kiowas never pausing, and he angled back along the broad trace the horses had made hurrying to water late yesterday. Into him, suddenly, charged the awareness of what was happening, or had already happened. Not only could he take her back because she belonged to him, but also he was free. He could leave the Kiowas.

"Is wrong?"

Plunged in thought, he flung up his head. "Nothing's wrong." Only there was something; it dulled his voice. Did he wish to leave the Whirlwinds yet? He breathed deeply. Heeling the blue horse into a running walk, he settled down for the long ride to the *hacienda*.

The grayness of the early hours dissolved, seared off by the brilliant high-desert sun. Paul followed the broad pocking of the trail. Behind him, because Star had a longer stride than the mare's, Bianca Chaves rode without complaint or awkwardness. He seldom glanced at her. Those times when he did, he found her eyes fixing him, a more than ordinary interest behind them, and finally he said, "Do I frighten you?" Impulsively touching his bearded chin and cheeks, he felt a smile spreading across his face as it had not in a long time.

She formed her lips to reply, perhaps in jest, that rare quality that he had so missed among the grim warriors. For another moment he saw the expression animate her small-boned features; then it fled and she cried, "Look!"

He whipped front, seeing brownish dust staining the plain that hadn't been there moments earlier. Low and fuming. Quick, bold strokes coloring the landscape. Gripped by a cold premonition, he halted. The light stain became a dense patch of brown and the patch became a roiling cloud, within it the hazy shapes of horsemen. His heart pumped faster. She said it for him:

"*Soldados! Soldados!*" She kept shaking her head, and his insight crystallized that she was afraid he intended to leave her here.

He whirled the blue horse and when the mare, skittish, turned and veered sideways against the frantic reining of its mistress, Paul quirted the dun across the rump until she straightened out running, surprisingly fleet, forcing the gelding to let out.

A long, hard, bolting run. Paul scanned the plain. To his relief the dusty cloud was smaller, certainly no nearer. He led on, in the alternate lope and running-walk. By afternoon, now following the fresh tracks of the *caballada*, he could see no trailing dust.

He picked a place to rest off the pitted trail, in a patch of switch mesquite where he could observe the long back stretches, which he did at length, quartering his gaze back and forth before dismounting. She stood slumped in weariness, grateful for the pause.

"*Indio*," she said, nodding. "You are like an *Indio*. You look, look. Look everywhere."

"A good thing since I have only a knife, don't you think?"

After they had drunk from the water paunch, Paul sat a while, reflecting. He said, "There's a fort some distance from the *Rio Grande*—Fort Stockton. We'll ride there. I'll see the authorities about sending you home. You understand? You savvy? You comprehend?" He was, he realized, talking with his hands like a sign-making Indian, and he broke off, damning his lack of Spanish.

She was sitting on the robe, the loose folds of the nightgown covering all but the tips of her too-large moccasins. That floppy gown bothered him. Somehow he was going to have to do something about a dress for her.

"*Politico?*" she said, distrust threading into her voice. "You take me to a *politico*, yes?" She was holding her head high, which he recognized as her one positive sign of defiance, that and the smoldering eyes.

He understood. She was thinking of Juarez. "No—no. No *politico*. I mean I will take you to the soldiers—the *Americano* soldiers."

Fear leaped into her eyes. "*Soldados*—no. Never."

"What I mean," he said, squirming in his anxiety to make her understand, "is the *Americano* soldiers represent the *Americano* government—my government—which will talk to

187

your government—the government of Mexico—about returning you to your home. See?"

"No—is bad—very bad—gov-ern-ment," she said, her full lips pouting and separating the last word. "Too much *politico*. Very bad. My father . . ."

"Your father—the *politico*," he nodded wearily, rising to look again. Her small, clear voice pulled him about, and he saw her incredulous expression:

"You—an *Indio*—talk to gov-ern-ment—mine —yes?"

"I'm not an Indian. I'm a white man."

She laughed outright, a spontaneous laugh as tinkling clear as a tiny bell. "*Americano*, yes. Only you look like *Indio*, yes."

He continued to watch her face, fascinated by her transformation, her doubt erased, the high, small nose wrinkling, the dark pools of her eyes sparkling, all alight, gay, the small face of fine olive skin simultaneously childlike and womanlike, for she was both.

He left her to move past the horses and look again. Nothing stirred the emptiness, that splintery-bright sunlight. He watched until his eyes tired, until he was certain. But they're back there, he said to himself, and turned to go.

Sunset flamed red and yellow, lavishly vivid, the desert aglow, by the time they caught up with the camped Kiowas, the Spanish horses grazing, herded in tight, ready for rushing flight to the north.

Paul rode straight to his old captor. The Kiowa betrayed not the slightest surprise. "The soldiers aren't many hours behind us," Paul reported.

"You saw them?"

"This morning. We couldn't go around them to the *hacienda*."

"I knew you couldn't, *Tejan*. The Mexicans are like hungry wolves trailing a band of buffalo. They never give up. You don't always see them. But let a calf stray or an old bull get careless—and suddenly they close in and the buffalo is caught." His tone was instructive, reflective, pleased. "You are learning, my friend. Someday you will be a wise Kiowa. A great horse-taker."

Paul glanced around, concerned. "You're going to camp here all night?"

"Now, *Tejan*, you know we Kiowas have more sense than buffalo calves. Let the Mexicans follow us. If they're that foolish, tomorrow they will die."

"You mean we'll fight them?"

"My friend, you are thinking like a white-eye again. We're going ahead after we've rested. Except we're taking a different way back. No water until we come to the Great River."

"But the horses . . . without water?"

"Without water tomorrow—and into the next day, stopping to rest now and then. Some horses will die, the weak ones. The best ones will make it. Those are the horses we want, anyway."

How needless and cruel, Paul thought. On second thought, he could see the practical logic behind the plan, the hard, primitive sense, based on successful practice. By simply enduring, the Kiowas would escape; also there were too few of them to stand in an open fight.

"My friend, make certain your water paunch is full. You'll need every drop," Straight Lance said.

Taking the mare's reins, Paul led the horses to the spring and handed Bianca Chaves down. He felt sorry for her. Fatigue lay darkly over her face. But she glanced down at his hand still on her arm, as though he were performing an unexpected gesture of gallantry. Her lips moved, conveying a teasing smile. *"Un caballero—yes,"* she said, which caused him to smile.

She crouched to drink and Paul did likewise, dipping his face into the cool abundance of the sweet water. He heard her washing her face and hands and he saw her drying herself with the hem of the long gown. She stood refreshed and strengthened, all traces of fatigue gone. He went to filling the water paunch. He staked the horses away from the spring and spread the big robe and opened the food pouch. They ate with ravenous pulls at the rich, stringy meat.

Just before dark he wandered out to the horses, brooding over the brutal ride ahead. Tomorrow and into the next day, Straight Lance had said. Coming back, he found her curled up asleep. The late twilight laid a shading of ivory over her face, and her smooth features suggested the delicacy of carved shell.

As he watched, she moaned a little and a sudden sympathy bit into him. God, how young she was! She had fallen asleep without pulling up the robe; therefore, he drew it over her, carefully, so as not to wake her. It came to him that she hadn't complained or whimpered once during the day, and he recalled what the Kiowas said about the Mexicans. How close they were to the Indians themselves, like distant kin; how quickly they became as Indians.

He stretched out on the robe and for a moment everything stood out in his mind—the merciless morrow, the relentless Kiowas, the punished horses, now the sleeping girl—all combining to create the mocking sense of unreality that haunted him from time to time—after which sleep drugged him.

No more than moments had passed, it seemed, surely, when he heard the sounds of breaking camp, the Kiowas moving and talking, the silky rustling of hoofs in sand. He touched the girl's arm. She sat up and rubbed her eyes.

"We're leaving," he said.

Mounted, the two of them waited. The night wind was rising, a humming voice whose breath carried biting chill.

A Kiowa yipped. At that signal the Spanish horses went jostling off through the velvet darkness, and Paul and Bianca Chaves followed the hoof-meshing sounds, which soon hardened to a rolling beat on the hard plain. Dust rose; he tasted its acrid grit. All at once his mind was swarming with imagery. The *caballada* a dark wedge flying northward, he and the girl as moths fluttering beneath the white haze of the fickle moon, or mythical creatures being carried away to a dusky world where a strange destiny awaited them. He felt the lift of exaltation.

Several hours, and they rested and went drumming off again. Much later, a pallid glow flushed the eastern sky, letting in shafts of fawn light. Still covered by night, Paul saw the advent of day speeding toward him. Light spilling and running like quicksilver. And the world turned golden, hard after it the bold eye of the sun. Still, the horses ran.

By afternoon the horses were beginning to drag, to rebel when the Kiowas pressed them, to quit the bunch more often, until sometimes the Indians had to quirt them into obeying.

Paused again, the muzzles of the blue horse and the mare crusted white. Paul gave Bianca Chaves water, and while she rested he walked the horses, leading them out and back. When he decided they had cooled off enough, he rationed water into a rawhide pouch for each horse.

As for the Kiowas, they merely turned their used-up mounts into the *caballada* and, expertly using horsehair ropes, lassoed their next mounts.

Paul was tying the rawhide pouch behind the mare's saddle when he heard a horse clatter up. At the same instant Bianca cried out sharply and behind him Bear Neck's taunting voice hissed:

"Nobody but a fool white-eye would waste water that way when there are plenty of horses. Now you'll have none for yourself or the woman there who is rightfully mine."

Paul, with a start, came about and instinctively touched the knife at his belt.

"You are slow, *Tejan*, like an old buffalo bull ready for the wolves. I could have killed you just then."

"Why didn't you try again?"

The flesh-heavy face feigned zealous sincerity. "Your memory is also slow, *Tejan*. *We are brothers*. Wasn't that what Straight Lance said when he stopped us? Just when you were weakening? Just when I could feel your strength slipping? When I was about to kill you?" He smashed his right hand downward. "Brother! Straight Lance is no brother of mine. He's yours—and you a white man—a *Tejano*. When we fight for the last time, Straight Lance will not be around."

In a flash of hoofs he rode for the *caballada*.

Paul, following him with his eyes, did not move until he heard the girl's light step at his side, and her voice, older and wiser than he thought possible:

"He will try to kill you again."

"Bear Neck is a braggart and a coward."

"The more to be feared. A coward will strike from behind . . ." She was gazing up into his eyes in that appealing way she had, at the same time shy, at the same time direct.

He said, "They're on the move again," and finished his tying.

After that, they seemed to ride across a never-fading plain of smoky fire, the brutal mace of the sun hanging to Paul's left, the strung-out horses bobbing northward, pennant manes flying, tails streaming, leaving a wake of saffron dust. The glazy world shed splinters of yellow sunlight. The wind sobbed, as hot and dry as a panting dog. He saw a gray horse quit, and lashed back. Another, a sorrel, head drooping, on trembling legs, refused to go on despite repeated quirtings, and finally the Kiowas left it to perish, a forlorn animal of blaze-faced beauty gazing after its vanishing companions, its gentle eyes dull and begging. Paul looked away.

Now he and the Chaves girl rode on the left flank of the horses, out of the choking dust. The sun hung at four o'clock or so. Once more he turned to look behind, and this time he marked the first blot of dust, so near it startled him. Far back there, he glimpsed toiling horsemen, and it struck through him what was happening. The soldiers were making a last determined run, recklessly spending the strength of their mounts in a final dash.

The Kiowas pressed on, howling the horses faster, quirting the laggards. The sun sank lower, smothering in a bed of copper. Although the trailing dust drew no nearer, neither did it grow smaller. The desert light closed down. A mauve veil obscured the dust and the struggling horsemen. New sounds struck: Paul heard the faint popping of rifles, muted and futile at this distance. And then he heard them no more.

During the long night at each rest halt, Paul gave the Chaves girl water and allowed a trickle for each horse, saving back the last for her in the morning; for himself he took only a swallow. In that victory over self, the insight became clear that even before this he had learned to endure like a Whirlwind Kiowa, willing his mind to resist the craving of his body.

Just when Paul thought the night would never end, patches of gray kindled the eastern wall of darkness, and to his right he saw the Kiowas walking the listless horses into daylight.

As he turned and peered backward, dreading what might yet lurk there, dawn burst full strength, a yellow rush of light, and he saw the plain empty of either dust or toiling horsemen. The race was won.

Chapter 13

Several more hours had passed when Paul spied the great fortress of the mountains, shrouded in haze, jutting up in broken battlements and castles, aloof from the smoky hell of the desert floor. Still later, he saw the beaten Spanish horses throw up their heads and pick up their feet and, noses high into the hot wind, hasten their going. He knew what those awakenings meant: water. They smelled the *Rio Grande,* the Kiowas' Great River. In no time at all the horses were pouring forward, in a dead run, the Indians unable to halt them had they wished; instead, joyfully trailing, whooping like herd boys.

And the *caballada,* running hell bent, instinctive, wild-eyed, packed, crazed, snorting, trampling brush in its path, overrode the chorusing voices. Some miles onward Paul saw the glittering ribbon of the river unwinding down from the northwest, and soon afterward he saw the horses surge into the shallow water and swiftly dip their heads and stand as motionless as statues.

A short while and the trailwise Kiowas rode among the horses and quirted them across the river, and held them there a spell before letting them drink again, after which they herded them into loose bunches for grazing.

Paul watched the sun set the bald peaks on fire, crowning them orange and pink and crimson. Purple darkened the slopes. He led the horses to the river, led them back, and staked them fast. Swiftly the sun dropped from sight. On the robe Bianca Chaves was already curled in sleep. He slumped downward. His body became a leaden weight before he touched the robe and he seemed to sink through its softness into the ground, while his whole being yet swayed with the steady motion of the blue horse, Star. A sigh escaped him. He dropped like a stone into sleep.

The hungering smell of meat cooking reached him; sitting up, he saw that someone had taken a deer. Straight Lance waved him over, and Paul cut off a portion. Carrying a brand from the fire, he started a blaze and cooked breakfast, his first warm food since leaving the American side of the river six or seven days ago. Or was it eight, nine? He couldn't say. Days were as sections of a telescope, sliding and overlapping, each the same, marked by sun rising, sun setting, endless motion, scattered waterings, scant food, and darkness and wind and dust.

Lassitude settled over him. Idly noticing her tentlike gown again, he grimaced and cut off a piece of horsehair rope and fashioned a belt for her, knotting strands of buckskin at the ends for tying.

"*Gracias.*" She clapped her hands in delight and

drew it around her waist, and burst into peals of laughter as she held the ends of the belt out in front of her. "Is too long, yes."

Paul laughed with her. "My apologies. I guess I was thinking of a much older woman."

"A fat one?"

He declined an answer and busied himself shortening the belt, and when she tied it, again delighted, she said, "Is very beautiful. *Gracias*."

"You need a dress," he said. "That can be arranged at Fort Stockton."

Her look of pleasure vanished. *"Be arranged?"*

"I mean there will be officers' ladies at the fort. They will look out for you. They will find you a dress."

Feeling stiffened her face, a close-eyed suspicion that thinned her even features. *"Soldados—no!"*

"But these soldiers won't harm you. They will protect you. You can stay at the fort until you go home." Of a sudden he quit, recognizing that she did not and could not comprehend yet. To her, all soldiers were the same.

He bathed in the river. The wind and sun drying his body produced a languor that soothed his senses, brushing out the hurry and dread of the past days. He dressed slowly, consuming much time.

Climbing the slope, he saw her facing the river, watching; seeing him, she came to meet him, small, slim, graceful, her walk swaying. An awareness of a gap in his life these long months wound through him, pulsing fast, and he increased his step to reach her sooner.

"You gone a long time," she said, disapproving.

"It's a lazy day."

"Bear Neck watches me. Is wrong. I'm afraid. When your friend rode away, I came to find you."

Paul scowled. "Rode away? Where?"

"That way," she said, nodding, indicating the mountains.

"Deer hunting."

"You come with me, yes?" she said, her head high; without waiting for his reply, she turned downriver and Paul followed. She picked her way through a dense jungle of reeds to the river bank and trailed along it, pausing often to gaze at the slow-gliding greenish water. Where the browsing river had formed a back pool and rocks, white and smooth, marched like flagstones into the shallows, she hesitated and said, "Now—you look so," and pointed upriver.

To humor her, he folded his arms and struck an exaggerated watchfulness, and heard her drawn-in gasp of pleasure when she splashed in the water. Spray flecked his neck; more of it, and more. He pretended to turn in annoyance. There was an immediate shriek, though the splashing ceased. But when he turned front, more water stung his back. He ignored her and presently he heard no sound, not even splashing. Tiring of his pose, he adopted a slouched attitude, eyes fixed upstream, amused, determined to wait her out.

Something flitted past his ear, a white pebble. He started to turn; instantly she shrilled, "No—no—you watch for *Indios*—yes!"

"Then better quit throwing at me," he growled, feigning irritation.

Still another pebble flew past his head, still another. Hands on hips, he assumed a threatening voice, "I'm going to count to ten. Then I'm going to look. You'd better be dressed. One . . . two . . . three . . . four . . . five . . ." He paused. "Six . . . seven . . . eight . . . nine . . . ten—" Hearing no protest, he hitched slowly about, surprised to find her fully clothed, reclining on a flat rock, sun-drying her glossy black hair.

Her teasing laugh floated up to him, "I fooled you, yes?"

Light-hearted, they laughed together—and he hadn't laughed with abandon like that in so long. An inane, quaking laughter that started around his middle and shook him until he had to clench his sides, turning him all loose and resistless, legs wobbly. Weakly, he dropped to a rock and faced her.

"Why, you didn't even take a bath," he mocked her. "All that time you were just sitting there sunning."

For rebuttal, she handscooped water and dashed

it against his face, and he in turn splashed her and she shrieked her outrage, and they kept up the barrage until both were streaming wet, then ceased, silent for a waiting moment, too out of breath to go on, then slumped in laughter. Shaking her head, brushing and combing with her slim fingers, she turned her face to the warm sun to dry her hair.

Paul, watching her and listening to the humming river, noticed again the finely drawn formation of her face. How unfortunate, he thought, that he couldn't sketch her before he took her to Fort Stockton. Never had he seen hair so black, so black it was blue-black; it cascaded to her waist, and the sun picked up its myriad of tiny glints like crushed light. Time meant nothing. He seemed afloat on a drowsy sea, eyes half-shuttered, and the rock on which he lay, bathed by the sun, felt as warm as life, cast up on a glassy shore.

When they rose to go, the forenoon was slinking away. Paul led the way along the sandy bank and through the tall reeds, parting them, rank on rank, for her to pass. Seeing her up close, he saw again how small she was, though not slight, not frail, and how her hair, in thick, glossy braids, made her look even younger than she was. As she passed him, he looked down into her face.

"*Gracias*," she said, and in the deepness of her large eyes, intent on his face, he recognized the expression he had noticed other times. He smiled at her, vaguely pleased, for there was liking in her eyes. She spoke, and her voice might have belonged to a child, "Hungry, yes? I am . . . just a little."

"There's some jerky left," he assured her, eager to please her, this first time she had asked him for anything. "I'll get you some. When we reach the sand dunes, there'll be deer. All we want." Immediately he caught his miscalculation. The sand dunes lay north of Fort Stockton. By then, she would be safe, in the quarters of some Army officer's watchful lady. He moved on ahead of her, his forehead ridged with a frown.

He came alert at sight of a figure waiting near the blue horse and the mare. A burly shape that could be only Bear Neck. Behind him the resting Kiowas lolled like fat wolves, watching. Farther on, Paul saw that his captor hadn't returned, and understood what was coming. His steps no faster, but deliberate, he advanced on a straight line to the Kiowa.

"What do you want?" Paul clipped.

"Now we fight."

"That's behind us—settled."

"No—we fight again. While our war leader isn't here to protect his beloved white brother."

"I won't fight you again. I tell you it's settled."

Bear Neck exhaled scorn, Kiowa scorn: haughty, despising, taunting, derisive, hating.

In place of anger, Paul felt a weary disgust. Unlike Straight Lance, Bear Neck would never change because he couldn't. His uncomplicated mind, insensible to change, always impelled by dark moods, always in shadow, moved along simple, gouged-out channels. And one was hate, hate for all whites, for any white man, above all a *Tejano*.

He heard Bianca come up and post herself near his side. Hardly had she done so when Bear Neck sprang across and seized her arm and twisted it, forcing her sharp cry.

Paul pounced on him a split moment after, and felt Bear Neck wheeling, ready, almost in unison, prepared for the customary knife fight. Paul's fury flamed; it soared higher and higher, then burst. Instead of digging for his own knife, he drove his fist into the folds of tallow layering the bronze belly, ramming all his strength behind the punch; and when Bear Neck brought down his hands to protect his stomach from a second blow, Paul smashed him in the face, two quick blows. Bear Neck reeled. He fell ponderously, and Paul snatched the dropped knife and flung it away.

"Now—" Paul hacked, "we'll fight my way."

And he kicked hard, laying the inside of his right foot against Bear Neck's head. When the Kiowa, down, tried to stagger up, Paul deliberately kicked him down again; and as Bear Neck wrenched upward again, Paul seized him by the hair and jerked him to his feet and flung him to the ground. Bear Neck rolled and caught himself, trying to push up. Paul booted him in the stomach, and the young man's cry was still in his throat when Paul, kneeling, clamping both hands, began choking him. The dark eyes bulged to their whites. Paul squeezed harder, liking the pain he caused. Harder. Harder. Under him, Bear Neck was growing weaker.

"Paul!"

Someone was calling his name. *Paul! Paul!* From a distance. Strange-sounding. He relaxed his grip a trifle, but as Bear Neck struggled and gasped, Paul renewed his grasp.

"Paul!" Screamed this time.

He continued to choke the sweaty neck.

"Paul—Paul!" Her voice.

Of a sudden he let go and Bear Neck flopped free, head arched back, wheezing, sucking for wind, and Paul, staring dully, no longer understood himself.

His movements unsteady, he stood clear of the twisting form, longing to rid himself of the Kiowa's musk. And heard his own wretched, wrenched-out accusation, "Damn you—oh, goddamn you—get up and go."

He was dripping sweat, the stink of murder fouling his nostrils and a strange brassiness on his tongue. A sense of uncleanness swept him.

Head down, he turned blindly for the river, aware of the girl a step behind him.

He scrubbed his face and chest and arms and neck, and afterward slumped on a rock, his eyes downcast, his breathing shallow. She spoke, close at his shoulder.

"I was afraid, yes—afraid if you killed him, the *Indios* would kill you."

Turning his head, he met her eyes and saw the openness of her feeling for him.

"Thank you, Bianca," he said, leaning closer. "That's what would have happened, all right. Because I was going to kill Bear Neck, damn his savage heart. I had all I could take. I realize now just how near I came. Thank you."

She said no word, her upturned face softening, a thoughtfulness rising to her fine eyes and her never-failing expression of intentness, her gaze not once leaving his face.

He pulled back and said, "In a few days you'll be at the fort, safe from all *Indios*," and the words, somehow, became an encroachment, shattering that quietest of moments, and he wished to call back what he had said for another time.

Her face dulled. She turned her back to him.

To humor her, he took her hand and drew her about, feeling the warmth of her and seeing her, on tiptoe, suddenly tilt her face for him and the light shading back into her face. He froze.

Then, not looking at her, though still holding

her hand, he led her up the pebbly bank for camp.

On the third day northward from the Great River, the Kiowas watered their horses at the spring west of Fort Stockton, and while the raiders rested, Paul went to Straight Lance.

"I'm taking the girl to the pony soldiers' fort," he said. "Their chiefs will talk to the Mexicans and see that she gets home. I will catch up with you at the Little Great River."

"Be careful, *Tejan*. The soldiers often send out small parties to kill us. Listen to me." Paul smiled at his manner and the patient tone he used when instructing a green young brave. "Don't come in from the west. Circle around. Come in from the south. Usually there are fewer soldiers that way. Watch for dust signs. As soon as you sight the fort, send her ahead, alone. I'll be glad when she's gone. You and Bear Neck fight too much."

"I believe I know how to look out for myself by now. I also have another reason for being careful."

"Is there another?"

"Didn't the trader, Wrinkled Hide, tell you?"

"He told me nothing except how generous he was," the Indian snorted. "How precious his cheap goods were. How poor our good hides were."

"Then I'll tell you. He showed me a thing, a piece of paper, on which the *Tejanos* mark their words and pass messages. They will pay one thousand dollars to the man who brings me in dead or makes me a prisoner. They call me a white renegade, a bad white man, because I live with you Whirlwinds. They believe I led that raid against the settlement the time I was shot."

The Kiowa appeared pleased. "So you can't go back and live with the white-eyes?"

"Not in Texas, certainly, and not elsewhere if the *Tejanos* knew."

"Ah, that is good, *Tejan.* Your real home is with us, anyway. You have no other place to go. The whites will kill you."

"But soon I'll have to slip back to where I came from, far to the east."

"If so, why not keep her as a wife? Why take the chance of getting rubbed out today? Keep her, my friend. If you don't like her, you can always get another woman when we raid Mexico again during the Moon-of-Deer-Horns-Dropping-Off."

"I don't want to do that. Since she's my woman, I've decided to take her back." Paul left him. A step beyond and he heard the other call sharply, "Watch like a Kiowa—not like a fool white man!"

It had been a long, dusty ride to the spring, up through barren, monotonous country today, once they had left the ragged mountains and the wide valleys. So Paul rested the two horses awhile longer and was unmounted when the Kiowas raised a yipping chorus of departure. A warrior on a handsome chestnut horse swung out, letting the van of the *caballada* tear past him. It was Straight Lance, and he was gazing at Paul.

Something caused Paul to wave. Dust from the passing horses smoked higher just then, obscuring horse and rider, enveloping them; when it settled, the chestnut had vanished, as if plucked north-ward by the fleeing mass.

Paul, turning to her, hesitated and said, "Let's go."

She was faced away from him.

"Let's go," he said.

She didn't move, and he saw that she was pouting and pretending not to hear. Watching her in detail, his attention growing closer and sharper, he was bothered by an unwillingness he could not discard. "You have to go home," he explained. "You can't stay with me. You know that."

"I know."

"Then why—?"

"Is because . . . is because you don't want me?"

A swift heat prickled his face. "You will see your people again soon after the American authorities at the fort send word to your government."

"My gov-ern-ment and your gov-ern-ment, yes," she replied humorlessly.

"Yes," he said, "come on," and when he stepped to the horses, she, to his surprise, moved with him, as obedient as a gentle child. He lifted her to the hide saddle and mounted, bounding to the blue's back, and heeled off fast.

After the first rushing momentum of his departure had worn off, he reined down to more careful going, his eyes sharp, scanning the barren land folds for movement. She, trailing him, displayed not the faintest interest in the surroundings. He halted to look at her, frowning as she continued to affect indifference, and he asked, "Are you all right? You aren't sick?"

She shrugged. Her smoky eyes, studiously avoiding his face, seemed to focus on a far-away landmark.

He dug a forefinger into his bearded chin, lost for words, and went forward, gravely dissatisfied.

He rode through a series of gravelly washes, through a scattered tangle of switch mesquite. Such a long time passed, he felt, though he knew he had used up only an hour or so, when an instinct told him to turn north for the fort; and a longer time, watching like a Whirlwind Kiowa, his trained senses examining each denuded nub of barren land across the unchanging sea of sameness, traveling on into the enormous, swallowing hush of the desert, the drumming of unshod hoofs the cadence of their lonely passing.

He rubbed his burning eyes. No—that couldn't be the fort so soon. That miscellany of drab buildings the color of burned umber, lying athwart the cauterized landscape. But it was. He could see the flag. His heart sang. "There's the fort," he called back to her. "There it is!"

She had her look. Quite a brief look. Her expression dulled and she gazed away to the east, her head tilted, meaning, anew, that he had rejected her.

And just then, as he had feared all along he might, he saw a furrow of dust; blinking against the glare, he followed it with his eyes instead of taking flight, assessing its meaning like a Kiowa, and his senses relayed: dark figures on horseback. A small detachment of cavalry toiling from southwest to northeast, probably returning from a futile scout on the War Trail. In a short while the troopers would pass between Bianca and him and the fort.

Hastening, Paul dipped into a scoured wash, left her with the horses, and posted himself on the north side to watch.

He thought the soldiers would never pass. From his vantage point, he could see the droop of their weary horses, the slack-bodied troopers riding in columns of two. When the detachment reached the outer buildings of the fort, he scrambled back.

"I'll take you closer in," he said.

"Is bad—they will shoot you for an *Indio*."

He shook his head and rode out of the wash, leaving her to follow. When he came to the place where the soldiers had passed, he halted, watching figures moving on the parade ground, and said, "Tell the first soldier you meet to take you to the fort commander. Tell him your story. How it happened. There'll be women there. Wives of officers. They'll take care of you, I know." He waited for her to ride by him, only she did not.

"*Gracias,*" she said, keeping her chin high. Her lips had barely moved, but her eyes had a sadness.

It troubled him that he could find nothing to say to her. Nothing that would help her. Absolutely nothing. He could only stare at her in farewell, conscious of a stifling in his chest.

"Sometime you come to Mexico, yes?"

"I would like that."

A warning look knitted her brows. "Not like an *Indio*, no. Like yourself. Like Paul. Like *Americano.*"

"Like *Americano,*" he nodded, and before another moment he was promising, "I will come to see you, Bianca. I will. But now you must go back to your people. They're mourning for you."

He saw that understanding vivid in her face, and then her eyes changed, softly intent upon him, wide and luminous, near tears, the last of her pretense gone.

He jerked a look at the fort, not liking the sight of horsemen knotting there on the edge of the parade ground.

"Go," he hurried her. "They see us. Go now!"

She seemed frozen, incapable of movement; only the great, hurting eyes alive and alert. All at once he slapped the mare across the rump and she bolted forward, startled. Bianca pulled up.

She looked again at Paul, who gestured on to the fort. At that, she let the mare proceed.

Paul waited. When he saw the mare continuing, he reined along the trail the cavalrymen had followed coming in. A short way and he glanced back. Bianca was going on, and the troopers were watching.

He experienced a sharp relief for her, yet also the stab of isolation, for he had grown accustomed to having her beside him night and day; now, abruptly, he had dispatched her out of his life.

He rode down into a shallow wash, careless and off guard, his mind fixed back there on her, visualizing her reception. He passed through a scrabble of mesquite, following the trail.

Star's fox ears were twitching, by which sign Paul should have known. That was the only warning he had, and just momentarily, of the plodding figure of a blue-uniformed trooper materializing before him, leading a footsore mount.

The trooper discovered him an instant later. The other's jaw hung. Paul could see shreds of black tobacco on the man's teeth. A young trooper, filmed with yellow dust, sun-beaten, blue-eyed, a shock of sweaty-brown hair pouched down under his hat brim. And next in the blue stare, red from sun glare, Paul glimpsed himself as he had in the eyes of the frightened old man in the cabin at the Elm Creek settlement: a despicable white man dressed like a greasy Indian, dangerous and hated. A traitorous white renegade.

The trooper clawed for his holstered revolver, unheeding Paul's shouted, "No—no—!"

Paul was within a few feet of him, heel-jabbing his horse as he continued to shout. He felt the jar of Star's forequarters smashing the young man and he heard his sudden gush of pain, and saw the trooper spinning down and the revolver flapping out of his hand.

Paul yanked to a stop, his first impulse to give aid. But the racket of a horse pounding hard from the direction of the fort caught him, and he turned to see Bianca Chaves on the dun mare. She was waving frantically for him to go ahead, at the same time crying at him in her small voice.

He jumped the blue horse out as she swept even, the mare flying past in the lead. The trooper was weaving to his feet.

When out of gunshot range, Paul cut in and blocked her way, snapping his suspicion at her.

"Why didn't you go on?"

He expected her to avoid his eyes, but she looked at him straight. "I was afraid."

"Afraid? The soldiers won't hurt you. Now you go back."

Into her eyes leaped a naked feeling that he felt, that silenced him. "Not afraid for me. Afraid for you. The *soldados* are coming. Many *soldados*. Look."

Doubting, he turned to see. And there, past the arm-waving figure of the trooper, boiled the smoky dust of galloping horsemen. Paul began to distrust his earlier thoughts as to her safety. If he forced her to ride back now, the troopers might shoot her for an Indian.

"Don't make me go," she said.

"You must return to your people."

"Paul, don't make me." She was pleading in the softest of voices. "Later, you send me, yes? Not now. I'll never see you again if you do. You said you come to see me in Mexico—but no. You said that so I would leave, yes? You didn't mean it."

Her honesty got to him and he wasn't certain whether he had meant it or not, though he wanted to believe he had; perhaps yes, perhaps no. He spoke hurriedly, his eyes on the horsemen, who had reached the trooper and halted:

"There's still time and the mare is fast. Ride around the soldiers to the fort. If you ride straight to the soldiers, they may mistake you for an Indian. Go—go around."

Before she could plead again, he saw the riders spurt into motion and he heard a distant shot, after it a spattering that sounded like carbine fire. He had waited too long.

"We can't stay here—come on," and he saw her face light up, and already she was touching rein, and together they sent the horses at a dead run into the afternoon dazzle of shivery heat.

Chapter 14

That evening they camped in the vicinity of the spring west of Fort Stockton, off the hammered trace of the Comanche War Trail where pony soldiers might follow.

On the soft robe, gazing up at the glittery sky, Paul felt both peace and exhilaration; for the first time in days there was no hurry. He turned on his side. She was sleeping with knees drawn up, her dark head cradled in the fold of her arm. She had let down her long hair, and its blue-black luxuriance all but covered her. Asleep, she looked even smaller, more a child than ever. He rolled over on his back to watch the sky again, while sleep strayed over him like a caress.

As the night advanced, he heard the many voices of the wind rising and whimpering, and he felt their chill breath; yet, deep in his serenity, he could not waken enough to draw the robe higher, and he slipped back into bottomless sleep, still at peace.

He woke, warm and comfortable, to find the robe snugly about him.

"I thought you never get up, you sleepyhead," a laughter-filled voice chided him.

He yawned and looked around. Dawn was near. She stepped around from behind him, enjoying her surprise. "I could have captured you like an *Indio*," she teased.

He agreed with a nod and glanced down at the robe, knowing she had covered him. Rising, he drank from the paunch and scrubbed water over his face, wiping at the droplets beading his beard.

"Breakfast," he announced, reaching for the rawhide pouch.

After eating, they continued to rest on the robe, neither speaking, watching the flushing eastern sky unmask the first glow of the high-desert morning.

Some time passed before she said anything, then hesitantly. "You like me, yes?"

"Yes."

"*Mucho?*"

"Enough."

A frown pecked at her brow. "Is *mucho* or little?"

"*Mucho.*"

She reached out on impulse and touched his arm. "Is not like promise to come to Mexico?"

"I meant that, too," he said, hearing the solemn assurance in his voice.

Her frown vanished. "So you do like me?"

"Very much."

"Is not pity?" She was looking directly at him, with the honesty he couldn't avoid. "Not just sadness for me and my people?"

"No. I truly like you, Bianca. But you still have to go home."

"I like you, Paul." And her eyes were as coals warming his face.

He became aware of their gazes locking, of her finely made face smoothing, as it had that day on the river, rapt, waiting, giving. He took her hand and pressed it, leaning toward her, and she toward him, his eyes on her face, on the offering of her parted lips.

Sudden stamping of the horses jarred his senses; drawing back, he saw the gelding moving nervously and facing the trail, head high, those sensitive fox ears flicking. Striding across, Paul took the rawhide halter ropes and held the horses fast, becoming still at what he saw. A line of dusty cavalry, a detachment about the size of yesterday's, doggedly riding south down the main trail.

Motioning Bianca to bring their belongings, he led the horses out of sight and began walking them north. When he and the girl mounted, he cut northeast for the Little Great River, for the crossing where the skeletons of horses and cattle littered the alkali flats like debris from the ancient carcass of this merciless desert world.

Toward late morning, following the clutter of hoofprints and the brown droppings of the *caballada*, he set eyes on a solitary wagon, its cover flapping and whipping in the wind like a thing alive. A sickening stench reached him; closing in, he saw the team of mules dead in the traces, bloating under the steamy sun. A trail herd's chuckwagon. Looted, pans and pots scattered about; flour whitening the hoof-gouged ground. Little bunches of Longhorn cattle drifted in the distance. Paul could see the scene: the Whirlwinds, more concerned with their treasured horses, driving off the few riders and hastily sacking the wagon, scattering the cattle, killing a few and eating the raw meat on the spot, and rushing on.

He eyed the wagon curiously, the first he had seen since his stop at Fort Sill, Indian Territory. Was that a year ago? It seemed an age. Obeying a compelling urge, he climbed over the front wheel to the wagon seat. Inside, everything was a tangle of disorder: rough clothing, some short lariat pieces, two sweat-rimmed old hats, a pair of rundown shoes, the leavings of strewn flour, coffee beans and sugar. He moistened a forefinger on his tongue and touched a drivel of sugar and tasted. His mouth juices ran; a hunger came over him. His forager's eyes settled on a pair of blue denim trousers, a gray shirt, and rumpled brown coat, the better of the two hats, and a pair of high-laced brogans. Taking them, scenting the smell of white man's tobacco clinging to the garments, he realized that mainly the chance of finding clothing had drawn him inside the wagon.

Next he scooped up coffee beans and sugar, which he cached in flour sacking. His greatest prize he found under a gunny sack, a slab of bacon. He stuffed it in the sack and swung down, displaying his booty for her to see.

"Now," she exclaimed, "you will look like *Americano*, yes," and she struck a scornful pose of superiority, small, white teeth clenched, full lips curled to form a ludicrous sneer.

He roared at her caricature. "These are so I won't get shot when I ride in with you at the next fort."

"Fort?" He could see her gaiety retreating to gravity. "Is where?"

"On northeast. A long way, I'm afraid."

"A long way? Is good! Is good!" she said, clapping her hands, her face lively again.

His tolerant grimace said otherwise, and then he had to smile at her frankness. "We can't live like Indians forever, Bianca. We both have to go back someday."

A hot wind blew fine grit against their faces and she closed her eyes, and when she opened them, looking so genuinely young and unaffected, a rush of tenderness tore at him with its familiar conflict, but he did not touch her.

"Someday," she said, but her uncaring expression made that seem a distant thing.

Late in the day they caught up with the Kiowas on the Little Great River, the spent *caballada* scattered around the ford on the far side, and on the alkali flats, some of the horses down and dying from overdrinking the briny water.

It suffered Paul to see the agony of the horses. Yet there was no other water on the trail at this point, and he estimated, roughly, it was some sixty miles from the spring west of Fort Stockton to the river. Forewarned, he did not allow the blue horse and the mare, which had had water from the paunch, to drink their fill.

His old captor, jubilant at Paul's return, grasped him by the shoulders as Paul related what had happened, gripped him until Paul hurt. "See, *Tejan*? I told you the mean white-eyes would try to kill you. You are a Kiowa."

"At present," Paul said, "I am neither Kiowa nor white. The soldiers shoot at me because I look like a Kiowa, and your people won't accept me because I am white."

"They will, my friend."

"When?"

"After you've taken a white man's scalp."

"Then that will never be," Paul swore, and left him to find a suitable camping place, if such existed on these hellish flats.

Just before dark, he gathered up the bundle of white man's clothing. When out of sight of camp, he stripped off his buckskin pants and shirt. The denim trousers proved too large for his lean waist, and the sleeves of the gray shirt too short for his long-muscled arms. These many months of wearing moccasins had spread his feet, it seemed, and the brogans, when laced, felt like iron clamps. Shrugging into the brown coat, he found it too tight for comfort, inasmuch as he had broadened through the shoulders; and the sleeves of the coat, like those of the shirt, hung above his wrists. Last, he put on the hat; it fit.

He stood erect and straightened the coat, in that moment seeing himself in his mind's critical eye as he would appear to others, an unkempt country fellow in ill-fitting clothes. As the French would say, it was but to laugh; with a smile, he rammed his hands into the coat pockets.

Something lumped under his right hand. A soft leather sack, its contents feeling hard and small and flat and metallic. Taking out the sack, he caught the clink of coins; and fumbling the drawstring loose and reaching in, he felt their coolness. Gold coins, he saw, shaking them into his palm, and greenbacks, and some twenty-dollar gold pieces and some ten-dollar pieces, and a few two-bit and fifty-cent silver pieces. He started counting. Shortly he held more than three hundred dollars.

Stepping gingerly in the tight shoes, pulling on the stubborn coat, he returned to meet the greeting of her bright, teasing voice:

"*Americano*? No. I like you better as an *Indio*, yes."

"At least, I look like a white man," he reminded her. "No worse than some I've seen hanging around Army posts."

"Posts?"

"Forts," he explained.

"The fort, yes," she said, her smile fading, and the lightness of the moment was gone also.

Afternoon of the next day, coming up a long slant, Paul saw the sand hills spread out to the north as the likeness of a tawny sea slowly moving beneath a cloudless sky, and his mind closed on pools of clear water and green, waist-high grass, and fresh deer meat.

He did not don the white man's ill-fitting clothes that evening, nor the next, when the Whirlwinds clattered through the broad hills down to the Big Spring. After that, he left the garments untouched, virtually forgotten, incidental now, while he searched for new ways to please and entertain her, and while he listened to her gay laughter, which was often.

And this was a moment:

Riding off to themselves, at their leisure, the wind hissing through the manes of their horses, sometimes behind the Whirlwind Kiowas, sometimes on a flank, laughing, pausing when the whim took them, sometimes almost losing sight of the *caballada*'s dusty standard.

Hedges of dark clouds were forming when the Kiowas turned the band of horseflesh into the broad mouth of the great canyon. Paul noticed the lack of victory preparations. No chanting, no singing this time. Red Calf was dead.

As if chastened, the Kiowas rode quietly into the village behind the shuffling procession, past the watching families. Each man cut out his booty horses and drove them out to mingle with his other mounts.

Paul saw Straight Lance hesitate, then dismount in front of a lodge where two women stood, Red Calf's young wife and his old mother. The war leader said something, a halting speech of sorrow, and at once Paul heard the high-pitched keening shrill above the horse sounds. He wanted to look away, knowing what was next, but before he could the young woman started hacking at her hair and slashing at her arms and breasts. The old woman, Paul knew, remembering the ritual of grief, would likely hack off a finger to signify the loss of a son.

At his side Bianca gasped out her horror.

"It's their way," he said. "Come along."

He led off past the lodge to the accompaniment of rumbling thunder, which he suspected the Kiowas would term a bad sign, appropriate to the bad news they brought, and rode up to his hut. It looked smaller and more miserable than it had ever seemed, shrunken to three-quarters its original dimensions. During his long absence one side had caved in.

"This is where I live," he said. "I'm going to build you a hut of your own to sleep in tonight."

Her eyes contradicted his decision. Why build

another? This one is large enough for two. Didn't we sleep on one robe under the stars? Are you afraid of me now?

Ignoring her, he took his knife to begin clearing a place near his own hut, only to pause after some minutes when a rumbling shattered the sky directly overhead. He then resumed his hacking and pulling and stacking, aware that the air was growing hot and moist.

There was a sudden rushing of the wind whipping the treetops. Across, in the village, the Indians, experienced at gauging the temper of fast-striking Plains storms, were scurrying and calling children and closing tipi flaps.

At once he felt raindrops pelting his face and he could hear the wind rising furiously. Giving up, he unsaddled and removed his gear and led the horses into a stand of cottonwoods, tied them and trotted back and motioned her to go inside.

By this time the rain was drumming hard, and he scooped up their belongings and ducked inside. Forthwith, pushing, tying, he bolstered the caved-in section, while the rain came whipping and the wind ran shouting through the cedars and cottonwoods.

With the hut secure, he spread the robe and they sat upon it, apart, listening to the gusty, throaty roaring and the rain striking like bird-shot. A tiny trickle formed on the hard-tamped floor where the hut had caved. He crouched down and muttered with the mimicking sternness of a medicine man, "Water, go away." And the trickle, as if obliging, wavered and hied itself away from the robe. "See," he told her, pounding his chest, "I have much power." He laughed and she laughed with him.

A feeling drew Paul about. He met her eyes, smoky warm. And over him there descended a sense of comfort and of protection from the elements. The sturdy old hut was weathering the storm quite well. His laborious interlacing of the boughs had made it a tight refuge. He lay back and half-closed his eyes, listening, his mind at peace, reaching out.

"Bianca," he said presently, "I have to take you back—soon. After we've rested a few days. An Indian camp is no place for you."

The brunt of the quick-hitting storm was passing, spending its strength in useless charges against the canyon walls, while the rain was settling to a steady, musical tattoo. She was so long answering that he supposed she had fallen asleep, as he had become drowsy, lulled by the sounds and the half-light within the hut. A little later he heard her voice, clear and thoughtful:

"Is good to see my people, yes. But I want to stay here."

Her meaning shook him awake. "Why?" he asked, turning to look at her.

She was gazing right into his eyes. "I love you," she said.

His breath shortened. He turned to see the blue-green rain screening off the canyon, his face controlled, his body as outwardly calm as he could make it, though his pulse was pounding. "We can leave whenever we wish," he said, deliberately speaking around what she had just told him, somewhat unsteady with his words. "I know that's all right. I have that freedom now. I've earned it. You're my property in the eyes of the Kiowas. It will be safer for both of us to ride to Fort Sill—that's southeast of here, out of Texas, in Indian Territory, across Red River. Safer than riding up to one of the forts near the Texas towns where they shoot an Indian on sight."

He talked on, assuming that she listened, when he realized that she had moved and sat beside him, and was looking up into his face; and their lips were almost touching and he could feel the stir of her uneven breathing warmly on his cheek. It then seemed the most natural circumstance in the world to find her fitting into his arms as if she belonged there. He had never held her like this before. Loosely, for a lingering moment; his arms tightened then and her face blurred as he buried his face in her hair and they just held on to each other, for a long time, for a very long time, the feel of her like a smooth fabric. He drew back to kiss her, and the taste of her mouth burned his mouth with its giving sweetness. Feeling stifled him. He was exalted.

"I love you," he said. "Forever." Her eyes were glowing as she lifted her face to him, and he held her again and kissed her.

He had no sense of time, but vaguely he knew time had passed. Beneath him the pale oval of her face swam in false twilight, and her eyes were still closed, her lips just parted, maternal and full; teardrops glistened on her cheeks. Her breasts rose and fell softly. Something trickled down his beard and skipped off, and he discovered that he was silently weeping with the pain of loving.

And there was no other world than theirs, nothing but the spongy softness of the buffalo robe under them and the dim shell of the hut arching over them and sheltering them from the drum-roll of the rain.

Chapter 15

One autumn morning, when the plains had cooled and the coats of the buffalo were losing the sunburned look of summer and turning darker for winter, Paul surrendered to a restless hunger for news of the world beyond the fastness of the Whirlwinds' remote chasm. He informed his friend of his decision and returned to the hut, now amply enlarged for two. Bianca had gone to the stream. He began folding and stuffing the white man's clothing into a saddlebag.

A shadow fell across the light from the low doorway. He turned toward her, chastened by a certain guilt. She was barefoot, and he hadn't heard her.

"Why you do this?" she asked, her fear stronger than her puzzlement.

"I'm going to the settlements. Be back in a few days."

"Settle-ments?" she pondered, in her surprise faltering over the strange word.

"I mean a town. I won't be gone long." He was, he saw, speaking too fast to reassure her.

Her eyes widened enormously, hurt, shocked, afraid. She looked misshapen and too young to be having a child. And still, he perceived, she did not understand. "Why you go?" she asked.

"I need to go," he tried to explain, and sensed he could not. "I'll bring you some nice things. Remember the money we found in the wagon?"

Her troubled expression didn't ease. "I need no things. I have everything."

"I want to find out what's going on in the rest of the world. Remember, I've been here a long time."

"Here we are happy," she said simply, her voice sounding smaller and smaller. "Is good."

"I know." He finished packing and stood up. She hadn't moved. He could see an old fear alive in her eyes.

"*Soldados*—the *soldados*?"

"I will be dressed like a white man."

That appeared to calm her, though just a moment. Her face changed back, troubled once more.

"We have to go back someday," he said. "In a way, I guess this is getting ready for when that day comes."

"Someday," she acknowledged, with an inflection that said she would keep that time at a distance as long as she could.

Taking her hand, he led her out to the picketed blue horse, and threw on the saddlepad and saddlebag, and a robe and food pouch. He was talking as he tied on his gear, trying to reassure her:

"Straight Lance and Star Woman will keep an eye on you. I'm going to a town where he says many of the hide hunters come from. A place called Fort Griffin." Her absolute stillness alarmed him. He cut his eyes at her. She was rigid, her somber eyes steadfastly locked on his face, a terrible light in them, her hands balled. Her lips moved, and he hardly caught her words:

"You come back—yes?"

"My God, yes!" he roared, wrapping both arms around her, bringing her to him and stroking her hair, alternately patting and squeezing her. "I'll always love you. You're my wife—you'll always be my wife."

She felt lifeless in his arms, even when he kissed her. Shaken, he held her away from him to examine her face, his hands on the points of her shoulders. "Smile for me," he said, "just a little," and saw her try and fail, too miserable. But he had to go. He kissed her and held her fast, stepped free and mounted and heeled the blue horse away.

At a place where the canyon wall jutted out and shut off his last view of the hut, he turned to look. She was standing exactly as he had left her, so small a figure, so touching, her hands twisting together again, her distended body seeming over-burdened. For a painful moment he almost rushed back there, and would had she not waved. He waved in answer and reined sharply about, refusing his eyes another look.

On the third morning he crouched in scrub timber on a stony hillside and scanned the broad flat, the horses and mules and man figures down there seething like maggots in the brown flesh of the wheel-crossed earth, watching the army of countless wagons and tents and the noisy town, and the lip of the rocky bluff where the flag fluttered like a wounded bird in the hot wind above the fort.

He could dally no longer, not if he made his few purchases and put the place behind him before darkness. Riding to the creek, he donned the uncomfortable white man's garb, including hat and shoes, and left Star tied in the timber.

Coming in on the dusty street, the shoes cramping his feet and his body protesting the confine-ment of trousers and coat, he felt his senses sorting out each new scent and noise. He stopped short, his mouth juices running. Some-body was baking bread. And that sappy smell was fresh-cut lumber. From a tangle of parked wagons sailed the mournful strains of a harmonica.

Seeing so many whites, he found himself staring and dragging step. Their nearness made him tremble and sweat, sniffing wolfishly. He felt like an alien. Like a Kiowa. It had not occurred to him before now, but white men had a peculiar smell of their own. The mingling of unwashed bodies in heavy clothing, of armpit odors and dried sweat and strong tobacco, whereas a Kiowa was mesquite smoke and tanned hides and grease.

To his relief, he passed unnoticed, and he continued his journey up the street toward the foot of the bluff. These men, he perceived now, were also long-haired and bearded, hunters and skinners for the most part, judging from their talk. To his left spread the smelly confines of a vast hide yard, and he drew about, agape at the mounds of stacked hides. A long string of ox and mule-drawn wagons, their broad beds and frames suggestive of hay wagons, jammed the street, drawn up to unload more buffalo hides.

Onward, reaching the upper section of town, his wariness increased and he felt himself tensing against the onrushing bedlam of shouts and curses and hoarse laughter and bursts of music and the sight of men reeling whooping from the numerous saloons. He came to a standstill, as if resisting the unreal and bacchic world he was about to enter. Then, he saw, something unusual was up. Men stood in agitated knots before the Planter's House; everyone was armed, though that would not be uncommon in a frontier town. A detachment of cavalry hurried down the street. Men left the general merchandise store, waggling new rifles and sacks of shells. Women sauntered along the street.

The voices in front of the hotel became louder. He paused to watch. Beside him, a woman said, "Say, friend, how about buyin' a lady a drink? It's a hot day."

Paul, turning, took in the carelessly smiling face of uncertain age and the slack, red lips. His nostrils told him the powdered smell of her was much too strong. He backed away.

Her outright laugh stopped him. "Friend, you've sure been a long time in the sticks—that's plain. Some getup you're wearin'. But you look creek-washed clean."

He strode quickly on, behind him the unbroken stridence of her voice cursing him. And now, other than purchases for Bianca, he searched for the purpose of his coming and found it—a narrow frame building, looking crushed between a saloon and the general merchandise store. The modest board sign out front read: Fort Griffin *Echo*.

It was all he could do to control his eagerness. In moments he was inside, breathing the redolence of ink and paper. A stooped man of tired middle age, hands as begrimed as a chimney sweep's, sat humped on a high stool before a case of type, filling a composing stick. Around and beyond him the clutter of his spare shop, a paper-littered desk, his few cases of additional type, a stone, and a hand press. Only his eyes moved toward Paul.

"I'd like a paper," Paul said.

There was a metallic *snick* as the printer set down the tray-shaped stick, wiped both hands on his smudged apron, and slumped forward and peeled a paper off the stack on the counter. "That's two-bits." Paul paid. Before he could turn, the man asked, "You just haul in?"

"I came from the East," Paul said, feeling ill at ease. The inquisitive brown eyes under the green eyeshade seemed extraordinarily alert, capable of ferreting out any identity or untruth.

"I see. Had me fooled. I took you for a hunter, sure. Maybe one of the new civilian scouts at the fort."

"Just looking for prospects."

"Conrad and Hooks putting a new hide crew together. You'll find 'em at the Planter's."

"Thanks."

"If a man's willing to sweat and take his chances, Griffin's the place to shove off to the buffalo ranges. Bug-free hides bringing up to three-fifty. Buffalo tongues—cured, of course— fifty cents each." He fell into an overdrawn attitude of disdain, one eye cocked. "For the back-East carriage trade, y'know. Nothin' but the best." The brown stare changed, again appraising Paul, and something like local pride replaced the mockery. "Some fifteen hundred hunters and skinners operating out of Griffin this season."

"A considerable number," Paul said, curbing his impulse to talk.

"Be more'n that if it wasn't for the Indian trouble. Never been so bad. All the way from

Jacksboro—that's east of here; maybe you came through there—and on west wherever there's buffalo . . . Wonder you didn't lose that long, yellow hair of yours. Some Comanch' or Kiowa'd sure covet that."

"I'm sure of that," Paul smiled.

"You'd better believe it. Billy Fitch dragged himself in this morning, plumb from California Creek. Indians, as usual. Killed both his partners and the Frenchy skinner. Billy's over at the Planter's. Got two arrowheads in one flank, a ball in his chest. He won't make it. Fine fella, too. Everybody's all riled up."

Paul's gaze chanced on the wall, where a rough sort of bulletin board hung, on it, tacked, the latest copy of the weekly *Echo*, which Paul had, and an assortment of reward posters, old and new. He turned his eyes to a yellowed poster and on to the next. A moment. He jerked back to the old poster, feeling the sickening smash of something almost forgotten. He stepped to the wall, his eyes tearing at a poster identical to the one the white trader, Wrinkled Hide, had mocked him with in the village, one he still had in his belongings at the hut.

"My rogue's gallery," the *Echo*'s editor chuckled. "Quite a collection of the leading cutthroats and thieves in Texas. I seem to print more reward notices than I do newspapers. Setting type today on a new one out for our white renegade.

State of Texas has upped the reward from a thousand dollars to five thousand—in gold."

"White renegade?" Paul kept his voice merely curious.

"No less. A real, live white renegade. Worst kind. Seen last year on a raid at Elm Creek. Rangers figure he's the one behind most of our Indian trouble. They figure he organizes things, keeps the hostiles stirred up. Ranges far and wide. Clear to the Mexican border. Last spring he was spotted around Fort Stockton. Least he fits the description." He picked up a curved-stem pipe, tamped it, and struck a match, talking over the flame. "Some figure he was there to scout the fort—maybe rub it out. However, there was no attack. Reckon being seen tipped his hand."

Paul was able to speak calmly. "Aren't the Rangers crediting one lone white man with a great deal of influence? And there must be more than one white living among the wild bands." (Just in time, he had stopped himself from saying "white-eye.")

"One thing's certain—the Rangers and soldier boys are all on the lookout. So's every hunter, skinner, freighter, and cowboy. Five thousand is a heap of money, even for these times."

"If there's more than one so-called renegade, how would the Rangers know if they had the right man?"

"Anybody they catch with the Indians is worth hangrope, you can bet that. Can you figure a white man that'd turn against his own kind?"

Paul shrugged, noncommittal. "The description seems too general to me. No particular or identifying features."

"Closer'n you might think. Twenty-five or -six years old. Blond hair and beard. Blue eyes. Slender. Regular features."

"Fits a lot of men."

The other nodded amiably. "Could fit you to a T—you, a total stranger." He was grinning like a cat, eyes as bright as match flames. "There's one fact you don't know: An old-timer on Elm Creek was an eyeball witness. He *saw* this renegade. He *can* identify him."

"Just hope the Rangers don't hang the wrong man," Paul said, smiling, and departed. Between two buildings he found a quiet spot and prepared to devour the contents of the *Echo*.

There had been a recent murder at Worley Lake, fifty miles northwest of Griffin. . . . The body of an unidentified man found floating in Collin Creek. . . . A hunter found shot to death behind the Bee Hive Saloon. . . . A colored man found shot through the head, his body discovered on the bank where Collin Creek flowed into the Clear Fork of the Brazos. . . . An attempted robbery when the stage was passing through the rough country near the head of Ioni Creek in

Palo Pinto County. One Milo Hatcher, the special mail agent, had bravely opened fire on two masked men, who then "lit out for tall timber." . . . Company A, Twenty-second Infantry, had just arrived from Fort Wayne, Michigan, to relieve Company E, Tenth Infantry. . . . Some ninety-eight thousand head of cattle had passed through Fort Griffin so far this season to the northern pastures.

Paul's hungry eyes spied another headline, at the top of the right-hand column:

INDIAN INHUMANITY

News was brought to this office Tuesday evening by Mr. Eugene W. Miller, of Throckmorton County, that last week a party of forty-odd Kiowa Indians ran into Mr. Caldwell, of Henrietta, and Mr. Belcher, who has a large stock ranch on Pease River, while those gentlemen were en route from the ranch to Henrietta, and killing both of them. Two days later, about the same number of Indians killed two men between Harrold's ranch on the Little Wichita, in Archer County, and Henrietta.

The time and ferocity of the two raids confirms the belief of civil and military authorities that both are the cruel machinations of the depraved mind of the notorious white renegade directing war parties not only in these parts for more than a year, but as far as Fort Stockton near the Mexican border.

Colonel H. B. Irwin, post commander, issued the following statement to the *Echo* editor:

"The very nature of these well-planned attacks is indicative of civilized man's cleverness, combined with primitive savagery. We have valid reasons to believe that the forays were plotted by the same fiendish white renegade, likely the possessor of military training, observed in last year's dastardly attack on the brave settlers of Elm Creek. Meanwhile, the good and peaceful citizens of Griffin may rest assured that our zealous troops are constantly on scout, keeping the security of our fair frontier ever in mind."

The *Echo* congratulates Colonel Irwin, indeed one of nature's noblemen, and his men for their intrepid adherence to duty.

Thoughtfully, Paul raised his gaze from the printed page. Cleverness! As if only a white man could be clever. At least, for the present, the "notorious white renegade" provided the authorities a handy scapegoat for the young bucks, Comanche and Kiowa, they couldn't catch, runaways from the reservation near Fort Sill. In an adjoining column, lower on the page, he read:

THE RANGERS MOVE

Wednesday morning, Captain Arrington left here with his command of twenty men, carrying forty days' rations, under orders to proceed to the Little Wichita and on to the Red. From there he will make a scout to the foot of the Cap Rock.

The command will be gone from here about two months, which means the boys will live off powder and lead and prairie dogs, if need be. If Captain Arrington should run across the Indians depredating in the state, there will be hair liftin' for certain. The Captain informed the *Echo* editor that any white man caught with Indian bands will be hanged on the spot. Now, folks, this is the kind of "peace policy" we like to hear about.

He was preoccupied as he folded the newspaper and stuck it inside his coat, still not quite able to believe that such an absurd role had been thrust upon him. His unease over time returned, and he went out to the rowdy street, pausing there to observe the angry-voiced men in front of the Planter's House. A good deal of drunken talk, he gathered, with gestures, talk about going looking for the bloodthirsty Indians on California Creek. A man ran out of the hotel and called, "Billy's dead, boys!" There were shouts, a mad rush for horses. Paul watched them go spurring up the street, then entered the general store.

He drew still just inside the doorway, taken back at the laden tables and racks and shelves. Coming from the often meager world of the Whirlwinds, he had forgotten so much could exist. Thereupon, he purchased yards of several bright-colored cloths, needles and thread and pins, a pair of scissors, a small hand mirror, some soap, and some half a dozen women's combs. That was all, he thought, turning.

The slanting afternoon sun shone upon something in the case next to the long counter where the clerk was measuring the last of the cloth. Something silver-bright and dazzling bluish-green. An exquisite silver bracelet of geometric design, graced with turquoise stones set like sparkling jewels. And a picture rose to his mind, of Bianca smiling her delight at the glittering object on her slim wrist.

"I want that turquoise bracelet," he said. "How much?"

The clerk slanted him a look. "Twenty dollars." A look that frankly questioned Paul's ability to pay.

Paul's anger spun out. "Is gold good enough?" and he snatched out his sack of coins and clinked it on the counter.

"No offense," the man said, all haste. "No offense."

Paul paid him. As he closed the sack and pocketed it, a sensation of coldness seemed to breathe on his face from his left, and he turned his eyes.

A tortoise-shaped face was watching him, the mouth as hard as a rock slit. By then the clerk was placing the bracelet on the counter. Paul picked it up to inspect the handiwork and the green stones. It was even more lovely than he had imagined. Bianca would be filled with rapture. When he looked left again, the watcher had gone, and Paul dismissed him from his mind. Slipping the bracelet in his coat pocket with his other small purchases, he folded the dress goods and went out, harassed by the wish to leave the din and the close smells and the milling crowds.

He moved as fast as he could through the jostling, elbowing, drunken, profane mass, detouring when groups of idlers blocked his path. He did not know when the feeling he had in the store took a grip on him again, but suddenly it was there. He shot a swift look about, disturbed to discover the tortoise face not twenty paces behind him. He whipped front, only to crash into a long-haired hunter reeking of rotgut fumes.

The man, mumbling curses, stumbling, lifted his hands to grab Paul's shoulders. It wasn't difficult for Paul to ward off the clumsy grasp, to slip inside and shove hard. The hunter swayed backward, into the arms of a watching bystander, who merely threw him sprawling into the street. The watchers roared.

Paul dodged ahead.

Another man, not nearly so drunk as the first one, took quarrelsome amusement at the colorful bundle under Paul's arm, and called, badgering, "Takin' that calico to some Tonkawa squaw?"

Paul kept moving. Now was no time to be drawn into a senseless street brawl. Forthwith, he cut away, striding across the street. Before him a skittish six-mule team pulled a hide wagon. Paul had to stop. His heckler followed and tugged at the dress goods. "Where's that squaw?"

Paul could feel the blood pounding up his neck. He caught the forearm savagely, wrenching, and swung him in a short arc, and hurled him reeling toward the mules. The heckler, off balance, struck the flank of the middle mule, which spooked; then all the mules spooked, and they tore off down the street toward the river, scattering pedestrians and riders. Shouts rolled back, "Runaway! Runaway!"

Paul hurried on, losing himself in the crowd on the other side of the street, and slowed to a walk, thinking he had evaded his first pursuer. The crowd was thinning here, toward the lower end of the street.

A keen whistle shrieked behind him, and he

slanted around without slowing. There followed his tortoise-faced stalker, deliberately lengthening his steps even as Paul discovered him.

Paul jerked forward, ready to run.

At that moment a bulky figure stepped out from behind an empty shack. A moon-featured man whose pale eyes, boring into Paul, cast a watery gleam.

Paul veered for the open street, too late. This second man blocked his path, and a coldness shivered through Paul. He glanced back and front, hemmed in between them. He seemed stupefied, unable to act, even when he saw the second man lifting a short, leather-covered club to knock him down.

Retreating, Paul felt his back bump against the wall of the shack. Trembling, he braced to fight, his hand flitting to his knife.

With a leer that said he expected Paul to cringe or beg as other luckless men had, the tortoise-faced man charged him. Paul slashed at the melon- sized belly, missed, slashed again, and heard a cry as he felt the blade rip flesh. Sliding to his right along the flimsy wooden wall, he tried to duck the second assailant's clubbing swing and took a smash across his upraised left arm that glanced off the side of his head. A savage blow, nevertheless, that rocked him with pain, that half-blinded him, that knocked him banging against the thin wall. He dropped his precious bundle to slash back. The man jerked out of range. Now, teeth bared, both men rushed him, Tortoise Face hugging his slashed arm to his body, swinging a leather cudgel with his other hand.

Paul, down on one knee, tasting the salty blood of his streaming scalp, dug the blade into a flank. It belonged to the moonfaced man, who cried out and fell back. Paul, groping, retrieved his bundle and scrambled up fast, at last feeling the end of the wall at his back. Given one more moment, he could flee down the side of the shack.

Tortoise Face, as if sensing Paul's intention, bulled toward him, mouthing obscenities, swinging the club in short arcs to avoid the jabbing knife. And Paul, crouching lower, seeing the paunch wide open before him, kicked suddenly and felt his foot strike pulpy flesh. As the man doubled up, Paul buried the knife high behind his shoulder.

Paul had his moment now, and he sprinted between two shacks.

Just as he cut behind the shack on his left and into an alley, he heard a shot; but he felt no pain and he raced on toward the creek, running a zigzag pattern as the Kiowas did to present an elusive target. When he saw three wagonloads of hides creaking up from the river crossing for town, he ran across and got on the other side of the wagons, using them as a shield between him and the alley's end. Nothing happened back there. Reaching the trees, he waded the creek and ran pounding up the bank.

His rush sent the blue horse snorting side-long, eyes rolling. "So you don't like my white-man stink," Paul called, jubilant. "I'll take care of that." And he untied and caught the dark mane and flung himself aboard, the gelding stretching out before Paul had his seat.

Star was nervous and pent-up, wild to run. Paul let him. There were no shouts from the timber. No shots. No sounds. He looked up at the white-patched blue sky and felt an enormous well-being. He was free again.

Chapter 16

It was the cold time, which already the Whirlwind Kiowas were calling the "Buffalo-Scarce Winter," when Bianca cried out with a pain Paul had not heard before. Shaken, he ran to the village. Some hours later a tyrannical midwife named Medicine Woman poked her dark head out the door of the hut and spoke curtly, voicing the superior knowl-edge of her kind:

"A son—a strong son. I hope he becomes a brave man—braver than his father, who has yet to take the scalp of even one weakling white-eye."

A sharp fear severed Paul's jubilation. "My wife? Is she all right?"

"She is also strong. You have a good wife, *Tejan*. Better than any white man deserves. Worthy of some prominent warrior. Yes, your wife is all right."

Overjoyed, he took hold of the midwife and hugged her impulsively, getting a strong whiff of grease and woodsmoke. She broke free, striking at his arms, her dignity at stake. "Get away. Don't you white people have any manners?"

He laughed and hugged her again. That same day he gave her a fine robe and some choice buffalo meat.

He named his brown-skinned son Christopher, after his paternal grandfather living in Baltimore. Meanwhile, the boy needed an Indian name. It was Kiowa custom to invite a medicine man or leading warrior to bestow the name. Thus a child led a longer and more useful life.

When the naming-day ceremony came, in Straight Lance's tipi, the Kiowa laid admiring attention on the fat baby. "*Tejan*, your juices are strong, my friend. My heart would be full that I had such a son. Your son will be brave, I know." Taking a coal from the fire, he lighted his pipe; blowing puffs of smoke to heaven and earth and the four great directions, he began chanting:

"O sun, make this little one as wise as an owl, as swift as an eagle, as strong as a buffalo bull, as brave as a war horse. Have him always respect his old people and always help them, for they will be his conscience as a man."

For a moment, then, Paul wanted to cry out, to protest, that such a life for his son could not be, for soon Paul had to take his family away.

And then Straight Lance lifted the child, and again and again and again, each time a little higher, symbolizing growth, and addressing Paul and Bianca, he said, "His name is going to be He-Rides-Straight-at-the-Enemy."

Paul was overcome. Proud, grateful, humble, he gave his friend a good bay horse he had taken on the prairie, one bearing *Tejano* brands and there-fore that much more cherished.

Life turned bursting full. Paul, content, lived each day to its languid depths. Not unlike, he often mused, recalling bits of his schoolboy Tennyson, Ulysses' men partaking of the lotus plant, he virtually lost all thoughts of home and desired to remain here. . . . *With half-shut eyes ever to seem falling asleep in a half-dream. . . . To dream and dream. . . . To hear each other's whispered speech. . . . Should life all labour be? My first, last love; the idol of my youth. . . . I will take some savage woman, she shall rear my dusky race. . . .* At night, with Bianca and the boy beside him on the soft robe, listening to their sweet, even breathing, he would float off into sleep to waken to the voice of the stream whimpering between its low banks through the breathless summer darkness, and tears would rise to his eyes and his chest would tighten, his being drenched in the joyful yet painful awareness of love. At dawn he rose to another bounteous day.

All too quickly, the days seemed to pass like vapor through his sunlit world, gone, he brooded, almost as they formed, before he could savor enough of their rich bounty, each like a precious coin which, once spent, could not be repossessed.

With a sudden sense of fleeting time, he felt autumn in the air. The short, curly buffalo grass was burning brown and yellow. Of an evening he built a fire inside the hut to drive out the chill. *Now,* he kept telling himself. *Now is the time to go.* And still he delayed, loath to leave, the logic of his mind tugging him one way, his heart another; for once he left, he knew his life and Bianca's, she a stranger, nay, a foreigner, among the *Americanos*, would change drastically, never to be the same again, and he wanted to guard the present as long as he could.

One cool, bright morning, while playing with the boy outside the hut, he heard a single roll of sound, muted by great distance. A distant peal of thunder? No. His trained senses knew better. He stood and faced southwest, an immediate sense of foreboding raking him. Again he heard it. This time more distinct, a sullen boom, though still faint on the wind, and then knowing, comprehending, he lifted a hand as if to ward off something long dreaded. His mind darkened.

He was standing in that stiffened attitude, his body straining against the dying rumble, when Bianca came to the doorway.

"Is wrong?" she asked.

"It's nothing," he said, forcing a smile. "Take Chris while I go to the village."

Straight Lance was standing near his lodge, listening, a worried scowl on his broad face.

"I heard white hunters' rifles," Paul said.

A solemn nod. "First time this close. Let's go see."

With him and Bear Neck and others, Paul rode out of the canyon toward the firing, which wasn't steady, just a boom now and then.

Flattened out on a ridge with the Kiowas, Paul saw a wagon and a team of mules, a skinner toiling over the dark carcasses, dragging the skins to the wagon and throwing them aboard; in the distance a hunter, afoot, working over a bunch of shaggies.

Bear Neck was for killing them both at once.

"Not yet," said Straight Lance. "There must be more of them. Let's see where their camp is. Soon these white-eyes will get hungry and go in. Being cowards, they have to eat three times a day."

As the watchers settled down to wait, Paul, with a gibing expression, said, "You forget that I'm a white man."

"We've changed all that. You're a Whirlwind Kiowa now."

"I haven't yet killed a white man."

"You may yet."

On the littered plain, the dwindling bunch of buffalo finally took lumbering flight. Lugging heavy rifle and a sack of shells, the hunter plodded to his tied saddle horse, in a draw several hundred yards back, and rode to the wagon. There, sitting on the shady side, he smoked his pipe while the skinner continued to toil.

"See," mocked Straight Lance, "he loafs while

his friend works. Only a white man would do that."

There was laughter, and Paul joined in.

"Look!" a warrior said. "The white-eye who sweats is taking only the tongues."

"Why wait here?" Bear Neck growled.

"You will do as you're told or I will send you back to the village to cut wood for the women," Straight Lance said.

When the last buffalo was skinned, the great lumps of red meat dotting the prairie as so many glossy pumpkins, the two white men took off on a southwesterly course. The Kiowas followed. Later in the afternoon the line of a creek snaked ahead, and an array of wagons and knots of horses and mules, and mounds of hides stacked like hay, and row upon row of pegged hides, drying in the warm sun, resembling brown squares drawn on the lighter-colored grass.

And—Paul saw, with a start—riflemen posted at regular intervals around camp, the wagons, some twenty in all, circled just so for defense, and saddle animals and teams picketed nearby where they could be led quickly inside the circle. There was an air of military order. All business. No sport. Professionals, he thought, and was appalled at the hundreds of stacked hides and the hundreds more drying on the pegging grounds. These men would kill enough buffalo in one day to feed the Whirlwinds all winter. He ranged his eyes over the encampment again and counted thirty-one men; perhaps others were still out.

His attention kept gravitating back to one man in particular; even from here he loomed extra large. Constantly on the prowl, he was, curtly gesturing a man here and there; arms on hips, watching everything with a proprietary bearing. Now striding across to the man feeding the low fire under the broad wooden rack on which hung rows of drying buffalo tongues; now striding within the circle where two men were cleaning rifles.

"Let's charge them," Bear Neck blustered. By now the Kiowas, circling, watched from the lip of a deep wash, which provided a clear view of the camp.

Straight Lance didn't even bother to turn his head. "You are blind as well as foolish. Don't you see how their guards are placed? That all have the big buffalo rifles that shoot a long way? Six warriors would go down before we reached the first wagon. We're going back to the village to talk about this. These white-eyes will be here tomorrow. We may have to take them a few at a time."

Paul fell to brooding on the way back. He had delayed too long. By God, he'd better get his family out of here. He had a picture of them safely in Maryland, the boy playing around the spacious old house, his patient mother showing Bianca new ways. His heart seemed to swell and pound until it filled his chest. A decision firmed: soon. He would take them away very soon, before war broke out between the Whirlwinds and the hunters.

It was purpling dusk, the breeze in the canyon freighted with the smells of cooking fires when the Kiowas clattered into the village. A village of excited voices and anticipation lighting the coppery faces. Old Heap-of-Bulls, the camp crier, called to the warriors, "Get ready for a big hunt. Many buffalo northeast of us."

Paul felt an instant elation. Good news indeed during these lean times!

"We can take care of the white-eyes after we come back," Straight Lance nodded. "We'll fight better on full stomachs. In the morning we hunt."

When Paul told Bianca about the hunt, she turned completely still save for the clasping and unclasping of her hands, and she turned away, but not before he caught her familiar dread whenever he was to be gone on a long ride.

"Everybody's going," Paul said, "except the old men and enough boys to herd the ponies."

"Is long way," she said.

"We need meat to dry for our going-away journey."

"Journey?"

His exasperation struck. "We're leaving at last, Bianca," he told her flatly, seeing her catch her lower lip between small, white teeth. "There's going to be a big fight with the white-eye hunters when we come back. I want us to be gone then."

"You won't help your friends fight?" She looked surprised and disappointed in him.

"We're staying out of it. It's not our fight."

"Is not?"

He hardened. "You don't want me to go on the hunt. It's mainly because bringing back meat means we are leaving."

"We are happy here," she said, her face softening. "Far off—where you take us—I don't know."

"We'll be happy there, too."

Rather hastily, she took the water paunch to the stream, to be gone a long time.

Next morning he mounted the blue horse and, leading a gentle pack mare, joined the hunters. The early sun was burning off the last gray tatters of dawn, revealing the procession of hunters, which included about every male member of the band capable of killing buffalo, leading pack mules and horses, when Kills-Something, scanning the riders, said in surprise, "Not all the young men are here. Not even my son or Bear Neck."

No one knew why or seemed concerned. Everyone, Paul knew, was thinking of the buffalo. And Bear Neck had been a hard one to figure, always. Perhaps he would catch up later. Perhaps he was still sleeping. Whatever the reason, a

Kiowa was his own master, free to hunt or fight when his medicine or power so augured.

At the time of sun straight overhead, while the hunters were stopped at a creek, a young man, his body taut, his head canted, listening, his face agleam, exclaimed, "Listen! I hear bulls bellowing!" An older man nodded. Heads turned. Now all heard the low rumbling.

They hurried in that direction for some time before the bellowing sounded louder. With the others, Paul rode to the spine of a ridge and halted short, his heart pumping faster. On the tan plain below, as far as he could see, to the broken red hills beyond, stirred a dark-brown sea of buffalo. More buffalo than the murmuring Indians had seen in months. It was just past the Yellow-Leaves Moon and so the bulls still ran with the cows, and would until frost, when they left the herds and gathered in bunches and remained to themselves until breeding time in midsummer. His trained eyes said these buffalo were at ease, undisturbed by white hunters, browsing the short, yellow grass, and in long files leisurely traveling belly-deep trails to water and back to the feeding grounds; others lying about as the day warmed.

Paul, feeling a pang, an awareness of the passage of time, realized that within a few days he would be leaving these sights forever, and not only because he was returning to civilization, but because the slaughter for hides was inexorably destroying the old ways of the Whirlwinds. Watching now, he opened his senses so he would not forget—just how the shaggies looked in late fall, their hides turning darker and richer; the spring calves still yellow, their fluffy hair making them appear big for their age; how the buffalo got up to go to water, feet first like a horse; the cows, instead of the bulls, usually posted on the outskirts of a bunch as lookouts; the solemn dignity of the prime bulls, their mops of chin whiskers nearly brushing the short grass when they lumbered toward the trails veining the low hills; the horns of the two-year-olds just beginning to stand out and curve; the very old bulls getting thin, their brittle horns cracked, already congregating in forlorn groups because not even the Indians wanted their poor meat or robes; the saucer-like wallows pocking the plain. Now and then spirals of dust feathering up as a lordly beast dusted himself.

Soon, Paul mused, this would be gone from the face of the earth.

He continued to observe, wholly absorbed. A clattering of unshod hoofs on loose rocks broke his concentration. The Kiowas were changing course. The wind wasn't right, being from the Indians to the buffalo; if the hunters moved much closer the outside animals would catch the scent of danger. Thus, the hunters looped around to approach from the northeast against the wind. Closing in, they strung bows and drew dogwood arrows from skin cases, clenching between their teeth extra shafts, which they would shoot at the soft spot between the protruding hip bone and the last rib to reach the low-hung vitals, or saw to their ash lances, depending on a hunter's prefer-ence and how swift his horse, inasmuch as the lance required closer work than the bow and was, therefore, more dangerous, should the buffalo turn on his tormentor.

Paul carried a lance. Star, sensitive to knee pressures, would take him in and out however he wished with sure-footed swiftness.

Ready, leaving the youngest boys to hold the pack animals, the Kiowas spread out and loosened reins, walking their mounts forward. Paul, feeling the blue's eagerness to give chase, had to keep reining the gelding back. About two hundred yards now. Now one-fifty. A hundred or so, Star's restless hoofs husking through the curly, short grass. Just when Paul thought how unusual that the buffalo indicated no uneasiness, a cow on the edge of the nearest bunch quit browsing and turned her mossy-black head toward the line of advancing riders. For another moment she seemed to peer and puzzle, possibly too lulled to react, or possibly too curious.

But no longer, for as Paul watched, she tossed her great head and her stumpy tail swelled and she went trotting off into the wind, southwest, her abrupt alarm drawing several animals after her. And the Whirlwind Kiowas whooped joyously and let their mounts go and the fleet buffalo runners dashed away. And above the aroused herd fountains of dust sprang up, which the steady wind scattered as a brownish veil, through which Paul could see the cows forging into the lead, the bulls following at their heels, and the little yellow calves and the dark yearlings bobbing behind like forgotten children, while a peculiar throbbing rolled over the hazy plain.

Within moments the blue horse, running with the headlong relish of a racer, took Paul to the rear of the younger buffalo, then dodging through them, and into the gap between them and the trailing bulls. Paul breathed powdery dust and the moist gaminess of hundreds of fleeing animals. Picking a four-year-old bull, he kneed the gelding toward the jerking hindquarters, past them along-side the hump, so close Paul's left moccasin brushed the furry flank.

That touch seemed to enrage the beast. In time, Paul saw the horned head twisting to hook Star's chest, and with a squeeze of his left knee he sent the horse out a bit, clear of the curved horns. When the bull straightened out, Paul brought Star in again, and again the bull, sensing danger, twisted its head menacingly. Once more the blue glided clear. And then the bull, true to the unpredictable nature of its kind, slewed around, almost stopping, hooking wildly, viciously, its small black eyes shiny beads of seated fury. Paul let him go and swept ahead. His last glimpse was of the bull tearing straight across. Whipping around for another look, Paul heard a mighty thud as the bull, running blindly, crashed into the underside of a screaming pinto, lofting the churning-legged horse high, the young Indian rider sliding nimbly down its back.

Racing on, Paul found another young bull running straight. This time he kneed his horse alongside without touching the buffalo, and when the dark-brown shoulder bobbed just ahead and below him, Paul, two-handed, with a yell, plunged the metal point of the spear behind the shoulder for the lungs, forward and downward, and muscled it free streaming blood, and as he did his horse instinctively swerved clear of the wounded beast's charge.

A moment and the bull began to falter, blowing stringers of bright blood. Paul jerked up, poised to ram another thrust, while the bull lost further momentum, swaying uncertainly, wobbling. Of a sudden it flopped in a spatter of dust.

Blinking to clear his vision of the fuming dust, Paul raced on among the bulls. His next victim made one menacing lunge and ignored him to lumber on with the herd. Paul's thrust struck too far forward, and when the bull turned to charge, the blue horse pivoted like a flash in behind to give Paul another stab. He drove the spear downward, behind the shoulder. Blood flying, the dark beast tore into whirling rage, bumping and hooking his brothers. Suddenly the bull crashed down, done, and Paul had to haul hard on his horse, for Star wanted to continue the game. Paul thought: *Enough.* He had more meat now than he could pack back. There would be plenty for the old people as well.

When he slid down to commence the skinning, the herd was a dark mass rumbling away under the pall of dust. Here and there horsemen dashed about like gadflies. Scattered on the dusty plain, other Kiowas were down and butchering, while their trained runners stood by as sentinels.

Paul, rivulets of sweat greasing his arms and hands, heaved the bull over on its belly with hoofs spread. He slashed the brisket across at the neck and folded it back to remove the forequarters at the joint, then sliced the hide down the middle of the spine to avoid cutting the valuable sinews. Peeling the hide back toward both sides, he took the hindquarters. After some minutes, all that remained was the bushy head and bare spine and rump, after which he bagged the meat in the hides and loaded the pack mule, which a youth had brought up.

He cleaned his knife and sheathed it and wiped his hands on the grass and paused to rest before riding back to butcher his first kill. Glancing about on the dotted plain, he could see that it had been a good hunt. Hunting from horseback as the Kiowas always did meant the killing had to be fast, before the game scattered; also, they believed that meat spoiled when the slain buffalo was overheated from long running.

He paused in his musing, his eyes pinned on a spur of dust smoking up from the southwest, from the direction of the village miles away. Curious, he waited.

The rider halted where a hunter was butchering. Moments there and the rider galloped on to the next man. By the time the horseman had stopped a third time the first two Kiowas were hand-signaling for everybody to come fast and the man on the horse was cutting tight circles, the signal for danger. Paul mounted and raced across, his exhilaration of the hunt forgotten, a premonition beginning to cloud his mind. As he reached the group, Kills-Something was laying his warrior's harsh voice into the rider, a frightened boy herds-man:

"Are you a child or a man? Calm down. Start over."

The boy was trembling. Struggling to speak, he choked out, "The village . . . the white-eye hunters attacked the village. It was bad," he said, avoiding the elder's eyes. "Most of our people made it to the rocks. Some didn't."

A coldness clutched Paul. "Did my family?"

"I don't know," the boy replied. He kept wetting his broad lips, kept searching for the difficult words. "Bear Neck—it was Bear Neck. He led a raid this morning on the white-eyes' camp. He was killed in the first charge."

"Bear Neck—the fool!" Straight Lance raged, his neck column cording. "Who else was killed?"

The boy's deep brown eyes, appealingly on his chief, then on Kills-Something, bared the burden of one who must bring further misfortune. "One," he said, delaying, "was Quick Wolf." Kills-Something flinched, nothing more, even though Quick Wolf was his son. "And," the halting young voice continued, "Little Turtle, Wild Horse, Green Shield, and Bull-Lying-Down. They were very brave. They made two charges. Bear Neck was also brave, the young men said."

"A fool!" Straight Lance cried. "Always a fool! I should have known he'd do something crazy like that." Bitter and furious, he said to the boy, "And so the white-eyes followed the war party back to the village?"

The boy lowered his gaze and nodded.

By that admission Paul was pained to understand more. Had an experienced war leader been along, the young men would not have allowed themselves to be trailed home. Instead, breaking up into twos and threes, scattering in all direc-tions, they would have confused the

263

hunters and drawn them away from the village.

Now the warriors were tearing about, shouting to the old men and boys to bring the pack animals.

Over and over, through the long hours of afternoon, Paul prayed softly, as if he were in some sacred place, back in the white-painted little church where he had worshiped as a boy, where life had seemed so serene and all prayers answered. He seemed to move in a stupor, his mind caught fast on the rotelike supplication: *Please, please, Father, for they are only poor innocents.*

Time crawled. The sun appeared stuck on the molten shield of the sky, and his punished blue horse, though still swift, could not stride fast enough. No one spoke.

It was sundown when the Kiowas clattered into the canyon. Onward, they raced their used-up horses, and when they slowed down, it was as if some ill wind deterred them from their course, and Paul, stiffening, heard the dreaded wailing as only Kiowa women could mourn. He turned utterly cold, afraid now, affected by each keening note. It was Straight Lance who shot ahead first, after him Paul and Kills-Something leading the headlong rush of the others.

Gradually, through the screen of dust, Paul saw the low oval of his hut and people standing there, among them Star Woman. His heart bounded when he saw her holding Chris, an elation as quickly dashed when, with a return of the terrifying cold-ness, he did not see Bianca.

Down, moving on halting steps, he saw Star Woman avert her face. It was another moment before she could force herself to meet his eyes. By that alone he knew, seeing it so absolute across the mute sadness stamping the broad face, which he kept hoping would change and tell him it wasn't so, and which did not. And knowing, glancing from Star Woman into the grieving faces, he saw grief and sympathy for himself as well, and he thought, *At last I am one of them.* As from a long way off he heard Star Woman say quietly, "We found her over there," pointing to the brush. "They did terrible things to her. Old Heap-of-Bulls saw a man in a red shirt, a big man, drag her out of the hut. She must have fought very bravely as long as she could."

Brave—his lips moving soundlessly—*brave. Always you had to be brave.*

Woodenly, he ducked inside and dropped to his knees by the robe, his eyes riveted on the small face, on the swollen face, on the purple bruises, on the staring eyes that saw nothing. He took her stiff hand and his pressing fingers found the broken nails. Tears coursed down his cheeks and splashed on his hands, while massive sobs tore his knotted body.

He did not know how long he stayed there like that, just watching the still face, free of all pain now, lost to all love. As in a nightmare that became real with dawn, he remembered digging, gouging his knife into the flinty soil, digging for hours, it seemed, and afterward scratching her name with his own after it, and the date, on a piece of sandstone. October 1875? November? It didn't matter. Just so she wasn't forgotten as his wife.

Now he was stumbling aimlessly through a wilderness of dark and choking grief. Star Woman had the boy; that was all he knew. And that he was upcanyon, weaving, arms hanging, mouth ajar, throat and lips parched, almost blind, wandering, uncaring, driven by the terrible anguish that refused him rest. The day was bright and he could feel the sun bathing his bearded face, but the watery mist over his eyes gave him the weird impression that a greenish cloud obscured the face of the sun. He scrubbed at his eyes, at once frantic to see; his hand came away wet from his streaming face and the green fog merely thickened and he slumped to the ground, inconsolable, his hurt rising and falling, never ceasing. He stumbled up. From a distance the scrape of a rawhide moccasin sole reached him, and he turned on instinct, in alarm—and realized it was his own moccasined feet staggering forward like separate appendages from his tortured being.

Now and then he paused for no reason at all,

just paused, standing flat-footed, swaying, staring but not seeing, until his rousing agony smashed him on. An indefinite time passed; no longer did he feel the harsh sun. Why, it was evening. A chill breeze was slipping along the canyon floor.

Even after he could no longer see, he felt and bumped and scrambled over rocks and through thickets and around scrubby trees. Something shone. Water glinting. Little by little, his stupefied senses gathered that the moon was up, pale and sword-shaped. He took a step toward the water. That far and he wrenched back savagely, in merciless self-denial, and flung himself away, scrabbling faster, like a frightened night animal.

Without warning, he staggered and crashed on his hands and face. To his astonishment he felt no pain. The place was soft and sandy and cool; and because he hadn't the strength to rise, he just lay there, his breath wallowing thinly in his chest.

At once the mercy of exhaustion blanketed him, and he slept.

His own doleful moanings waked him. He groaned and turned on his sandy bed, and his sluggish senses registered a new sound, of coyotes wailing foxlike, disembodied in the night. For the briefest interval he listened to the shrill serenade, before the wave of his grief massed again and plunged him deeper into despair, sobbing, great tears like silent raindrops skipping down his bearded cheeks, bringing a rapid sensation of suffocation, and across his memory's eye the vivid likeness of her small-boned face. Forever young, forever sweet, loving, and innocent, an exquisite portrait in miniature drawn before his eyes. His pain deepened and he struggled to turn his head, but she was still there. He turned again. Her perfect face followed, unchanged. Any way he looked he saw her, the dark eyes lovingly intent on his as ever. *By the purling Great River we laughed and played. On the soft robe we lay and watched the jeweled stars winking over the sand dunes. In the little hut in the canyon we lived and made love. Is good. Is good.*

His brain was reeling. Why? Why? Why did it have to happen to her? To one so young, so innocent, so good, so tender, so trusting, so loving?

He wrenched up crying, protesting against unbearable pain; but the pain stayed and although he wished to flee, some fatalistic sense whispered there was no escape, really, and he slumped back, resigned, and after a long while a kind of compassionate sleep stole over him.

Morning. Streaks of dull gray, of soft pink. Mocking birds twittering a mad, sweet chorus. He listened, forgetting; when a mourning dove released its melancholy call, the knife of his grief, always close, struck him again. Bars of light now. Seeing the pool as he reeled stiffly to his feet, he felt the usual impulse to drink and wash, and was about to indulge himself when the iron discipline held him fast. And although his throat burned for water, he turned his back on his craving and stumbled off. Somewhere in the remote wasteland of his mind a thought whirled up and cast its shadow, evil yet tantalizing. He let it come close. Suddenly he seemed to find himself nodding, resolved. He would seek out a side canyon and there, alone, strengthless, like an old buffalo bull horned out of the herd, he would seclude himself and turn his face to the sky and wait for death. To manage that, however, he must leave no signs of his clumsy passage, for likely Straight Lance would send out searching parties in a day or two.

His weakness hindered him and he spent a good deal of time locating his refuge, a V-shaped little slash of a canyon slitting the high, red wall, thick brush and tumbled rock masking its narrow mouth. Low, like a crouching wolf, he slunk in, careful to break no branches, to walk on rocks, not to disturb the damp earth still soft in the shade of the rocks.

Beneath a pungent cedar tree he chose his place, the strong incense of the gnarled wood stifling his senses, and lay flat on his back, eyes closed. Insects whirred a brittle, sing-song chant that became as time itself, tediously passing, if at all, if not motionless, even though the hot disc of the sun moved. He opened his eyes to gaze at the broken sunlight through the branches, and closed them again to commence the long wait, aware of no fear, no caring; already his life seemed to be ebbing from his pained body.

His senses dulled; far later a rustling pricked his eardrums. Turning, he spied a horned toad, the mottled brown-gray head erect, alert for insects. As Paul watched without interest, the horny head sank lower and the squat body flattened, basking in the sun. Paul dozed, to be roused by his inces-sant agony. A comical little brown gopher scurried up, the beady eyes curiously on Paul, cheek pouches distended, the puny nose twitching.

Paul groaned and shut his eyes, insensible to time. When he opened them again a brown hawk was sailing back and forth across the blue-domed sky, a mere dot, and the smoking iron of the sun slanted past noon.

A sound. A distant boom. One small part of him seemed to hear it while the rest of him, protesting the intrusion, struggled to shut it out. Another boom, then two more. He was counting, his senses refusing to exclude the noise. That was four shots. And just then another sounded. His numb brain stirred, and cleared, and meaning crashed: hunters. Hunters' big-caliber rifles.

He lay there another spell, heedful in spite of himself, lashed by an accusing guilt. The hunters could be coming back, and he was here, out of danger, as he had been the first time.

He could lie still no more. Turning on his side, he pushed up and crawled out from under the cedar and swayed up standing. His head swam, his vision went black, and he fell drunkenly to the ground. Again he tried and flopped back, astonished and fearful at his lack of strength. Desperate, weaving up, he gripped a branch for support and held his feet this time, feeling his terrible, empty-bodied weakness. He continued to grasp the branch, and when the world righted itself, he took an uneven breath, a faltering step, and started back.

Now the hard way he had chosen mocked him. He stumbled among the rocks, but they gave him something to hold to and gain his feet again. Brush and scrawny cedars clawed him and tore his body, but they also gave him support. Strange, he mulled, that he heard the booming buffalo rifles no more.

On the floor of the winding canyon the day was growing old, wrapping itself in robes of scarlet and purple. Paul's throat burned, his legs untrustworthy. Now and then he fell. Was that the rustling of a pony herd? He saw no movement. He stumbled on some distance, and was beginning to question whether he had the strength to reach the village, when he came upon horses herded by a boy.

Paul motioned weakly and tried to call out. All that issued from his throat was a dry croak. The boy had an odd manner as he edged toward Paul. Some rods away he halted, and Paul saw recognition animate the dark eyes, and quickly an expression of shock fed by fear. Still staring, he whirled his pony and bolted downcanyon.

Bewildered, Paul followed. Although the boy knew him, he had shown fear. Why?

He experienced the clutch of a deeper silence as he staggered past the horses, which spooked to the other side of the canyon and bunched there, stamping nervously. The vast silence held until, simultaneously, with sudden relief, he saw the pale cones of the outer lodges and the murmur of the village became audible, and he saw people moving about, some of whom were advancing to meet him. Just seeing them touched him and brought warm tears to his eyes. These people were indeed his friends, and the one in front, hurrying toward him, was his old friend, Straight Lance.

"Where are the hunters?" Paul called.

"A small hunting party. They left when we rode out to fight." The Kiowa's voice tailed off softly, which was unlike him. And in his eyes, scrutinizing Paul's face, Paul saw understanding and shock, or was it more like horror and superstitious fear, such as he had seen in the boy's?

"What is it?" Paul croaked. Before him, the

bold warrior's face was wavering, dimming, twisting, unreal, like a trickster's false face.

"My friend," the other said, with sympathy. "You must eat something. We are getting a war party together. We were going to look for you in the morning. Come."

Paul couldn't speak, though his lips moved. His eyes were still on the mask of his friend's features, in these few moments grown unspeakably sad and dimmer and smaller. A gasp tore Paul's throat. Frantic, he reached toward the Kiowa, and when he did the sky tilted crazily and he could feel himself collapsing, sinking into a sea of murky darkness.

He felt water on his face, a cool balm, and a delicious trickle in his mouth and down his throat. He choked and swallowed. But he couldn't see the sky; everything was pitch black. And he was being borne away, farther and farther, through a world without light.

Consciousness came to him in a place of delightful coolness, his body rested, his mind serene. A lodge. It was daylight. He could tell because the skins were drawn up to let in the cool breeze. A chief's lodge of many colorful trappings. His eyes wandered to a trader's hand mirror suspended from a pole, from there to the entrance and outside, where hung a medicine shield, a sun and lance painted upon it. The medicine shield he had once touched for power. So this was the lodge of Straight Lance.

At his stirrings there was a quick movement through the doorway. He turned his head. It was Star Woman looking in on him. She left after a moment, but not until he had observed the fleeting expression of shock he was becoming used to, and which once more left him so bewildered. What was it about him that repelled the Kiowas, that made them afraid of him? His wasted appearance? His weakness?

He lay back, troubled and uneasy, even through the cruel haze of his grief, which held him fast again. His eyes went to the mirror, idly, and before he had time to reason why, he was crawling toward it. Reaching the pole, he pulled himself to his knees and looked into the glass, and the features he saw seemed those of some gaunt and sunken-eyed stranger. That grieving face, lined, drawn, aged, bearded, the sockets of the sorrowing eyes like beds of ashes. He continued to stare, transformed, shocked, horrified, and all at once he touched his hair and clutched it, as if he might alter what he saw. Nothing changed. Nothing. He let go and slowly sank down, under-standing why the Kiowas, despite their sympathy, had shrunk from him:

His face bore the slack imprint of aging that only grief could leave, and his hair had turned gray.

Chapter 17

He sat the blue horse, as motionless as a wooden image, around him the swirl of assembling warriors. Impatient to be off, he did not turn his head. As the war party set forth, he loosened reins and Star took position up near the leaders. Thereafter, Paul settled himself for the long ride, cool and self-composed, the outward signs of his grief dried out, while inside him lay the terrible breach in his life, bearable only because of the boy left with Star Woman, and the rod of vengeance that burned his vitals.

When thirsty, he took a swallow from the paunch; when hungry, he chewed dried meat, knowing he would require all his strength and keenness when they fought the hunters. One constant fear nagged him: that he might fail to find the right man or men. How would he know?

As the day wore on, he had but a vague conception of time; everything seemed moveless—the clouds, the sun, his numbed body; he had been riding some hours and yet he felt little time had gone by until he was riding up a hogback ridge and gazing down on the flat where the canvas tops of the hunters' wagons should be blooming on the prairie.

An instant bitterness of frustration rose to his

throat. Except for one forlorn wagon, the flat was empty.

Riding through the abandoned camp, seeing the clutter of hasty departure, the rows of pegged and stacked hides, he chafed when the young Kiowas, disgruntled after finding no loot in the wagon, tarried to make a fire underneath it. He called to Straight Lance:

"They're wasting time. Let's go."

The war leader's shout sent them mounting, and the older Kiowas, like grim cats, pounced upon a broad, rim-marked trail going south. An old trail, Paul fretted, made not today or yesterday, probably the afternoon after the attack on the village. The hunters were fleeing for the settlements.

When he lay down that night on his blanket, his spirit seemed to depart his tortured body and float above him, motionless, disjoined. The prairie darkness oppressed him. How he hated it! He dozed, waked by the wailing of coyotes and the rising chorus of the wind sweeping over the short grass. He dozed again, waked by a nearby choking and weeping and discovered it was his own and that his face was streaked with tears. He moaned and tossed, dreading the further hours of darkness, and slept no more.

Still, when he got up at fawn light, he felt no fatigue, only the fixation to move on, to ride, to catch up, as the pain smashed over him again. He ate sparingly of the tough, dry, stringy meat. He drank from the paunch, a brief swallow. And, yet, it was remarkable how keen his senses were, how tireless he felt. He was riding with the leaders when, past noon, crossing the head of a small creek and traversing a plain sloping southward, he saw the first long stringers of moving wagons, writhing like dusty brown snakes, and the swaying hoods of the wagons, and, closer, the blue horse in a dead run, he could see the drivers whipping the teams faster.

There was a gap dividing the fleeing column that puzzled him until, rushing much nearer, he saw the deep-sided draw. The onward wagons had crossed; those behind were delayed while men with spades and picks toiled at the crumbling steep bank.

Watching, Paul divined the opportunity: attack now, before they could cross. Cut them off before they could join the forward wagons.

Straight Lance waved the older warriors together. While they sat their war horses, he told them the plan: Those with the best rifles would ride along the draw's bank and kill the teams of the lead wagons; that would block the crossing. The rest of the Kiowas would attack from the other side and the rear.

Paul, then, circling with the front warriors, heard his friend calling to him: "All you have is a knife. Take my rifle."

"The knife is enough," Paul said. "Or my hands."

"*Tejan*," the Kiowa said, his eyes glittering, "you are taking a new road today. The Whirl-winds' road. You are going to fight in close. Remember, you are brave!"

Shortly, hearing the rifles popping, and the Indians yipping shrilly and jumping their horses out, Paul hastened Star forward. They were upon the wagon train in moments. He could see white men running about, snatching at rifles carried in leather boots hanging to the wagon sides. Straight Lance knocked a man down, the first coup. Kills-Something rode his horse over a teamster, whirled and dropped to the ground, and split the man's skull with his battle ax, the second coup.

Paul, not hesitating, swept in yelling and with the sound of his voice his craving for action became resistless. A white man on a gray horse loomed straight ahead, his face blanched, his eyes bulging fear. He aimed his handgun at Paul, who flattened out and kneed the blue horse in. An explosion jarred his eardrums, but he felt no pain. He reared up and slashed at the dodging shape, missed, struck again, and felt the blade strike flesh and bone and heard the man's cry and saw him pitch from the saddle, the third coup.

With the blue horse cutting and weaving through the dusty haze as in a buffalo chase, Paul glimpsed scarlet-and-white war bonnets bobbing amid the cottony blooms of powder smoke and heard the swish of war ponies. The whooping of the Indians shrieked above the shouting white-eyes. Young Blue Hawk, slim and brave and ocher and red paint streaking his face hideously, slid from his horse and raced for the wagons, eager for hand-to-hand combat. A white man lifted up a canvas sheet and shot Blue Hawk in the head. He dropped instantly, shot dead. Before the white man could turn, Yellow Horse, swinging a stone-headed war club, charged straight in and crushed the man's skull.

Another white man, hatless, ropes of greasy black hair dangling to his shoulders, was calmly snapping off revolver shots. Buffalo Head swayed off his horse and bounced in the dust. Two Tails and White Bird, their horses neck to neck, galloped in for the pickup rescue. But as Two Tails leaned low, he lurched, wounded, and grabbed a fistful of mane. A second white hunter, running up to join the long-haired one, fired his rifle and White Bird slumped across the neck of his horse.

Paul sensed as well as saw the indecision among the Whirlwinds, on the edge of faltering, of falling back into the old, circling strategy, which here would be fatal against the hunters' heavy rifles.

Wheeling the blue horse, he slid downward and

hooked his left heel across Star's backbone and looped his outside arm in the rope plaited into the black mane. Leaping out, Star had him upon them almost too soon as Paul hastily freed his arm and dove for the long-haired man. He felt the bruising impact, felt the man crumbling under him. They tumbled over and over, Paul grappling for a hold on the handgun. He got it with both hands and heaved to his knees, twisted it free, and shoved the barrel into the man's belly and pulled the trigger. There was a muffled blast. The bullet knocked the man backward. Shock sprang across the bearded face. Above Paul a scrambling, cursing, yelling, grunting struggle was taking place.

Up, Paul saw Eagle Heart hacking at the other hunter. And the din of voices and hoofs and guns became deafening. Crouched, he saw Indians, some afoot, swarming around the wagons, shooting, striking, fighting hand to hand.

Then, quite suddenly, the tumult tailed off to a hoarse whoop or shout. Paul, looking for another adversary, caught the flopping of the mules, shot down, tangled in the traces of the lead wagon blocking the path down the bank cut. And then even the shouting of the white-eyes ceased, leaving only the aftermath of the exulting whoops. It was over.

Paul was trembling. The hunter whose revolver he had taken lay at his feet. Eagle Heart was ripping off the other man's scalp. There was a distinct popping as the hide tore loose.

Afterward, Paul walked over the battleground to look for the man in the red shirt, "a big man," among the bodies sprawled around the wagons. The sight got to him. At once he lifted a withdrawing hand, sickened, revolted, and yet, when he remembered, there was no bottom to his indifference, and he continued his search. The skin on the foreheads and cheeks of the scalped white men, loosened and slack, produced a horrible impression, as if by some dreadful alchemy they had become prematurely wrinkled and aged in moments. His revulsion deepened. The place suggested an immense slaughter pen. He fought back the convulsive reaction to gag.

A red-shirted body took his eye. He turned the man over with the toe of his moccasin, his gaze like a file. It was, however, the face of an old man, slight of build, raggedly scalped, the loose flesh of the face as puckered as a prune's. He paced on slowly, until he had covered the line of wagons. No, a cold logic hammered, no. Besides, any number of men in the hide outfit could be wearing red shirts. Let down, he went to his horse. Star was quietly grazing, reins grounded.

Spent, he stood aside, a sense of detachment from the war party upon him for the first time. A good fight by Kiowa standards, though Blue Hawk was dead and Two Tails and White Bird, of the young men, and Buffalo Head lay wounded. And the spoils included Sharps buffalo rifles, plenty of shells, and lighter rifles and handguns.

He mounted and rode across to the war party leaders. Straight Lance cut him his keen approval.

"*Tejan*, you counted coup. You were brave."

Paul lifted a shoulder, his shrug saying it mattered not. Moments past he had no feeling other than the headlong tingling of danger. Now he was experiencing a deep and persistent depression, which must have told in his face, because the Kiowa, understanding, said, "It's proper to kill our enemies. They killed our people."

"It's not finished," Paul said, wishing it were. "The man I want isn't here. I'm going on."

"Good. *Tejan*, today you charged with only a knife, while the rest of us held back. Therefore, you have the honor of leading the way. Come!"

Four o'clock sun had passed by the time Paul spotted the dirty mushroom color of wagon canvas on the browning prairie. But not strung out fleeing. These wagons were drawn up, tightly circled, the saddle stock and teams picketed just outside the defensive corral.

He studied the enclosure while the Kiowas rode up around him, silent and hating. Finally, Kills-Something's bitterness spilled out of him, his voice like acid. "In honor of my dead son,

I want to lead the charge when we take their horses. Hear me, my friends?"

Paul's shoulders sagged. It was the old, loose Kiowa plan of attack. Rush for the horses first. Except it wouldn't work here, in the open. Today, Kills-Something's grief and hatred affected his usual sound judgment.

Paul rubbed hard at his forehead and edged forward among the leaders. They made way for him. He had forgotten: He had proven himself. He was a warrior. A Whirlwind Kiowa. He had killed a white man, perhaps two. He wondered where his satisfaction lay, his triumph.

While he listened, he continued to scrutinize the corral and its environs, puzzling over the wrongness there, the one piece that didn't fit, that eluded him. Eagle Heart, whose horse had played out, was suggesting engaging the white-eyes at long range, using the buffalo rifles taken at the draw.

"But we aren't used to the rifles and the whites are better shots than we are," Wolf-Appearing reasoned. "We'd still have to get in close to wipe them out."

Paul could hold silent no longer, though with tempers short he realized he must consider the feelings of all. "My friends," he said, "what you say is wise. However, look down there again," he said, turning his head. "Look hard. Does it not seem strange that the white-eyes have picketed their horses and mules outside the corral instead of within the circle? Friends, those horses and mules are bait, to draw us into the open where the white-eyes can use their buffalo rifles." A wordless pause followed. Even the bitter Kills-Something was quiet. Paul continued patiently, "Let's go in afoot as you did that time against the Utes. Go just before dawn. Cut the picket ropes. Stampede the stock in on the wagons. Follow them inside the circle. That way we can fight in close."

Straight Lance arched his head around at Paul, a perceptive light slicing into his stare. "*Tejan*, I am proud of you. It would be foolish to rush down there now. We will go in afoot just before dawn. Everybody stay out of sight."

A darkness seemed to pass from the savage faces. There were nods and murmurs of approval.

"Listen," Paul told them, "I want the man in the red shirt. Heap-of-Bulls saw him take my wife. There were others, too. But a red-shirted man took her."

"We'll kill them all, anyway," Kills-Something said. "What difference does it make?"

"I want that man," Paul said.

From the rocky ridge where he lay, turning at times to mark the furtive pygmy figures about the wagons, and the picketed stock, like plums dangling down there to lure the horse-hungry Kiowas, the afternoon hours marched by in tedious procession. Paul was glad when night swooped down and he could roll in his blanket, when he was that much nearer the finish. He dozed in fitful bits, waking impatient to get it done, his mind not free even then of the pain of his grief-dreams.

So many times had Paul risen just prior to dawn that he seemed to waken at some prearranged signal this morning. The Kiowas were likewise stirring, and with them he started down the long slope for the wagons, at his belt the knife and the revolver he had torn from the hunter. It was yet dark, the stars dimmed, the night voice of the prairie wind hushed.

Reaching the base of the slope, the Kiowas fanned out to Paul's left and right, and he realized they had given him the honor of leading them in. Strange, how his mind seemed anchored back in the canyon, not here.

With an effort, he willed himself to new alertness. Slower, much slower, at a stalking walk, the dim bows of the circled wagons and the dark swarm of the picketed stock emerging through the muddy darkness. A pause while the Kiowas, those master horse thieves, apprehensive lest the horses and mules snort alarm at the unfamiliar scent of Indians, brought forth pieces of clothing taken at the draw and rubbed their nakedness to smell like the white-eyes.

Out of the dissolving blackness ahead grew the

cropping of grazing stock, and like ghosts the Kiowas glided in among the tethered animals.

Directly ahead of Paul a blaze-faced horse ceased grazing and flung up its head, blowing suspicion through its nostrils. Paul became dead-still. A moment, a longer moment. When the horse dipped its head to graze again, he slipped forward and touched the withers, feeling the quivering flesh, and slid his hand, patting, down the shoulder and forequarters to the hobbled shanks. With quick motions, he slashed the leather hobbles and cut the picket rope and released the horse, turning it toward the wagons. Stepping to the next animal, a mule, he did likewise.

Around him the Kiowas were working even faster, it seemed, and presently he saw a vague mass of freed animals drifting toward the corral.

He checked himself to eye the changing sky. In a few more moments it would be rose-colored.

As he held his breath, waiting for the signal, it came: a blood-chilling *hoo—kaaa—yaaa*! The yell was like a trigger releasing other voices screeching on both sides of him as the terrified stock fled in blind flight.

Paul was running, swinging the revolver in his right hand, the knife in his left, a whoop ripping from his throat. Above the hoof-clattering he heard the splintering shock of the horses and mules smashing into a wagon and he heard it go over and crash and the thudding of solid flesh as they milled and jammed against themselves.

As he reached the overturned wagon, a figure sprouted almost at Paul's feet, a white man in buckskins. Paul clubbed him to the ground with the handgun and kept going. There was enough light for him to see stock running wildly round and round inside, some breaking out on the far side, some bowling over hunters huddling for a stand; to see Kiowas sprinting here and there, their piercing cries never ceasing, and now that their guns were empty, hacking and clubbing the buffalo-destroyers, fighting as he had never seen them fight, not just for the glory of close-in coups, of touching an enemy first, but for members of their families lost in the attack on the village.

The advantage of the dim light now became a hindrance as Paul searched through the powder smoke and dust and the confusion of running shapes for the man in the red shirt, moving along the wagon line as he did. He froze. Was that a red shirt over there?

A fleeing white man suddenly pivoted and swung his rifle on a line with Paul, very close, very fast. Nothing happened. The rifle was empty. The hunter dropped it and fled. Paul snapped a shot at him. The man cried out and slapped his thigh. Bear Above, racing across, cut him down with one ax swing and whipped out his knife to take the scalp. The hunter, Paul saw, wore a blue shirt.

A rush of young light exposed the corral's harsh detail, the terrified horses and mules circling through the dust and more breaking out now, the littered camp gear, the strewn figures on the ground. The red-shirted man had vanished.

Grimly, he started his search anew. A short distance and he became motionless, aware that the racket had lessened. Just one rifle was banging, and it across from him; and as he singled out that sound, it quit and he heard a brief, strangled cry over there.

Guttural Kiowa voices. Someone was shouting, "Kill the white-eyes. Kill them both," and another voice, calmer, Straight Lance's: "Take them to *Tejan*."

Paul, striding over, saw two white men struggling in the grasp of Straight Lance and Kills-Something, and young Dry Throat and Yellow Horse. Both whites wore red shirts. Both big men. One youngish and loose-lipped and pale-fleshed, fear oozing out his terrified eyes, his hands quaking. The other older and thicker through the shoulders, a brush-thicket beard covering his square face like brown moss, and hands like hammer heads. An arrogance about him even here. Paul's mind closed like a trap, remembering: the big man he and the Kiowas had observed when they spied on the hunters' camp.

This man was peering intently at Paul. "White—" he blurted. "Hell, you're white! Ain't you gonna help your own kind?"

Paul said, "You're not my kind," and advanced, eyes raking both men. "Which one of you took the Mexican girl from the brush hut in the canyon?" He could not, he found, bring himself to say the rest of it.

The older man slanted his eyes slyly toward the other and back.

"Are you the one?" Paul demanded of the younger man.

"No. Somebody had to keep camp."

Paul stepped nearer, seeing the frightened young eyes meeting his own, seeing the open fear, yet eyes that somehow seemed steady and earnest. Not once did the eyes shift, though it wasn't that. A man fighting for his life could afford to summon hitherto uncalled-upon resolution. It was a growing feeling that Paul had, not unlike gazing at a cross-section of a man's being. Strangely, without altogether knowing why, Paul believed him. And he said, "One of you is lying."

"Look here," the older hunter roared. "You're white—I'm white. Tell these heathens to let me go." Paul didn't answer. The arrogant voice thinned, desperate-sounding, on the verge of whining. He began waving his arms. "You're a white renegade, so you understand money. I've got plenty money back at Fort Griffin." He gestured wildly to the south.

Something attracted Paul's eyes, a flash of pretty metal incongruously on the hairy wrist, a blur of bluish-green. Striding in, he seized the thick wrist and his eyes locked on the silver bracelet he had given Bianca that tender day long ago, set with lustrous turquoise gems, given with love and worn with love thereafter every day as long as she had lived. He tore it free, his eyes searing.

The hunter sank back, almost to his knees. "I bought it—bought it off him. He *was* there!"

"You're lyin', Plummer!" the younger hunter shouted. "You took it off her. The boys said you did. They saw you."

"Let's kill them both right here, *Tejan*," Straight Lance suggested. "Take the buffalo rifles—drive in the stock—burn the wagons—go home. This has been a great raid, even though two of the white-eyes escaped on horses."

Paul shook his head in negation, then pitched Straight Lance the bracelet and revolver. "You and I," he told the white man, "are going to fight to the finish," and turning to the Kiowas, "Let the young man go free. It would serve no purpose to kill him, since the two whites who escaped will tell the soldiers."

Disgust rose to the copper-hued faces, but the Kiowas released the white man. For yet another moment he did not move, swinging his head from side to side, watchful, still doubting. Suddenly galvanized into action, he flung Paul his gratitude and started running.

The white man called Plummer moistened his lips. "When I kill you, will they let me go free?"

"*If* you kill me," Paul mocked him. "But, instead, I will kill you." And he called to the Kiowas: "We are going to fight to the death. If he kills me, let him go. Hear me, my friends?"

"*Tejan*, you talk like a fool white man now," Yellow Horse said. "But we hear you."

"I have no knife or gun," the hunter said, spreading his hands and shrugging.

"Nor I," Paul replied. "I intend to kill you with my bare hands."

"I'm innocent. I tell you I bought the bracelet. You let the wrong man go."

"A man's eyes betray him when he lies. Yours are lying now."

Then Straight Lance raised a warning, "This white-eye is as strong as a four-year-old bull. Let me kill him for you."

Paul's eyes were fixed on the hunter, watching him peel off the hated red shirt, a towering, muscular man. Sweat beaded his hairy torso. He advanced crouching, hands extended like a wrestler, bringing a heavy-bodied smell that infuriated Paul.

It was time. Never had he felt so tireless. From a flat-footed stance he leaped in, feinting, and out, in again from the side, aiming a kick. His moccasined foot struck a fleshy hip. The man sagged but held his feet. "Renegade," he hissed. "I aim to stomp you into the ground. I've killed three men that way."

"How many women?" Paul hissed back.

The hunter came with his words, hard-breathing, slow of foot. Paul used his fists. It was like hitting a horse, and the man continued to crowd him. Paul lashed out with a kick. The hunter crashed. Paul pounced upon him, grabbing for his throat. With almost ridiculous ease, the white man flung him off. Paul landed on his back, briefly stunned. Seeing the shape looming toward him, he spun away, feeling the brush of the boots stomping where he had lain and after him the hoarse voice, "See, renegade, see?"

On his feet, Paul set himself for the hunter to resume his plodding pursuit. But, instead, he charged with astonishing speed. Paul had time to glimpse the wedge of a fist before his head seemed to explode. Falling, he felt a heavy body flop upon him, felt his breath go, felt pawlike hands gouging for his eyes. Jerking his head from side to side and tearing at the hands, he drove his knee into the region of the groin and heaved sideways, free.

The hunter, dragging up after him, breathed, "Next time, renegade."

Paul circled warily to clear his head. The fight began to take on a wearisome monotony. The man would charge and Paul, more agile and lighter, would harass the flanks, kicking or swinging with his fists, forcing his opponent to turn and pursue.

"Goddamn you," the voice hacked. "Fight like a white man."

"I'm wearing you down," Paul sneered. "I'm going to finish you."

Also weary of the stalemate, Paul bluffed a kick, and when the hunter lowered his guard, Paul hammered the shaggy face. The man dropped back, apparently stunned. Paul, impatient to end it, rushed in and saw his mistake too late, as the long arms shot out and bearhugged him, beginning to crush the wind from his chest. Paul managed a leg around, tripped him, and they smacked down, heavily, like two logs slammed to earth, above them the high cries of the Kiowas urging Paul on.

Paul didn't know where the knife flashed from, inside a boot, under the broad belt? All he glimpsed was its menacing glint above him. Pain fired along his ribs. And pain gave him strength. Crying out, he forced the knife hand upward with both hands, inches away and no more. Neither able to budge the other, until the hunter, all at once, brought his left hand across to add leverage. Paul strained for strength as the point of the blade moved closer to his throat. Only his right foot was free, and he beat his heel against the base of the other's spine and felt the pressure lessen against his arms. Swinging over, he locked his feet together and clamped on a schoolboy scissors, squeezing with all he had.

The hunter was gulping for air. Paul squeezed harder, slowly hoisting the heavy body upward. For an endless moment the heavy body hung midway; then Paul gave a lurch and flopped him over. At the same instant, Paul twisted the knife backward and with all his body he drove the blade into the hairy slope of the heaving chest.

There was an ear-splitting scream. Paul pushed harder, to the hilt. When he felt the man go limp, he flung up to his feet, while the hunter dug at the handle of the embedded knife.

Paul stood over him, humping for breath. He saw one hand slide away, saw the other cling to the handle; one by one the dirt-crusted fingers loosened, and the hand slid down. That was all.

Paul stumbled to a wagon and leaned there, holding his blood-greasy ribs. Something moved through his mind. Suddenly he slumped forward and retched, crying, crying for her, whom the killing could not bring back. It was done, brutally finished, and he felt no release whatever.

Chapter 18

Dawn was near. Here, upcanyon, he could see the timid tatters of light braving the high red walls, as bright as crimson shawls draping the ragged rim. A burst of twittering birdsong announced another cool, clear day. Hours ago, waking out of his grief-dream, at last able to move without grimacing pain after the fifth day of the big fight, he had come here to find peace of mind, though knowing he could not, and it entered the dark crypt of his mind that that was to be denied him for a very long time, if perhaps not forever.

There was distinct movement behind him and he recognized the even, balanced tread. Without turning his head he said, "My friend, you are walking with heavy steps this morning. Heavy for a new member of the Koitsenko, The Ten Bravest."

The Kiowa squatted down across from him, his gaze for a moment resting keenly on Paul. He glanced away, turning somber eyes to the ground.

Paul understood that look. Paul's hair had turned snow white and he appeared gaunt and aged. Such a change, so sudden, bothered the superstitious Kiowas, who read therein mysterious portents.

"I resemble an old man," Paul said, smiling faintly, "as old as the camp crier, Old Heap-of-Bulls, whose hair is merely gray. However, I feel strong enough to ride. I am leaving today with my son."

"Do you feel strong enough to fight?"

"Fight?" Paul asked wearily, dumfounded. "Again?"

"Soon. The white-eye hunters who escaped must have reached the settlements. Many hunters are coming to fight us. Wolf-Appearing saw them late yesterday while he was out hunting. All night he watched their fires. They are bold and noisy. They are drinking much crazy water."

"How many?"

"Wolf-Appearing says there are ten times as many as we fought."

"It's time to leave this place. To take your people across the Great Sand River and go to the fort, near the mountains where you captured me."

The Kiowa opened and closed his right hand, drove his fist hard to his thigh. "Live on the reservation? Never be free again? Be tied up like mules? Dig holes in Grandmother Earth? No," he said, but he sounded unsure.

"You have to think of your people, of the children. The way the white-eyes are slaughtering for hides, soon there'll be nothing left to eat on the plains. Then what?"

Straight Lance lurched to his feet, his eyes

296

gleaming combatively. "I haven't seen these new white-eyes myself, and sometimes Wolf-Appearing's eyes get big—he sees more than is there. I want you to ride with me. We'll scout these white-eyes together."

They rode through vacant, silent country. Where usually this time of year there would be a plethora of buffalo, their hair turning heavy and seal-brown for winter, there was not a single moving animal. The emptiness depressed Paul.

"There they are," said his friend some two hours later.

Paul, searching the browning distance, wanted to refute his eyes: so many wagons and teams and men stirring around them, a giant swarm, some wagons stringing out in motion, others waiting to fall in behind—a small army, he said to himself.

"They're breaking camp," he said, his voice jamming hard. "Heading this way. You have no choice. You have to move the village." Having said it, he was prepared to overcome the Kiowa's objections.

To his surprise, the Kiowa spoke quite calmly, "Yes—we have to move." Unwillingness swelled the high-boned warrior face, unwilling-ness balanced by resignation.

They whirled their horses running.

There seemed so little to take along, Paul found later, far less than he had supposed: the bracelet, his white man's crumpled clothing, which he would need when he re-entered that other uncomfortable world where people swathed their bodies, his few weapons, a buckskin shirt made by Bianca, another pair of moccasins. An insight tore him: how little one actually needed of material things for true happiness. He kept only his recent hide paintings, a small, tight roll, for they were his best work, done after he had brought Bianca to the canyon; the others he abandoned, as he was this phase of his life. Again, Star Woman took the boy.

Soon the scolding women, making the *travois* loads ready, and aided by the eager, obedient children, had the cedar lodge poles down and tied into two bunches by means of rawhide ropes passed through holes, then bound on each side of the patient horse so that the upper ends rested against the animal's shoulders. The tipi cover, folded into a compact bundle over the poles behind the horse, formed a litter upon which other household belongings were placed and on which the smaller children rode.

Trailing southward out the mouth of the canyon, guarded by the main body of warriors, the dust-raising pony herds following, the villagers bore southeast. After the *travois* procession cleared the canyon, warriors, using cedar boughs, brushed out the tracks.

From afar, Paul saw the vanguard of the hunters, resembling a column of ragged cavalry, sweep into the canyon. It was some minutes before the last horseman passed through.

"They'll pick up our signs before long," predicted his friend and ordered the young men to tie poles to their horses and start numerous diverting trails.

As the hours snaked by and Paul observed the dry country through which they were passing, an understanding became clear: His friend was deliberately taking the waterless course to make travel hard for the hunters.

Next morning, nevertheless, dust tails yellowed the sky behind the caravan, and Paul saw why as he pinned his aggravation on the hundreds of Indian horses and ponies scuffing dust that even a bleary-eyed greenhorn hunter couldn't miss.

It was strange, he mused, how the white-eyes, instead of closing the gap, continued to hold back, staying about the same distance. Their smaller number also puzzled him. What had happened to the swarm of several hundred hunters? Perhaps some fifty trailed the Kiowas today. He doubted that the others had tired and given up the chase. Whatever, it defied reason, and he could find no satisfactory answer except the foreboding nagging of one.

Apprehensive, he went to Straight Lance. "You have noticed there aren't so many white-eyes trailing us today? Is it possible they have circled around during the night to get between us and the river?"

"Who knows what a fool white man will try?" the Kiowa said, troubled. He became uncommunicative and Paul, seeing his mood, left him alone.

The hot wind was picking up, terse, abrasive, dry. Sitting the blue horse on the right flank of the plodding procession, Paul had the feeling that he was seeing something historic. This, the last wild band, was coming in to surrender. He read it in the stark faces, cast like bronze, in the demeanor of the silent children, thirsty today, yet taught never to cry or complain.

By late that afternoon the water in the paunches was running low, and grim warriors, eyes bloodshot, tongues swelling, went along the line, their actions a threat to any man who might drink.

When evening came, Straight Lance called the older warriors together. "We are being driven like cattle. Tonight we will run off their horses. We will charge in three waves. First, those dragging the bells, then the dry hides, then those with the bull-roarers."

Star Woman gave Paul a raw, stiff buffalo hide tied to a lariat. "It will make much noise when you drag it," she said. "I will look after your son."

Other warriors were tying lariats to belts and muffling the clappers with blanket rags. Others, particularly the young men, carried the bull-roarers or noisemakers.

Guided by a moon as lemon yellow as hand-worked buckskin, the Whirlwinds circled in to the north side of the hunters' camp, discernible as a low mass marked by the dull-glowing eyes of campfires and the picketed horses.

Kills-Something, tonight's raid leader, said, "There are some Tonkawa scouts with the white-eyes. But don't bother to take their hair tonight. Just scatter the horses good, take what you can, and hurry back to camp."

Paul, with the second wave of warriors dragging the dry hides, saw Kills-Something burst to the front with a screeching howl, and then all the Whirlwinds yelled, sounding like hundreds of Kiowas charging the camp.

Star needed no urging. He was bounding away even before Paul kneed him forward, dragging the bull hide, and the crashing and skittering sent the Ute horse flying faster with each lunging stride. Ahead, the bouncing bells raised a clanging din; behind Paul whirred the maddening bull-roarers.

Quickly, Paul heard picket ropes snapping and the rolling racket of fear-crazed horses beating away, and broken hobbles flopping, and a popping of shots from the camp. He had a glimpse of Straight Lance, who seemed to disappear all at once.

A figure on horseback, running against the current of the Kiowa charge, suddenly loomed before Paul—a screeching Tonk scout. On instinct, late, Paul tried to swerve the blue horse, but the Tonk refused to give ground. Paul called on all his strength to rein clear. Star obeyed, turning, but likewise late. Paul felt the jolting impact as the horses collided. Star went to his knees, staggering, but humped up and ran on limping, leaving the Tonk horse and rider floundering.

It ended shortly. The volume of the crashing charge dimmed of a sudden, with loose horses scattering like the wind.

A sense of wrongness bothered Paul as the main body of the Whirlwinds circled beyond the camp. He called loudly, "Where's Straight Lance?" No one answered. He called again, louder. Just then Yellow Horse, riding up, said, "His horse went down right after we hit the pony herd. Let's go back for him."

Paul cut the hide loose and went back with Yellow Horse, guided by the shouts of the white-eyes calling to one another, and by the cones of their leaping fires. These foolish hunters had built up their fires and withdrawn behind them as a man would to protect himself from wolves, though the flames only outlined their figures.

Paul felt his contempt rise. Any Indian herd boy knew better.

Paul flattened forward as did Yellow Horse, and

slowly, their mounts like two aimless strays from the spooked picket bunch, they let the horses amble neck and neck toward the camp.

Under the hard moonglare there materialized the shapes of a downed horse and a man lying nearby. The horse didn't move, apparently dead, but neither did the man, and Paul bit back his fear. He remembered the Tonk, but then that was farther on. The drifting horses were about fifty feet away when the man raised up. A weak and searching voice called softly in throaty Kiowa, "Here I am, my friends."

Paul stifled a whoop. At the same time Yellow Horse quickened his mount. Together, then, they jumped their horses out and together, reaching down, grabbed under an armpit and lifted Straight Lance off the ground without dragging a heel and cut sharply eastward away from the camp, careening down a long swale before the first buffalo rifle bellowed.

Straight Lance's racer had tripped over a picket rope, he said. Unconscious, he had lain there until the unshod hoofs of approaching Indian horses had roused him. Paul helped carry him to a *travois* where he lay until morning, when he sent a youth to bring a mount from his pony herd. Over Star Woman's objections, he had himself lifted to his pad saddle.

Noon sun, hot and windless. That was when Paul noted, at last, the dim stir of motion behind the *travois* column, the dusty ruffle of riders again, though fewer in number than yesterday. And it flew into his head that last night's raid, although a success, still hadn't put all the white-eyes afoot.

About the same time, to his dismay, he discovered on both flanks large groups of horsemen, far out, riding parallel to the Indians. This sent the older warriors hastening the cavalcade straight for the river, the only open route left. Later in the day, at a glistening vein of sweet water, they watered the thirsty stock, filled the empty paunches, and pushed on without resting.

Still later, Paul, his pulse quickening, fixed eyes finally on their destination: the low, irregular wall of the north bank of Red River, which the Kiowas called the Great Sand River, and for good reason, lying across there in easy pitches enveloped in heat haze, yet some miles away. On the far side stretched the safety of Indian Territory.

Motion took Paul's attention. Kills-Something, leading the scouts, was cutting his pony in tight circles and riding back and forth: *Enemy close. Very close.* When Paul got there, Kills-Something was pointing.

Paul sat quite still, struck anew by the sense of doom that seemed to follow these luckless people, watching riders rising from the creases of the rolling grassland, positioned between the Kiowas and the river, blocking any escape.

As the warriors gathered, the vindictive Kills-Something was for charging the white-eyes immediately. Others favored caution. Wrangling rose. Straight Lance, still weak from his fall, was the last to ride up. He said, "Put the women and children below the rise while the rest of us stand guard here and see what the white-eyes do. Get ready. Look!"

Five riders, Paul saw, were coming this way. One, a Tonk scout, was holding aloft his rifle with a white cloth on the end of the barrel. Behind him rode two yellow-leg cavalrymen and two civilian white-eyes.

Straight Lance started off to meet them. When Paul followed, he was motioned away. "Go back. The white-eyes want your hair. Why tell them you're here?"

"They already know. Remember the young man I let go?"

"I told you we should have killed them all."

"You will need an interpreter."

"That Tonkawa scout will do."

"Would you trust him, a tribe that eats the flesh of humans?" Paul replied, and kept riding after him. Kills-Something followed.

The whites and the Tonk had halted about midway between the hunters and the Whirlwind band. A wave of scorn filled Straight Lance's features as he checked his restive mount. The two civilian whites kept their eyes pegged on Paul, their stares a cross of hostility and rapt curiosity. One put Paul in mind of a gross frontier merchant such as he had seen at Fort Griffin: brown hat and brown coat and vest, a gold watch chain looping low, dangling an elk's tooth; sheathed in shiny black boots, a neat-bearded, overfed man whose paunch jellied against the saddle pommel.

The second white man bore the nondescript markings of the typical hunter: rawboned, long, shaggy hair, wide-brimmed hat the color of raw earth, blackened at the sweat band. He possessed a keen-eyed competence and self-confident physical strength, backed by the long-barreled Sharps rifle across his saddle.

All this while the Tonkawa scout was nervously watching the Kiowas, who abhorred the cannibalistic Tonks and called them *Kia-hi-piago*— "Eaters of human beings." This Tonk had a slablike face, broader than a Kiowa's, and thick braids like black snakes hung below his shoulders. He wore a leather jacket decorated with porcupine quills and carried a bull-buffalo hide shield on his left arm, and he kept the nose of his Henry rifle hovering on his two Kiowa enemies. And because he was a Tonk, a despised pariah, and survived because he was a competent scout, Paul knew that it was he who had expertly guided the hunters around in position where they blocked escape across the river.

The two cavalrymen—one very correct, very young, too young, in fact, to support a full beard, very conscious of his duty, wore the plain shoulder straps of a second lieutenant, the other a first sergeant whose face bore the weathering of an old soldier—observed Paul with somewhat less naked interest, but with searching inquiry, nevertheless.

Paul regarded the whites like a Kiowa, haughtily, his head high, for they were his enemies as well. The young officer came to the point, his tone clipped:

"This gentleman," indicating the paunchy man, "is Mr. Fowler, and that is Mr. Sims. This is Sergeant O'Hare. I am Lieutenant Dowd, Fourth Cavalry, Fort Griffin. May I ask your identity, sir?"

Paul almost smiled through his arrogance. "The Kiowas call me *Tejan*."

"*Tejan*?"

"Means Texan in Spanish."

"I mean your given name and surname, sir."

"*Tejan* will do. There's a far more pressing matter here than mere names. Why don't you let these people through? They're causing no harm. They haven't fired on you. They're headed for the reservation to surrender."

"Lieutenant, I'll ramrod this powwow," Sims,

the hunter, flared before the other could reply, and he slung around at Paul: "They jumped the boys below the Cap Rock. Poor Ned Plummer's outfit. Nigh wiped 'em out—that's why."

"Those same *boys,* as you call them, first attacked the Kiowa village in the canyon," Paul said, his bitterness keen. "Those same *boys,* as you insist on referring to them, killed women and children and old men—including my wife, a citizen of Mexico. I repeat: my wife—raped—murdered. That's why the hunters were attacked."

The lieutenant glanced sharply at the civilians. "My commandant wasn't apprised of this . . . rape, women and children killed."

Sims looked bored and impatient. "Sure, Plummer hit the village. Sure, somebody got hurt—*after* the heathens raided Plummer's camp. Wasn't that the way it was, Fowler?" Fowler nodded and Sims went on, flat and loud, "Lieutenant, ask this white man, if he'll tell you the truth."

"Some of our young men did attack Plummer's camp," Paul said readily. "Except there were no women or children there; even so, it was no excuse for what happened at the village."

Fowler was playing with the elk's tooth, rubbing it between right thumb and forefinger. "Another fight won't solve anything. Let's get down to the nubbin, gentlemen. I," he addressed Paul, "am Benjamin P. Fowler. I buy and sell hides. I have general stores at Fort Griffin, Jacksboro, Fort Worth, and Dodge City. My word is my bond. I've come with these gentlemen to bring peace to the frontier. It was at my insistence that the Army detailed Lieutenant Dowd and a platoon to come along."

Paul's sarcasm leaked into his voice. "You mean peace would save lives, I suppose?"

"Exactly. You see the point."

"And improve business, especially if the Kiowas are run off their hereditary hunting range?"

Fowler's momentary affront faded, then swelled. "And why not? You, sir, are a poor one to question my motives. You are a white renegade, sir. The worst kind. Stirring up the wild bands. Not only have you lived among the Indians for that purpose, but you have taken part in their bloody raids against the settlements." He was furiously fingering the elk's tooth. "You were seen at Elm Creek, around Comanche Springs about the time a trail herd was wantonly attacked, and half a dozen other trouble spots. So, you see, you are also wanted by the federal authorities for exciting the wild bands, to be seized wherever the government can pick you up." Paul kept silent, maintaining his fixed Kiowa haughtiness. "Mr. *Tejan*, or whatever your real name is, our terms are these: You surrender to us and we'll permit the women and children to pass through."

Paul's arrogance became a fixed grimace. "And the Indian men?"

When Fowler hesitated, Sims pointed at the wooded line of the river. "See them cottonwoods, *Tejan*? We aim to hang you an' every greasy Indian buck down there—that's what."

"Oh, there's going to be a trial," Fowler said, but his tone sounded lame, without conviction.

"I can imagine what sort of trial," Paul sneered, making the harsh sign for rope around neck.

"Gentlemen." There was a stir among the horsemen as Lieutenant Dowd wedged between Fowler and Sims. "My orders are to escort Mr. *Tejan* to Fort Griffin, where the properly constituted civilian authorities will take him into custody. He will have benefit of legal counsel. There will be a trial by jury. Nothing was said about the Indian men, gentlemen. Neither you, Mr. Fowler, nor Mr. Sims here is a duly appointed or elected official."

Paul made a pushing-away gesture. "Our people are tired. They've come a long way. The children are hungry. We'll talk again in the morning."

"Morning, hell!" Sims stormed. "We'll take you right now."

"I think not," Paul said, having caught Straight Lance's warning eye, and motioned about. "We have Sharps rifles—Plummer's rifles—and we know how to use them. Look around you."

Indeed, the Kiowas made a menacing sight, posted here and there on the slight rise, forming a half moon around the white men and the nervous Tonk. Which was stretching the blanket, Paul knew. Never really excellent rifle shots, the Whirl-winds were even less expert handling the heavy, unfamiliar Big Fifty Sharps and the .40-90's, and the .44-90 Remingtons. Vernier peep sights and double-set triggers seemed to mystify the Kiowas additionally, inasmuch as they'd had so little time to learn their precise use.

Sims drew back. Fowler paled. The Tonk didn't move, but his alert eyes flicked left and right, as gauging as a wolf's.

"Now," Paul said, "I have a counter proposition. If I surrender to Lieutenant Dowd, all the Indians get through—that means all the Indian men."

"Like, hell!" Sims gritted, his jaws working. "You're surrounded, an' there's a good two hundred hunters between you an' the river. We'll hang them bucks even if you don't give up."

"Not without a fight you won't. You'll think you stirred up a den of wildcats. Plummer found that out."

Fowler pulled on his beard. He appeared to be searching for a modicum of judicious bearing. "Mr. *Tejan*, you represent the nubbin of this thing. I am not an unfair man. Let's . . . ah . . . parley about this again in the morning, here.

Come along, men." He turned his horse somewhat hastily.

Sims tossed him his damning contempt and followed, as did the Tonk and the cavalrymen, off galloping.

Already Paul felt himself dismissing them, not seeing them in detail though his eyes were upon them, his mind on the morrow. By God, he had bluffed them a little, for a while, all but that hardcase Sims, damn his bloody heart.

He heard a horse move up and his friend's guttural voice, uncommonly soft. "I understood enough, *Tejan*. You talk hard. If you surrender, all of us can cross the river. Then they'll hang you."

"I am very tired, my friend," Paul said heavily, and he rode back to be alone.

It was dark again, the clawing, blanketing, hated darkness that never let him rest. He felt alone, even among his friends. Up there, in majestic isolation, the stars likewise traveled their solitary paths through endless space, each to its own destiny. His thoughts kept circling back to Lieutenant Dowd, green and proper, also conscientious and soldierly. Could young Dowd, with his mere handful of men, provide safe escort to Fort Griffin? If so, what then? The trial? A mockery, the outcome foreordained before a jury of hunters and cowboys? He released a drawn-out groan and stirred again, thinking of these driven people, his mind hard-fixed on the women and children, particularly them. Long later, it seemed, his mind ceased its mad whirlings and weighings and fearful reckonings, and became still, uncluttered and resolved, evoking a grateful peace unknown to him these past days. Fowler was the key. A man of reason. Backed by the lieutenant, possibly he could guarantee passage for the Whirlwinds, if Paul gave himself up.

He tossed, he half-dozed, waked by grass-shufflings and whisperings. Open-eyed, he sat up. Although the sky was still dark, the advance gray scouts of daylight were already prowling the east. The shufflings and rustlings forced his attention closer about him, and he saw dark, moving masses and, just audible, caught single, muted words hushed in warning; and steps coming, and he knew whose they were before he heard the voice:

"We're getting ready to go, *Tejan*."

"Go?" Paul stood.

"Yes, all of us—and you. If we have to die, we'll all die as one people should, together, fighting."

"I'm willing to talk again this morning. To give myself up, if the white-eyes will let the band cross the river."

"You will listen to me. I'm the war leader. That talk is rubbed out. The white-eyes would only take our weapons and hang us."

Paul spoke thoughtfully, "There are two hundred hunters between us and the river."

"I know that. Many of them are drinking the crazy water. We'll drive our pony herds through their camp. Follow after them, close."

Paul rubbed his forehead. "Stampede the ponies through?"

"Is there another way? Come. And take this war club, my friend."

Paul mounted, and although he couldn't see much, he knew how the Kiowas were working it: the women and children and old men in the center, behind the herds of ponies, the experienced warriors on the flanks and at the rear, closing up any stragglers. Paul took his place in the darkness, trusting his horse, sensing more than seeing the forward motion of the herds being gradually bunched, hundreds of ponies streaming onward.

His blue horse halted. A brief spell of waiting and Star stepped out, in a slow walk. Ahead, barely, Paul could glimpse the bobbing shapes and hear their rustling hoofs, softly, softly, faster, faster, though not yet drumming, and the raspings of the *travois* poles. A child wailed, instantly hushed. Faster, the unshod hoofs beginning to drum.

His throat throbbed with excitement, and as of old his senses responded, rekindled once more, the scene sketched across his sight: the dark wave of the ponies rolling ahead, and the faintest dove-gray glow, as if filtered through stained glass, streaming through from the murky heavens.

Up there, Paul spotted the dull circlets of the hunters' fires.

He wasn't prepared when it did come, even while knowing it would, the first curdling whoop that goaded the ponies off and racing, scudding ahead, a wild cloud sweeping low over the prairie, outlined in brackish, spectral light now.

Immediately the tempo changed to a hard, staccato racket and rumbling that shook the earth under Paul, much faster, unbroken, the falsetto cries of the women interlacing the yelling and screeching and whooping of the men and boys.

Paul tasted the pungency of dust; it flowed up about him, a powdery fog that blurred the horses and the huddled women clutching the small children like so many bundles. Through the confusion ahead a shot banged. He had been expecting that sooner, and was puzzled at the delay. Moments afterward he heard the lead ponies striking the camp. Yells. Shots. Terrified yells, at once shut off; those men had been ridden over and under. And up ahead, incongruously, it began to sound like a shinny game as flying hoofs kicked and trampled tinware and sent it skittering and rolling.

But the women and children, on slower horses, and pulling *travois* poles, began to lag, and a gap opened between them and the onrushing horses. On Paul's left, gunfire speckled the semidarkness. A warrior riding flank swayed and vanished. Paul got only a glimpse. It looked like Eagle Heart. When Paul tried to cut out to pick him up, oncoming loose horses blocked him off and forced him back into the headlong mass.

Then a knot of horsemen bolted in from that troublesome left flank. Hunters on horseback. Screeching like panthers, the Kiowas wheeled to meet them, Paul among them. In a whirlpool of horses and jabbing lances and swinging war clubs and rifles going off, and there, right before him, a bearded face beneath a flop-brimmed hat and the long barrel of a big Sharps. Paul kneed the blue horse, which spun like a war dancer, inside the arc of the swinging barrel. As Paul crashed the war club downward, the bearded face fell away and the hat sailed off like a brown leaf. More hunters pressed in. Before many moments, Paul saw, they would smash through to the slow-moving column of families.

At that, some part of him seemed to go berserk, and he had no fear whatever. A screech ripped from his throat. He dashed into the white-eyes, his suddenness causing them to mill, confused. He continued swinging the war club, kneeing the nimble horse this way and that, knocking one man from his saddle, trampling one unhorsed hunter. There was no limit to his swiftness and furious strength as he and the blue horse cut and pivoted as one, Paul screeching and howling every breath, flailing, charging, until he realized Star had paused, sides heaving, warily looking for the next enemy.

Meaning crashed. No more hunters milled about him. They were falling back, and the warriors were following the last few families through the camp. In fact, they were through. He took after them at a dead run, riding in daylight, bold daylight, glimpsing horses scattered everywhere.

Yonder, as if through a struggling dream-vision, lay the hazy destination of the wooded river. Some Indian ponies were yet streaking northward, trailing them, the Whirlwind People, yet bunched, casting fearful backward looks.

He slowed, and when after some minutes he came near the river and saw the people crossing, gingerly picking their way over the sandy footing, in a loose, strung-out line, and he saw, nearer, warriors gathered on a knoll overlooking the crossing, he rode elated up to his friend, only to turn puzzled at the latter's frowning concentration.

"Look," the Kiowa told him. "They're coming again. Like wasps."

Paul looked and went cold. A fast-closing fist of horsemen. Unless checked, they would reach the river before all the families crossed.

"It's a good day to die, *Tejan*," the Kiowa said. A terrible look was working into his face.

"No—" Paul protested, hating the resignation, the fatalism. "No—" The Kiowa belief of always having to die, of always having to be brave, that nothing else mattered, had often vexed him because it seemed so needless at times. His friend was singing, his voice high and sing-song:

"O sun, you remain forever, but we Koitsenko must die.
O earth, you remain forever, but we Koitsenko must die."

He sang it four times, the magic number. Paul recognized the song of the warrior society, The Ten Bravest.

The Kiowa shook his lance and kneed his mount.

"No—" Paul shouted, falling into English, and grabbed his friend's bridle. "By God—no—"

The Kiowa seemed in a hypnotic state. He clapped heels to his horse, but Paul held on to the bridle, swinging the horse's head around, and shouting at the top of his voice, in Kiowa:

"Dying won't help your people now. They need you—your power. We'll get them across. They need you more than before. When they cross the river, all the old ways will be dead, my friend. A new way will start. Grandmother Earth isn't dead; Grandfather the Sun isn't dead. Only the old ways are passing—they have to change."

"But the white-eyes are coming." Straight Lance was both bewildered and angry.

Paul had run out of Kiowa philosophy. He flung around. Kills-Something and Yellow Horse and Wolf-Appearing all had buffalo rifles, as had some of the others.

"Listen," Paul called. "The white-eyes expect us to rush out and charge them as usual. We won't be that foolish. Get off your horses. Spread out and use the buffalo rifles. Kill their horses. Come on. Be quick."

At the first boom nothing happened. But when all the Kiowas started shooting, a horse flopped down, and another.

"Don't fire so fast," Paul called "Fire slower. If they come much closer, then fire as fast as you can."

Although two more horses fell, the hunters didn't slacken. A third horse broke down; still, the white-eyes charged, shooting as they came. Kills-Something gave a crooked lurch and jerked backward, his wide-boned face spouting blood. He was dead when Paul picked up the Sharps, eared back the big side hammer, dug a shell from the sack Kills-Something had dropped, and fired at the lead horse.

The butt of the heavy rifle slammed Paul's shoulder and the target horse suddenly was leapfrogging wildly, like a wounded buffalo bull, one foreleg dangling. Paul continued to fire methodically. It seemed impossible to miss that solid mass.

Now the hunters appeared to hesitate. They slanted off, arching around in a ragged turn, almost broadside. All the Kiowas were shooting, their lighter rifles also rattling while the hunters kept angling away. Dust bloomed as horses and riders went down.

Paul's left hand burned from the barrel of the Sharps. He reloaded, but held his fire, watching, lips pursed, expecting the white-eyes to circle and reform and charge again, watching, as stride by unwilling stride, instead of facing about, they turned for camp.

He watched them grow less and less, as horses and riders became as single figures. Not until then did he and the Kiowas hasten toward the river.

Chapter 19

Through the leafless cottonwood bottoms, across the sandy flats, breasting the shallow stream stretching like a copper tongue below the reddish brows of the broken bluffs. Up the loose earth of the sloping bank where the elders and the women and the big-eyed children, as silent as little owls, rested on drooping horses.

Paul looked back. Moving dots, far in the distance; nothing more.

The older warriors muttered, not trusting the white-eyes, even from here, and they urged the families to hurry on to the reservation.

Paul lagged at the rear, in him already a sensation of wishing to hold back. And he thought: *I'm like them. I don't want to go in either.* Before him the yellow carpet of grass rolled northward at a gentle pitch. No buffalo, not even a phantom antelope or two. Under the wide sky the emptiness and the stillness felt all the more oppressive, prophetic of what awaited the Whirlwinds.

The sun slanted at late afternoon when the agency buildings became visible on the rolling plain, and beyond them the clutter of the stone fort on the slope east of the stunted Wichita Mountains.

He pulled up, and so did the Kiowas, and in

that moment he sensed their thinking: There marked the end of the old, free road, the buffalo road, where always the wind blew and sometimes the dust made a dim moon of the sun by day, and one had the memory of landmark peaks and buttes and gemlike, sweet-water springs. It was hard for them, he knew.

As one, the Whirlwinds turned to him, knowing he couldn't go on to the fort with them. No one spoke. They waited for him.

He seemed to have lost his voice. Finally, he said, "It was a good fight, my friends," and his throat filled and he could say no more. It was his way of telling them good-bye. He saw that embedded in their weary faces.

"Your power is strong, *Tejan*," Straight Lance said. "I saw you fight."

Paul shrugged. "I have no power."

The Kiowa shook his head in denial. "I know where your power comes from, my friend. It is your heart, which is good. That is your power, *Tejan*. We are brothers. From the time we captured you we were brothers. I know that now. That is your real power."

Paul raised his eyes. "I want to leave my son with you," he said, and he rode to Star Woman and took the plump, brown-skinned child, embraced him and kissed him, inhaling his moist sweetness, and gave him back. "Ride with me to that clump of timber," he told his friend.

There, Paul dismounted and passed him the Sharps and the rawhide reins. "I'll walk to the soldiers' houses dressed like a white-eye. When I leave there, I'll be a white-eye again." He saw pain come to his friend's face and he heard him say:

"I'll take good care of your horse. Someday you will ride him again. You will, *Tejan*!"

"The blue horse is yours. I have given him to you."

The other stared morosely at the reins in his hand. "Just as we grow to love you, you must go away. Why is this? But listen!" He was suddenly the war journey leader and horse-stealer of old, breathing confidence and encouragement. "You can live in the mountains where the white-eyes will never find you. I will bring you plenty of good food. And when we leave the stone houses, you can come to live with us again. Come on!"

"I belong back there," Paul said. "To the east. There are things I must do."

"You'll come back someday?"

Paul hesitated. "Someday, my friend."

Too quickly there was nothing left to say. Their glances met and held, and it was Paul who had to look away.

Alone, he took his knife and hacked his long, white hair short, so it hung just below his hat like a white man's. Now, clad in his crumpled white man's clothing, and carrying his rolled-up bundle, he struck eastward to the Army road. There he turned northward toward the fort, an hour or two away.

Approaching the outer buildings of the fort, he began scenting the foreign smells and expelling them and feeling a guardedness. Nothing had changed. Everything was just as he remembered, to the boxlike hotel where he had sketched the shiftless Shadler and his Indian wife.

Paul, unobtrusively, entered and bought his fare with the gold, and came out to wait on the porch for the stage, conscious of a decided unease: He was a hunted man. Arrival of the northbound stage was yet an hour off. Evening haze thickened. He heard bugles blowing the clear, sad notes of Retreat at the fort. He held his stiff, listening attitude long after the music had gone, distracted, worrying about the Whirlwinds. By now they had surrendered and he had heard no shots. Could they follow the new road?

Restless, he stepped inside. Coal oil lamps shed sallow light. The place stank of too much close-ness and the lingering passage of countless passengers. Two white men, one a drummer, the other a booted cattleman, lounged in cane-bottom chairs. Paul stood.

Presently, bootsteps rapped the porch. A man entered. Paul took one look and the observation exploded, "My God, another Shadler!" For, like Shadler, this man had all the excessive frontier trimmings and trappings, the long hair and buckskins and the blustering air. He sauntered over to the innkeeper's desk.

"Well," he boomed, "I saw 'em come in. The last wild bunch. Kioways. I could tell that right off." He paused significantly.

The innkeeper lifted one brow. "If there was trouble, we didn't hear it."

"Naw. No trouble. Colonel had six troops posted around, all primed, you betcher boots. Fight's gone plumb outa them Kioways. They wouldn't swat a horse fly." Paul felt his blood leaping. He was edging toward them when he remembered where he was, and he took himself in hand and paused, listening as the boastful voice continued: "There was one thing. The white man—the white renegade ever'body's on the lookout for—wasn't in the band."

"Wasn't?" The innkeeper set his silver-framed glasses back a notch on the high ridge of his nose.

"Got killed. Seems there was a big fight with buffalo hunters south of the Red. The Kioways claim they buried him along the river. Colonel wants me to take a looksee down there tomorrow. Good riddance, I say. A no-good white man that'll turn against his own kind. That keeps the hostiles stirred up."

"Wonder who he was? Some deserter?"

"Hard tellin'. But the Kioways had a name for

'im, all right." The long-jawed face bore a strained recalling. He looked up suddenly. "Yeah. *Tejan* was his name. They called him *Tejan*."

Paul, unable to stomach more of the gasconading, returned to the porch. The sky was darkening to heavier shades, and he smelled the wind freshening out of the darker mountains. Was that mesquite smoke? In the great, red-walled canyon it would be full dark by this hour and so still, so peaceful. And, like a stab, he felt all the goodness, the pain of so much tenderness, of so much complete loving, all of it drenching him and filling him once again, standing in him like deep, still water; just for those moments and it began to ebb and elude him, retreating before the rattling racket of the stage charging up the grade.

He took a step to go and halted instead, checked by a keening coming from the direction of the fort. A sound as old as time. An elder's quavering prayer-song. Paul brushed at his eyes as the awareness wrenched through him that he too was crying, crying silently for these Wild Ones, because he had lived and fought with them and shared and grieved with them, and thus understood them.

He stood there, motionless, until the hostler led out fresh horses and hitched up, and the drummer and the cattleman boarded, and the driver called.

Then, brushing once more at his eyes, he went to the stage. A white man.

Epilogue

Here in the effete East I am known as Paul Latimer Benedict, celebrated western artist and distinguished portraitist, lecturer of note on the Plains Indians, the Kiowas in particular. I eschew long hair and buckskins, however, as the stagey trappings of pseudo-frontiersmen. I need them not. Because I have truly lived, because I *know;* because I have loved and been loved and experienced the fierce grasp of friendship.

I have no family. Only my work, my burned-in memories. Enough, most times. Yet, when spring comes and the wind sobs out of the southwest and the sky turns the keenest of blues, a thousand images spring to life. A deep unrest seizes me and I know that occupation of the mind is not enough.

Someday, perhaps, I shall go back among the Wild Ones. I must. For from them I learned that we are all part of the whole of humanity.

Center Point Large Print
600 Brooks Road / PO Box 1
Thorndike, ME 04986-0001 USA

(207) 568-3717

US & Canada:
1 800 929-9108
www.centerpointlargeprint.com